10-1-2018

# THE ROCK WON'T MOVE
## The Prequel

Best Washs,

*[signature]*

# THE ROCK WON'T MOVE
## The Prequel

### A Story of Forgiveness

## WM. HANK PERRY

Xulon Press
2301 Lucien Way #415
Maitland, FL 32751
407.339.4217
www.xulonpress.com

Scripture quotations taken from the King James Version (KJV)
–*public domain.*

Printed in the United States of America.

ISBN-13: 9781545624296

To Alex and Jacob,
Loving you has been so much fun.

# CONTENTS

# Letter from the Author

*So, here we are again… God having willed it.*

I f this opening remark makes no sense, then you have probably stumbled onto this book before having read the first "Rock" book. If that is the case, you should know there are now two books that share the main title of *The Rock Won't Move.* That is because, well, they both contain a magnificent rock that people would like to move but can't.

Pretty clever title, huh?

But why two books?

The metamorphosis, by which one book became two, is quite a riveting tale, but you will have to read the Author's Letter in my first "Rock" book (subtitled *A Love Story*) to find out why—it's just too long to retell. I am not heartless, though, and for the benefit of first-timers, the abbreviated version of that change went something like this: when I submitted my original manuscript to Xulon Press for their critique, it was one book with two separate and distinct storylines occurring at the same time. One story was taking place during the American Civil War (this book), and the other story was taking place in our modern time. Having two concurrent stories in one book confused everyone (except me), and my Xulon editor suggested that I separate them, which I did.

Now that everyone has been caught up, there are a few distinctions that I wish to clarify. First, it was not long after the division of these two stories that I noticed a profoundly different underlying theme to them. To my utter surprise, I discovered one to be a love story, and the other was more a story of forgiveness (hence their subtitles: *A Love Story* and *A Story of Forgiveness*). Again, this only became apparent to me in their separated forms. I believe this particular nuance was hidden from me, either by accident (on my part) or intentionally (on God's part). I prefer to think the latter.

Since you are now holding the book subtitled *A Story of Forgiveness*, I thought it would be an opportune time to share with you one of my lifelong challenges with this benevolent gesture. You see, I suffer from a disability (don't we all). When I was just a child, I lost complete hearing in my left ear as a result of the high body temperatures produced by the mumps... or was it the measles? In any case, back in those days there was no urgent care facility down the street. There was no ibuprofen to help reduce the fever that plunged me into a coma-like state. There were only cold compresses applied to the head by a frantic parent, while the patient lay stewing in his own bed. When I awoke, I was gleefully surrounded by a superabundance of gifts from well-wishers, but had no hearing on one side—a fair exchange for a kid.

As one might expect, age has now taken its toll on my good ear—precipitously. I have tried hearing aids, but they do not perform well with my active lifestyle: that is, they constantly fall out when I am at work or at the gym; they pick up every other sound, except for the voice of the person standing in front of me; and the battery life is approximately ten minutes. Interestingly, however, because of my hearing loss (a "thorn in the flesh," as the apostle Paul would say), I have discovered three basic types of people based on how they have responded to my impairment.

The first type of person has known for years (sometimes decades) my hearing limitations and yet will begin a conversation from another room, or will continue speaking as he/she walks away from me. Shortly thereafter, I get casually admonished for ignoring an exchange that I had no idea ever happened in the first place (i.e., I am deemed to have selective hearing).

The second type of person has known for years (sometimes decades) my hearing limitations and yet will persist on speaking to my bad ear. When I turn to ask him/her to repeat themselves, my request is met with a disappointed sigh, as if slow-wittedness or senility was the true reason of my need for clarification; not the fact that the ear was as good as a foot at hearing (i.e., I am deemed too high-maintenance).

The third type of person has known for years (sometimes decades) my hearing limitations and will make every effort to face me or to be on my good side. He/she will even go so far as to apologize to me for having to repeat themselves (i.e., I am deemed imperfect, just like everyone else).

I hold absolutely nothing against the first two groups of people, and forgive them without even thinking about it anymore. I only wish forgiveness would come to me as rapidly, and as effortlessly, with all of my perceived injustices.

So, where was I?

Oh, yes. To help further differentiate these two books, for which I stubbornly insist on using the same main title, I have affixed the qualifier *The Prequel* to this one, for reasons you might already suspect. The events that are occurring in my first book are totally dependent on the events having already occurred in this book.

Caveat: it is not my wish to be a stinker, but to be quite honest, the ending to this story would have a much greater impact if you were to read *A Love Story* first. That's just my opinion, and you know what they say about opinions.

It may appear that by using a considerable amount of ink to examine the seemingly mundane issues surrounding the naming and sequencing of my writing, I have been beating a dead horse; perhaps, and it would not be the first time I have been accused of this effusive trait. On the other hand, it has allowed me to bring my first book to your attention, in the hopes that you might find it enjoyable to read as well. More importantly, it has allowed me to expand on a deeply-rooted conviction of mine for starting to write in the first place. Again, I began this self-analysis—my personal metamorphosis—in the Author's Letter from the first book. In that letter, I make the case that this improbable, new vocation of writing was God's plan for me all along, and I now believe it is shaping up to be some sort of ministry.

How does writing a fictional novel become a ministry?

I remember beginning this idea of ministry in my own home with my two young sons. Of course, I didn't call it a ministry, per se—I was just trying to be a good dad. The idea was to become more Christ-like, not perfect; just an ongoing process of maturing into a man of spiritual integrity. As the boys grew older, and had learned as much as they were going to learn from dear old dad (for they were now attempting to teach Pops a thing or two), I brought the idea of ministry to a whole new level. That effort took the form of starting a Boy Scout troop from scratch (my two boys had already earned the rank of Eagle Scout).

The fundamental idea was simple: go out into the community and actively recruit "fatherless" boys or, more accurately, boys without a dad in the picture. Anticipating the financial hardship these families might be experiencing, I was going to make it known to the single moms that all expenses would be paid, so long as their sons behaved in a manner befitting a scout—not perfect: just trustworthy, loyal, helpful, friendly, courteous, kind, obedient, cheerful, thrifty, brave, clean, and reverent (Unfortunately, the Boy Scouts of America® have watered-down the biblical meaning of "reverence" and completely forgotten how to live "morally straight"). That much-needed ministry was received by my church with arms wide open, but had to be abandoned when my personal life spiraled out of control.

Why would God take away such a promising ministry?

I suppose because it was *my* ministry, not *His,* which brings me to my point. My life as some noble Christian son, brother, friend, husband, father, scoutmaster has never been my testimony—at least not a very good one, from what I can tell. Though I have now added *author* to that list, I do not believe my standing with God has been changed, or enhanced, much because of it. I am still the regular Joe in need of a Savior, as before; yet, since accepting Jesus into my heart, it has been my fondest wish to have some noticeable impact for my Savior. At this point in my life, it does not matter to me if this impact has its way within my close circle of friends, or one stranger at a time–if necessary. With this book, I may have been given that opportunity.

This book is simply a story with Jesus at the beginning, Jesus in the middle, and Jesus at the end—kind of like our lives, whether we recognize Him or not. It is my hope that you enjoy reading it so much that you will recommend the book to a friend, and that friend will recommend it to a friend, and so on; until it lands on the lap of a person who does not know how important Jesus really is, who will then read it and is somehow moved by it. That's the ministry.

Is it His ministry?

May it be true this time, is my prayer.

So, here's the thing: if you believe this book brings glory to God, then use it. Start a conversation with it. Talk about the loving and forgiving Jesus that you know.

In Him alone,
Hank

# 1

# The Battle

On April 12, 1861, Fort Sumter became the Civil War's first battlefield. It was an unfinished fortress in the middle of Charlestown Harbor in South Carolina, occupied by a small number of federal troops. They would surrender to the Confederates in a matter of hours with no fatalities, but it was enough to start a war. When word of the event finally reached the United States Military Academy at West Point in New York State, many of the students there felt an obligation to enlist into their states' respective armies. Some would fight for the North and others would fight for the South. It was inevitable that some would have to fight each other.

For two of these bright young cadets, that scenario became a tragic reality. Neither of these two men had any living relatives and, over the course of their three years together at the Point, they had become like brothers. Both were exceptionally gifted and were allowed admission into the Academy to study civil engineering, after achieving perfect scores on their entrance examinations. Once admitted, they excelled in whatever challenge was presented to them and were destined to graduate number one and number two in the class of 1862. In addition to gaining valuable knowledge, they would also come seeking to learn the discipline that would normally be taught to a son by his father, which was also of great worth to them.

The bond they had developed prior to the declaration of war was so strong and genuine that one sincerely promised to fall on his sword before taking the life of the other. Without hesitation, the other promised to shoot himself dead before his friend's sword could be fully unsheathed. Neither, however, expected the hostilities to last much longer than the summer break. God willing, they would both be back to finish their studies by that time the following year. Just before departure, they prayed for the others' good health and success in the battlefield—if it did come to that. That implied, of course, that the other's success would necessarily have to come at the expense of their own success. The names of these two cadets were Benjamin Franklin Hillary of Pennsylvania (Northern army) and John Philip Turner of Virginia (Southern army).

For the next two years, both men would serve their commanders, their states, and their countries, courageously and honorably, before fate would reunite them once again. That unforeseen and improbable meeting would occur on May 30, 1863, in the silent, rolling pasture of a southern Pennsylvania hillside. It would only be considered a cockfight compared to what would eventually happen a month later in a dull, little town twenty miles northeast by the name of Gettysburg. Unfortunately (or fortunately), neither Turner nor Hillary would know who it was they were fighting until the cursed work of soldiering was complete.

There was no great name given to their battle; it could have been called the Battle of Rock Creek if you were from the North—they liked to name their battles after a nearby river. If you were from the South, however, this might have been a little tricky because they liked to name their battles after a nearby town. The closest town to this battle was Gettysburg, and that name would soon be purchased with a sea of blood and immortalized forever. In reality, this unexpected engagement of two relatively small raiding parties would probably have been looked on more as a skirmish than a battle and, like most skirmishes, a minor footnote leading up to the day of the great battle. Tactically, this skirmish was of no serious consequence to either side except, of course, to the hundreds who would perish that day. Death would come swiftly, but leaving only one side to bear the entire loss of life.

The Union force of nearly a thousand Pennsylvania cavalrymen, with light and mobile-horse artillery, was commanded by Colonel Benjamin Hillary. His orders were to rove the territory between Frederick, Maryland, and Chambersburg, Pennsylvania, and discourage the enemy from crossing the Potomac by all means available. The Confederate force of nearly eight hundred Virginia cavalrymen was commanded by Colonel Philip Turner. His troops were said to be as swift and cunning as those of Major General J. E. B. Stuart's cavalry, and were fresh from General Lee's stunning victory in Chancellorsville, Virginia four weeks ago. His orders were to gain entry into Maryland and Pennsylvania to "see more and be seen less". That meant they were there simply to be the eyes and ears, in advance of Lee's aggressive campaign to enter into enemy territory and destroy the Army of the Potomac once and for all.

Apparently, the thrashing that General Hooker's Army of the Potomac received in Chancellorsville, at the hands of General Lee's Army of Northern Virginia, was enough for Turner to move freely through Maryland and into Pennsylvania without any interference. It had been raining for days, which hampered his progress through the Pennsylvania wilderness, as he tried to avoid the main roads. More importantly, however, his horses were making deep and permanent ruts in the saturated ground. This unintentional, yet clearly visible, act of trailblazing made Turner understandably uneasy. He could look back and see the deep scars he was making as far as the eye could see—and so, too, could his enemy. If the harassing rain continued, he dared not go much farther, although his intention was to get as close to Harrisburg as he could before turning back. Turner could not help but sense it was time to consider other options. He quickly revised his plan: they would camp for the evening and then, in the morning, travel a short distance east to observe any activity around the town of Gettysburg, instead of going farther north to Harrisburg. With the good Lord's help, they would be crossing the Potomac back into Virginia at that time tomorrow. In the meantime, he dispatched a small team to retrace their paths to see if anyone was following. They would return in haste before dawn.

* * *

Meanwhile, Colonel Hillary's troops were on the move. His scouts had no problem picking up the fresh trail left by Turner and his men. From all the signs, he knew the rebel intruders were fast-moving cavalry, even in this damnable rain. His enemy appeared to be approximately equal in number to his own, and at least a day ahead of him. Since his opponents lacked the burden of carrying artillery, there would be little chance of ever engaging them without luck. Hillary's only hope of boosting his luck of engagement was to advance through the night and hope the enemy had settled in someplace. He quickly calculated that his men could pick up most of that time using the main roads, before detouring back onto the much slower path of his prey.

* * *

The reconnaissance team sent out by Turner rode as fast and as long as their horses could bear before sunset, covering some twenty miles. However, had they not slowed their pace when they did, they most certainly would have driven right past the very thing they were seeking. Because providence would be in their favor this day, they decided just then to rest their horses on a well-camouflaged ridge. They dismounted and began a discussion on whether it was best to go on or return to camp. That discussion was cut short, however, when one of the men thought he saw some movement way off in the dimly lit valley below. Between the trees, the rain and with the waning light of day, it was hard to tell at first, but now it was unmistakable. There was Hillary's cavalry, pressing as hard as they could muster toward their position, with no obvious interest in slowing down. Turner's trail had been discovered.

At this pace, Turner's men estimated Hillary's troops could potentially reach their camp by dawn if that was, in fact, their intention. So off they flew into the night. Once again, the circumstances were in their favor; darkness provided cover, and they had traveled this way twice in less than twenty-four hours and were familiar with its many obstacles; and of course, there were five of them on horses built for speed and endurance. They arrived back at camp well before dawn to wake Colonel Turner. It did not take long for Turner to conclude he had but two options: fight or flight. Well, he certainly wasn't a guy to shy away from a fight, especially when he had the advantage of occupying the highest ground available and the real element of surprise (if it was true that his scouts were not spotted). Even so, they would have to hurry if his plan was to succeed.

The plan was bold: Turner would divide his army and attack the enemy's flank by surprise. His officers would have thought him crazy, if not for the fact that it was a similar strategy Lee had employed successfully against Hooker at Chancellorsville a few short weeks earlier. It would involve leaving two hundred of his men, including himself, exposed to the direct line of fire of the enemy's cannon, while the other six hundred men made a wide-sweeping tactical march to hit the enemy from both the left and right flanks. The risk, of course, was that these six hundred men would arrive back to the battlefield too late to save the two hundred from certain annihilation. If this plan was to succeed, the enemy must believe that all eight hundred of Turner's men were hidden somewhere behind the wide, modestly elevated ridge in a last-ditch effort to save themselves. The evidence, intentional or otherwise, left by Turner should help add to the deception. This would include the trail of an adversary without artillery approximately the size of their own, the remnants of a camp hastily abandoned and left standing, and the echoes of a few random rifle discharges from nominal fortifications along a minor ridgeline, slightly over a mile long. All of this should present to his enemy the exact location of an easy target that was both surprised and desperate.

* * *

Due to all the scouting reports, Hillary arrived on the scene before dawn knowing exactly where the enemy had set up their defensive position.

*So, they have decided to fight,* he thought without any feeling of arrogance or conceit. The rain had finally relented, and he expected visibility to improve by dawn.

*This should do well for aiming the Howitzers,* he concluded.

Hillary's men were tired but eager for battle. He gave orders to maneuver the four guns into an area well out of the enemy's rifle range and prepare to engage in one hour. His plan was to weaken the enemy's position and resolve with a barrage of cannon fire, lasting approximately twenty minutes. This should encourage any survivors to surrender or meet his men in the open field for battle. As his men rested and ate a little, Hillary was continuously watching the enemy's movements and appraising the situation in his mind. From time to time, he would see an officer ride down the length of his troop's line, loudly barking orders.

*What were his men shooting at and where has he hidden so many horsemen on such an insignificant hill,* he wondered, *unless…?*

Uneasily, Hillary asked his sergeant for his telescope. Without removing the glass from his eye, he asked if he had seen any other horsemen, except this one lone rider.

"No, sir," came the response. Hillary's heart sank.

"Oh, my God… What have I done?" escaped quietly from his lips.

"Turn the cannon now!" Hillary screamed, but it was too late.

* * *

Dawn was approaching, and by now Turner's enemy had every weapon at their disposal aimed on the ridge he now occupied. He had made several passes on horseback to give the illusion of preparation and to inspire his men. It was all he could do—the plan was set.

*Lord, let them come and come soon... or they will soon be without a commander*, Turner prayed silently for the return of his six hundred men.

Suddenly, a sharp booming sound came swiftly to his ears, and he bowed his head and asked his Savior for forgiveness and mercy. A moment later, after realizing that it was not the sound of artillery and that he was neither dead nor injured, he lifted his eyes to see a swarm of gray off to his right pounce on top of the enemy's left flank. The booming sound he heard was that of his men's rifles being discharged several hundred at once. Immediately following that event, an equally violent attack on the enemy occurred to his left. His sharpshooters must have dropped the cannoneer first, because their guns sat still and silent. With great enthusiasm, Turner gathered his two hundred men on the hill.

"It is now our turn to join the fight," he exclaimed with a shout. "Charge!"

The battle was essentially over in minutes. Hillary and his men were so focused on the enemy being in front of them that those who perished in the first few minutes didn't know what hit them. The surprise was so extraordinary, so contrary to the senses, that many would die with tin cups in hand rather than weapons. In the resulting chaos, a sort of madness fell on a few of Hillary's men, causing them to shoot their weapons aimlessly, accidentally wounding many on their own side. Those with some sense as to what was happening thought only of escaping the slaughter that quickly enveloped them. In less than an hour, half of Hillary's troops lay dead or wounded, while the other half were fleeing on foot or by horse in whatever direction they could find a gap. Turner's side would indeed suffer many career-ending injuries but, incredibly, all his men would survive.

Turner had the presence of mind to know that they were still in enemy territory, and there was no time to savor any victory. As soon as he believed that the enemy was no longer a threat and the battle had been won, he gave orders to suspend any further hostilities toward any enemy wishing to leave the battlefield peacefully, unarmed and by foot. He also ordered the disabling of the cannon and the spreading of any gunpowder they were unable to take with them. His final command was the regrouping of all his men for the expeditious trek back home within the hour. Turner immediately began studying his maps for the quickest way back into the Shenandoah and home, only to be interrupted by his sergeant, Joseph Parker.

"Sir, we have found the Yankee commander..." he stated, as if there was something else that needed to be said.

"Is he alive, Sergeant?" Turner asked, noting the incompleteness of the statement.

"He is badly wounded, sir," he said. Again, the sergeant's response lacked the conjunction *but*.

"Well, make him comfortable and send my surgeon if necessary. There is no purpose to be served by our meeting now," Turner stated, as if to say the conversation was finished.

"Yes, sir," Parker said with some hesitation. "But, before I go, sir... That is, I think you should know, sir... He is calling out your name, sir."

"How would—?" Turner cut short his reply when a sudden, bone-chilling thought stopped him cold.

*Who would know my name out here?* he asked himself, as he began to think the unthinkable.

"Take me to him at once, Sergeant," Turner commanded forcefully. The private standing with the sergeant was instructed to find his surgeon and bring him without delay.

"Yes, sir!" the private answered, noting the urgency in the colonel's voice and fully aware that this directive had better happen, and happen quickly. He was off in a flash.

Praying to God Almighty that his supposition was wrong, Turner instead found his most cherished friend mortally wounded, and in the arms of a young, Northern private.

"Benjamin!" he cried out. "I had no idea. Forgive me. Please forgive me, my dear brother." Those within earshot were stunned upon hearing this greeting.

*Could these two colonels really be brothers?* they thought.

Turner moved in quickly, but gently, next to the Northern private who was being so careful and tender with his wounded friend. Thinking the two might actually be brothers, the private moved slowly from his spot to allow the smooth transition of his beloved colonel onto the lap of the rebel commander.

"Is that you, Philip? Is that you, brother?" Benjamin wheezed with labored breath. It was obvious to all that the Yankee colonel had lost his ability to see clearly and was hanging on to life by a thread.

"Don't try to speak. I am here now. My surgeon is on his way, and he will mend this horrible thing I have done to you," Turner said, through the tears that were now forming in his eyes. He cradled his friend in his muscular arms and gently stroked his matted hair.

"I asked Jesus to bring you here... and you have come," Benjamin said weakly. "Blessed the Lord... blessed is our Redeemer." Turner said nothing, but now began to slowly rock his friend back and forth involuntarily, like a loving father would comfort his child.

"Philip?" Benjamin began again.

"Yes?" Turner responded without trying to stop him this time. He now knew the full extent of his friend's wound, and that it would soon take his life.

"Don't let them cut off my legs. Promise you won't let them take my legs. Promise me." Hillary pleaded, as he started to become somewhat delusional now.

"I won't allow it, dear brother," Turner promised.

*Oh, dear Benjamin, if only you had taken that minié ball to a leg instead of the gut, my surgeon could cut it off and you would be allowed to live,* he thought, lamenting.

Turner's sergeant was taken aback, as he watched his courageous commanding officer fall to pieces before his eyes. He thought it was his duty to remind the colonel of his obligation to his men and his country. His commander must quit behaving so foolishly and allow this man to die as the others had done, brother or not.

"Sir?" Parker began. "With all due respect, sir, we have delayed much too long. Your orders have all been fulfilled, except the last concerning our departure from this miserable place. 'Within the hour,' you said." Turner seemed not to be paying attention to anything the sergeant had to say. Benjamin began to weep softly.

"They... call me," he said, almost inaudible now.

"Who, Benjamin?" Turner asked, while holding him closer. "Who is calling?"

"Angels... above," was his slow, almost breathless response. Turner now knew the end was near and could hardly contain his unfathomable sadness. What could he possibly say that would comfort his dying friend and let him know how truly loved he was?

"Then go to them, my darling brother," he gently whispered into his friend's ear. "I release you into the arms of our Heavenly Father. He will make all things well again."

Just then, his private arrived with the colonel's surgeon, but it was too late. The patient was gone. Turner buried his best friend's face deep into his heaving chest. He could restrain his terrible grief no longer as great, anguished sobs began pouring from his aching body.

"Dear God, why have you given me the only brother I have ever known," he cried out, "only to take him from me this way?"

The men that now gathered around him could not help but appreciate the torment their commander was experiencing: a man unknowingly taking the life of his brother in battle. After several minutes elapsed, Turner's officers, believing the scene had played itself out, walked behind him and patted him on the shoulder to show their sympathy, as well as their readiness for departure. Sergeant Parker, who was also greatly moved, came up last and gripped the shoulder of his commander.

"Sir, we must be going, or we shall all die here," he said, as compassionately as a soldier could do at such a time.

"I will bury my brother—here, now," Turner replied without looking up.

"Then you will need to bury us all," Parker responded defiantly.

"There will be no need for that, sergeant," Turner responded calmly, as he reached into his coat pocket, pulled out his set of maps, and handed them to Parker. "You will assume command of these men and lead them back home, as if I had also died here on this spot."

"Sir, this is insanity. No good can come of this," Parker objected passionately.

Turner laid Benjamin's head gently on the ground, straightened his friend's uniform, and folded his arms across the lifeless body in an unsuccessful effort to conceal the impact of the bullet. Turner remained kneeling, bowed his head, and silently prayed for all those who fought and died so honorably that day. Now, slowly rising to his full height of over six feet, he straightened his own uniform, now stained with his friend's blood. With broad, muscular shoulders, he was a magnificent figure that towered over those closest to him. Appearing unmovable and unshakeable, he looked out over the battlefield and then into the eyes of his men. For many standing there, he took on the appearance of a man much older than his twenty-plus years and, had General Thomas Jackson not been given his moniker at the Battle of Manassas, they would have certainly nicknamed their commander "Stonewall". Finally, he addressed Parker.

"You must leave now, Sergeant," he stated matter-of-factly. "I will bury my brother and die with him here, if that is God's will."

Suddenly, from behind the circle of Turner's men, a lone voice called out.

"I will bury him!" the voice shouted.

Slowly his men parted, creating a lane between Turner and the direction from which the voice came. There stood the young, Northern private who had been comforting Colonel Hillary when Turner first arrived. Turner had quite forgotten about him, as had everyone else apparently.

"What did you say?" Turner asked.

"I will bury him proper, sir," the young soldier said again, using his normal voice.

For a brief moment, Turner appraised this young soldier. His first observation was that the young man before him was most certainly still in his middle teens. Second, he must have had a deep affection for his commanding officer to risk his own life to stay by his side during battle. Then Turner suddenly realized that, during the course of the events whereby he relieved this fellow of that duty, the young man still did not leave. Most assuredly, he was offered safe passage from the battlefield with the other Northern soldiers, and yet he still chose to stay. Evidently, he was simply jostled farther and farther away from his commanding officer whom he... what?

*Why did he stay?* Turner thought.

"What is your name, son?" Turner asked, politely.

"Nathan, sir... Private Nathan Walker, sir," he corrected himself.

"And why would you offer to bury my brother, Private Nathan Walker?" Turner pressed.

The private looked down at the peaceful body of his commander.

"Colonel Hillary, sir... he would talk to me, sir. When I was feeling like a kid, scared and all, he would make me believe I was a man, sir," he said, mournfully. Then, bringing his eyes up to look at Turner, he completed his reasoning. "Not just talk from an officer. More like a father, if you understand my meaning, sir."

Turner took a moment now to reflect on the young man's words. The sincerity and depth of affection was undeniable, but it was in that one word—*more*—that he expressed back to Turner all the feelings he ever had for Benjamin. They did, indeed, share a special bond with this man, and together they suffered a great personal loss. Having come to this conclusion, Turner also believed this young man could be trusted. He walked over to the young private and grabbed his narrow shoulders with his powerful hands.

"I believe Colonel Hillary was as much a father to you as he was a brother to me, Private. I accept your offer to bury my brother." Turner then walked purposefully back to where Benjamin's body was peacefully laid, kneeled, and gently reached inside his good friend's coat.

"I was going to allow this Bible to be buried with my brother. It was his greatest possession," Turner said thoughtfully. "I believe now that he would want you to have it."

The young soldier looked down at the book being presented to him, as if he recognized it and that it was of tremendous value. Looking around, Turner's eyes came to rest on the large remains of a dead oak standing alone along the perimeter of the open field.

"There," he said, pointing to the oak. "You will bury your colonel there. Count off ten paces from that dead tree and bury him deep. Cover the spot with every rock you can find. I will return after the war, God willing, and take my brother to be buried with me and our family." Turner then turned to address Sergeant Parker.

"Sergeant, may I have my maps back, if it pleases you?"

"It does, sir," Parker said gladly.

"Are the men ready to ride?"

"At your command, sir," Parker said, as he gave a signal for his men to mount up.

Hillary then turned back to the young private.

"I will not forget you, Private Walker," Turner said earnestly. "I will add a petition for your health and success in battle to my daily prayers. Perhaps we will meet again on friendlier terms. Good-bye and good luck."

That being said, Turner mounted his horse.

"Deep," Turner added, looking at the carnage all about him. "Bury him deep, Private. We don't know how long this damned war will go on." With that, he was gone.

Incredibly, Turner would return to Pennsylvania in a month as commander of one of General Lee's light and mobile horse artillery batteries in the great battle at Gettysburg. Once again, he would prove his valor and skill in a conflict where six thousand would die in the bloodiest battle in American history. He would not be counted as one of them, nor would he be one of the half a million men consumed by war before his beloved general, Robert E. Lee, would be forced to surrender to General Ulysses S. Grant.

Turner would, in fact, be one of the few to survive the Great American Civil War without serious injury, except for that in his own mind from being a witness to so much mutilation and death. To many, these irrepressible thoughts would abuse their lives far worse than any physical calamity. To Turner, however, the thought of God preserving him for some other purpose drove him to accomplish many great things. This noble legacy would begin when he returned once more to the site where his good friend still lay peacefully beside a large, dead oak.

# 2

# End of War

When Philip Turner, now a Major General, first saw the somber expression on the face of his beloved general as he rode his horse, Traveler, slowly past his adoring men, he knew the fight was over. The date was April 9, 1865. The place was a small Virginia village by the name of Appomattox, and General Lee had just surrendered the entire Army of Northern Virginia to General Grant, from within the sitting parlor of Wilmer McLean's country home. Turner heard rumors that the Confederate capitol of Richmond had fallen days ago, and that President Jefferson Davis had fled to the Carolinas; it must have been true. He had trusted the Great Grey General with his life for four long years now, and he knew that for a brilliant soldier like Robert E. Lee to give up, no other option existed. Still, there was only one other occasion during this bloody war during which Turner's heart had sunk so low, and that was two years ago this coming May in the pasture of a southern Pennsylvania hillside.

Turner's melancholy turned to astonished joy, however, when he heard the terms of the surrender. Instead of treason charges and imprisonment, General Grant immediately paroled his great multitude of "prisoners" and allowed them all to return home, along with their horses and personal belongings, in time for spring planting. Confederate officers were even allowed to keep their side arms to mitigate any unnecessary humiliation. Turner did not know it yet, but the events of this day would eventually result in the remaining Confederate armies surrendering within a month on similar terms, and the restoration of a deeply battered country would begin.

Turner had actually been planning for this day in earnest since the battle at Gettysburg two years before, and when it finally arrived, it came shockingly fast. It made little difference to him whether the South won the war and he was allowed to put his ambitious ideas into practice immediately; or if the South lost and he languished in prison for a few years before implementing his plans. All that mattered, if he survived, was to be able to apply all his energy and engineering talents into rebuilding the decimated infrastructure of the South. For the last five years, he had been a soldier by occupation, but he had never stopped contemplating the future with an engineer's vision and a dedicated patriot's spirit. So, as he passed through each Southern town ravaged by war, or crossed an essential bridge or railroad depot he would later have to destroy to slow his enemy's progress, he cataloged his findings and outlined, in detail, what would be necessary to rebuild them. In fact, it came about that the sheer volume of his writings and drawings (contained in various-sized notebooks) became so large and cumbersome that he had to find other means to transport this work other than in his personal saddlebags alone.

Of all Turner's investigations, the information of greatest significance dealt with the North's immensely effective railroad and telegraph operations. These were all privately held companies before the war, but soon after the fall of Fort Sumter, the federal government assumed control over them—and rightly so. The side with the ability to transport men, equipment, and information to the battlefield quickly did not always win the battle, but clearly held the advantage. It seemed strange to him that, as a cost-saving measure, the Federal United States Military Telegraph Corps employed mostly civilian operators in the field; only the supervisors were military. Turner quickly discovered that, with the simple hint of a prolonged internment and food deprivation, these underpaid and unappreciated civil servants would eagerly divulge every secret they knew (and then some) if they thought it would buy them favor. Occasionally, he could even get a captured military supervisor to talk freely about his business with enough amiable chatter between engineers—and some alcohol. Despite his best efforts, this invaluable information went mostly unused by the South's Confederate Corps of Engineers. Even though the South's Corps of Engineers was equal in size to the North's, its members were forced into spending all their time constructing defensive fortifications around their own cities, instead of maintaining Southern railroad and telegraph lines. Knowing what he knew, any engineer worth his salt would conclude the end result of this war was inevitable.

Now that the war was virtually over, Turner believed that these useful enterprises must soon be transferred back into private hands, and whoever provided the best solutions for keeping these once–federally supported businesses profitable, especially in the South, would be generously rewarded. It was obvious to him that this was somehow supposed to be his service to the Lord—God's calling—for which He had spared his life. Nevertheless, his ambitious ideas would take money and influence. With the Confederate money in his pockets now worthless, and being on the losing side of the war, these two essential resources were as far away from him as the East was from the West—unless it was truly to be God's will.

Then there were the other two pieces of unfinished business. One was to complete his last year at West Point, and the other was to reclaim the body of his dear friend, Benjamin, or at least know for sure that the gravesite had been preserved. As for West Point, he had been warned that the academy would not be accepting applications for readmission from those fighting against the North and might never allow him back. As for Benjamin, he knew he must be patient. The war might be over, but traveling into Northern territory too soon after its conclusion would certainly be risky. Even so, he still carried the map that showed the exact location of where the unforgotten body of his friend rested in Pennsylvania, and this was the promise he most wanted to fulfill. After turning these thoughts over in his mind for a few days, Turner decided he would attempt the trip north in spite of the risk.

Before being allowed to leave, however, Turner was obligated under the terms of surrender to certify that the men in his regiment would never again take up arms against the United States and then collect whatever government property they had in their possession. They were able to keep their rifles and pistols, if they were personal property. He was then given authority to sign the parole pass that promised his men safe passage home, as well as provide them food and shelter at federal installations along the way, if necessary.

Turner had less than five hundred men now, but most had been with him since he was first given the command four years before. He knew that every man left standing had just been granted a new lease on life, and wanted desperately to get them back to their families as quickly as possible. So, to oblige these natural instincts, he was willing to sign the pass for each and every one of these brave soldiers—from memory—and have them delivered like mail. The word came back to him that all of his men, with only a few exceptions from the newcomers, wanted to say their piece standing before their beloved commander. So, he met each of these men face-to-face. He began every meeting by warmly expressing his deepest appreciation for the soldier's valor in battle and the sacrifice each made to his country. With those who needed to talk, he listened patiently; with those who wept, he wept with them; with those who dropped to their knees and asked forgiveness for the things they had done to stay alive, he knelt beside them and gave thanks to God above for His endless mercy. For some, the only solace was to receive a bear hug from a brother-in-arms; some simply saluted and thanked him for delivering them from hell itself. There were as many ways of saying good-bye as there were men, and Turner gave each time to say what he needed to say. He felt it was the least he could do after all they had done for him. The experience was so exhausting, and Turner was so humbled by his men's affection that he collapsed on his cot and cried himself to sleep when all was said and done.

It was now early evening on April 14, five days after the surrender, and Turner was awakened by Joseph Parker, now his lieutenant. It was Parker who was asked to assume command of the regiment in Pennsylvania before Turner accepted Private Walker's offer to bury Benjamin two years ago. It was also Parker who would block anyone from disturbing Turner's sleep today. Parker could not help but notice the lack of rest his commander experienced while meeting with his men around the clock for three days. Turner had been allowed to sleep all night and all day.

"Good evening, sir," Parker said, giving Turner some idea of the time of day. "I've brought you some supper. It's an amazing thing with these Yanks... just when you think you've eaten everything they have, another train rolls in loaded with the best damn vittles you've ever set eyes on. That's not a lie."

"What time is it, Lieutenant?" Turner asked abruptly.

"A little after six in the evening, sir," was the response.

"Oh Lord, forgive me," Turner mumbled to himself, ignoring the offer of food and groping around for his trousers. "I spend two days trying my best to get these boys homeward without delay, only to add to their delay with self-indulgent sleep. I should be court-martialed!"

"It's been three days, and any delay was their idea, if you recall, General," Parker corrected his commanding officer plainly. "You needn't worry about the men anyhow, sir. I had your ledger with the names of all those you paroled listed upon it transcribed, knowing you like to keep records of this sort. I then brought the original to the Federal captain in charge of such matters early this morning. He accepted it agreeably, since you had the forethought to sign the document in advance. In fact, he did you a kindness and signed your parole pass himself, after being made aware of the particulars for my delivery in your behalf." Parker handed Turner his parole pass and continued.

"Having successfully discharged, in my mind, the obligations put upon us by our benevolent captors, I immediately sent word out to those wishing to leave that they may do so at their earliest convenience," Parker stated firmly. "I then ordered anyone interrupting your sleep to be shot dead... sir."

"Joseph, my dedicated and irrepressible lieutenant." Turner sighed and sat back down on his cot, half-dressed. "Nothing gets by you, does it?"

Parker grinned but said nothing. They had fought side by side for four long years, and had developed a strong mutual respect and understanding for each other's strengths and weaknesses. There were numerous occasions when Turner thought he had lost Parker in battle, only to have him reappear in the nick of time. For Turner, losing Parker would have been equal to General Lee losing Stonewall Jackson—or even losing Benjamin all over again.

"Well, it appears that I am a commander without a command, Lieutenant," Turner mused. "I will take that plate of vittles now and, unless you must leave immediately, it would do my heart good to hear a little more about your family. As I recall, your home is just east of here, is it not?"

They began a peacefully uninterrupted conversation that would last two hours or so. Having no kinfolk of his own, Turner enjoyed listening to Parker's stories of growing up on his family's Virginia farm with his three brothers and one sister. Parker was a middle child, who would assume much of the responsibility for running things when his two older brothers went off to become cadets at Virginia Military Institute before the war. All of his brothers would eventually go off to war and, as far as Parker knew, all were still alive.

Turner knew Parker carried with him an old family photograph, and he asked to see it. He had seen the picture of a mother and a father with five young children on horseback many times before. It was taken as a result of a chance meeting between Parker's father and a traveling photographer, who passed through their small town on his way to Richmond many years before. It had been a long time, but Parker remembered vividly the transaction involving a couple of horses, of average quality, for a full set of pictures, handsomely framed. Parker horses of average quality were head and shoulders above any other to be found in Virginia, and, in the end, both his father and the photographer believed they received a fair deal.

Turner gently took the picture from Parker's hand, as it was in poor condition by now, and gazed at it once again. As with all the other previous meetings when viewing this picture, Parker's reminiscences centered mostly on his love and devotion to his parents or the military careers of his brothers. However, on this night, it was as if Turner looked at it for the first time. As he scanned the picture in his hand, Turner found he could not take his eyes off the young girl standing next to a pinto-colored yearling. Turner discovered in their talk that he was actually two years younger than Parker, making him about the same age as this young girl. Turner wasn't sure why this mattered to him and why had he not noticed her before.

Turner handed the photograph back to Parker and sat, eating unhurriedly and listening attentively. They grew food on the Parker farm, not cotton, as some of their neighbors did. They owned no slaves and hired only God-fearing men to help work the fields and manage the cattle. Parker's father, a deacon in the church, did not allow drunks and vagabonds to spoil the pot. His mom was the town's school-marm and, as a result, her children would learn to read, write, and think resourcefully for themselves at an early age. Although the farming operation provided good food for the table and some profit at market, it was the farm's horse business that sustained everything. The Parker farm was well known for raising some of the finest horses in the South, and this is where Parker and his siblings spent most of their time: riding, training, and learning the family business. It was said that George Washington's favorite horses were purchased from Parker's great-grandfather.

It was getting late, and they both knew the time had come to end their long-standing professional relationship. It was determined that Turner's official duties would last another week or two before he was given permission to leave, but Parker was prepared to leave early the following morning. Although it was never mentioned in any conversation, Parker knew the burden on his commander's heart was to return to that Pennsylvania battlefield to retrieve the body of his brother. He had seen the maps lying out from time to time and how they were almost as worn from constant handling as the picture of his family. He also knew that such an adventure, so soon after this bitter war, would be asking for trouble. Since there was never any mention of home or family other than Benjamin, it made perfect sense to him that a stay at his family's farm, for whatever duration he could convince the general to agree to, before attempting a trip north would be a good thing. After a few more minutes of lighthearted bantering, he proceeded with his invitation.

"Sir," Parker began.

"Please, Joseph," Turner kindly interrupted. "From this moment forward, it will not be necessary to address me as a commanding officer, but as a friend. Will you call me Phillip?"

Parker smiled and was about to begin his invitation again using Turner's first name, but he stopped short. The proposition that his commander could be his friend suddenly confused him; it finally dawned on him that he knew absolutely nothing about this man. Any discussion between them about family went back only as far as life at West Point with Benjamin and no further. Any intentions of life after the war were written in books and tucked away.

In fact, now that he had a moment to think about it, any discussion that would shine light on his commander's life was always carefully redirected back to him. This redirection occurred again this very night. After two hours of conversation, Parker knew no more about his general than he had the night before—or two years ago. Shouldn't friends know something—anything—about the other so that, in times like this, they could offer something more than platitudes and a place to stay before the other went off to who knows where?

For years, Parker watched his commanding general take a pack of undisciplined country horsemen and turn them into the only thing that would keep them alive: cavalry soldiers. Turner had led him and his men out of so many situations where they had no right to live to talk about it, that Parker thought of him more as an angel of God Almighty Himself than a simple man to befriend. In those same years, Parker also watched Turner take on the many burdens of hundreds of broken and hopeless men and fix them up, good as new, over and over again.

*What would cause so many men deprived of food, rest, proper clothing, and personal safety to put off for three entire days the thing they wanted most in life?* Parker thought.

The only answer was their need to take one more sip from the well that had never failed to give them strength and hope, never emptied, and never asked for anything in return. Turner was that well.

"Joseph?" Turner gently injected himself into Parker's thoughts.

"You ask a great thing," Parker said hesitantly. He was ashamed to admit that he was as selfish with his commander's profound wisdom and kindness as the rest of them.

"What do you mean?" Turner inquired, not fully understanding the effect his offer of friendship was having on his lieutenant.

Parker raised his head again and peered deep into his commander's eyes. Even as a young boy, his dad would tell him that if you wanted to know what someone was thinking, you should look deeply into their eyes. Eyes can't lie: eyes will validate or betray you, reveal goodness or uncover evil, confirm truth or expose lies. So, Parker searched. When he saw what he was looking for, he continued.

"No man is without burdens, and yours must truly be great," Parker stated intuitively. "So why is it that you know all about me and my burdens, yet I know nothing of you and these burdens you carry?"

It was Turner's turn in the hot seat. He was now being asked to reflect on a simple, but significantly meaningful, question, put forth earnestly. Parker was right, of course. Turner did carry many burdens, and until recently, he believed the majority of them were the result of this terrible war and would diminish rapidly with its conclusion. They did not; if anything, they only intensified. Without the distraction of battle, he must now learn and accept that he was, once again, alone in this world. In some respects, however, his lack of a family might have saved his life and the lives of his men. There had been no cherished loved one to preoccupy his mind, and he never once suffered from homesickness. There was only war and the next battle to survive.

There were, of course, the many names and faces of men he had come to know, and then lost, and that troubled him greatly. He found that writing down their names in a journal helped him to forget them sooner, or at least recover enough to get his mind back on the business of killing the enemy before they killed him and any more of his men.

This recovery technique was very useful, and he discovered it purely by accident. He started listing the names of those he knew who had died in battle, even before he was given his command. When others were writing to their loved ones back home, he would write to the loved ones of his deceased comrades on small scraps of paper and stuffed them in his Bible. His intention was to have something of an answer to the basic, "What happened?" "When?" and "Where?" questions, in the event he was to ever meet up with a distraught family member. He soon realized that this was not enough, and so he began entering these names into a journal, along with his personal reflections of the person. He would recount the talks he had with them, any names mentioned, and how courageous they had been in battle. Some accounts were only a paragraph, some several pages long. Whenever he delayed in entering these names into his journal for too long, it would make him uneasy and less effective as a leader. After the entry, however, no haunting memory remained.

Still, he did not consider these men his friends, and as much as he needed and wanted true friendship, he knew that any close relationship of this nature during times of war was impractical. He had already felt the sting of losing one friend and the debilitating effect it had had on him. Life and death were rendered too randomly to risk that again. Now that this war was over, was it time to let down his guard?

If so, he could think of no one he felt more comfortable befriending than Parker.

"Sir?" Now Parker gently injected his presence into Turner's thoughts.

"Once again, nothing escapes you, Lieutenant," Turner said with a sheepish grin.

"Necessity has helped form me into this creature you see before you... and a poor friend I am, I'm afraid," Turner admitted. "I cannot say with certainty that I would have changed how I have approached these last four years, but if my actions have prevented us from becoming good friends, then I will consider it one of the greatest regrets of my life."

Parker continued his surveillance of Turner's eyes as he spoke. This only confirmed what he already knew to be true: his commander was speaking the truth, and he was truly the honorable man he had presented himself to be.

"If, however, you can total up all your grievances with me, then you might find I fall within the seventy-times-seven forbearances prescribed by our Savior," Turner continued. "And, with the benefit of a clean slate, I will from this point forward present my life as an open book, for whatever it is worth, and strive to be considered worthy of your friendship."

Parker had broken the stubbornness of many horses in his lifetime and experienced a unique feeling of relief and gladness the moment it happened. He was convinced that he had little to do with Turner's conversion, yet he could not help feeling those exact same emotions now. However, having had to endure his commander's self-imposed isolation and aloofness for four long years, Parker was not about to let this young man off so easily. He began to slowly pace the room. With head down and hands clasped behind his back, he walked back and forth in front of Turner, as if contemplating the next move on a chessboard; a practice his general employed many times in front of him before making a final battle decision. Every so often Parker would hesitate, as if to say something, but then continue on without a sound. Finally, after what seemed an eternity, Parker stopped and addressed his commander.

"I will agree to your offer of friendship on one condition," Parker said sternly.

"Of course, Joseph. If it is within me to do, I will do it," Turner responded willingly.

"You must agree..." Parker hesitated again. "You must agree to a stay at our farm for a considerable length of time before pursuing your trip up north."

Parker's scowl suddenly turned to a relaxed smile, then to a suppressed giggle, and finally into uncontainable laughter. When Turner realized he been so kindly abused, he, too, followed the procession from grim apprehension to ecstatic delight until they were doubled over in laughter. Joy returned to both men, and it felt good. It took some time to regain their composure, but as Turner thought more about Parker's invitation, he tried to recall when he had ever divulged his plan to return to Pennsylvania to anyone.

"You claim you do not know me, and yet you have shown tendencies that prove otherwise many times over, Joseph," Turner replied. "Regardless, I will agree to your demands cheerfully and with much gratitude, but I must first ask a favor of you."

"If it is within me to do, I will do it," Parker responded curiously.

"I would like to know... that is to say, might I ask for..." Turner corrected himself politely. "Yes, that is better," Turner continued awkwardly. "May I inquire of you that which you can most certainly provide, without any sense of impropriety or fear of misuse on my part?

"Wait... perhaps I should say it in a different fashion," Turner offered, now in visible discomfort. "With all due respect, I have on my mind the need to know some

44

precious information that, once entrusted into my care, shall be treasured as if it were pure gold.

"No... that is not exactly right, either," Turner babbled on in a losing battle to force himself to be understood. "I simply mean to say that, if you were willing to address my inquiry with the same courtesy as I myself am attempting to provide, I would be most grateful to you for it. You see?

"Well... of course you can't see," Turner chuckled nervously. "I don't believe I have made my desire clear to you yet.

"Did I say 'desire'?" Turner quickly asked apologetically. "I do beg your pardon. I did not intend to use such a word that might carry with it more than one meaning and may have, in error, implied an ill-mannered or immoral disposition..."

"Stop!" Parker demanded loudly in frustration. "Good Lord, man, have you lost your mind? For heaven's sake, if you have a favor to ask of me, then let's hear it and be done."

Stunned by this reprimand, Turner sat down heavily on his cot, as if to take a much-needed breath of air. He sat there, churning one thought after another in his mind with the same unsatisfying results. Hesitantly, he spoke once more.

"Your sister... I do not know her name," Turner muttered softly.

Thinking Turner had started off on some other tangent, Parker grabbed the chair from under the small writing table and, in one motion, spun it around and sat down facing his commander. There he waited, impatiently, as Turner sat looking back at him.

"And?" Parker asked, after a moment or two of awkward silence, but Turner said nothing.

Parker was about to give up hope of any sensible response when it finally dawned on him what Turner was asking.

*Of course! How could I be so dense?* Parker thought. *In battle, this man was as clever as a coyote, but in matters of love, he is apparently as helpless as tumbleweed in a tornado. This whole exercise was simply a good man's effort to discover the name of a desirable woman... and the focus of that attraction is my sister.*

Parker grinned approvingly and leaned in towards Turner.

"Her name is Margaret Jane," Parker answered, now speaking in his role as his sister's older brother. "Sometimes she likes to be called Jane, others times MJ; depends on the day of the month, if you know what I mean." Turner responded with a quizzical look. Parker continued.

"Anyway, if I am not mistaken, I believe you two are close in age. I have mentioned your name many times in my correspondence back home, Philip."

An appreciative smile had not been on Turner's face long when he heard the pounding sound of a horse at full gallop and closing in fast on their location. Both he and Parker stood and reached the tent's doorway at the same time the unknown rider was pulling up hard on the reins to get his horse to stop abruptly.

"Major General Turner, sir?" the rider inquired with a salute.

"I am he, Sergeant," Turner said, returning his salute.

"General Lee requests your presence immediately, sir," the sergeant spoke in boldness.

"What is this about, Sergeant?" Turner asked.

"We have received word that Mr. Lincoln, the Northern President, has been shot this very night, sir," the sergeant said cautiously.

"My God, no," Turner exhaled.

# 3

# Peace and Joy

T he following day, it was announced that the United States president had succumbed to his wounds, and a Union manhunt had begun for a man named Booth. The assassination did not change anything with regards to Grant's pardon, however, and Turner's men were still free to leave. Parker remained in the area of Appomattox Court House a few more days, meeting with friends of the family. Because of his family's long history of raising some of the finest horses in Virginia, the Parker name was well known and well respected in just about every town and village between Richmond and Lynchburg. Therefore, spending an afternoon here or an evening there, while keeping the encampment as the central hub, was easily attainable for him. Besides catching up on some of the relatively trivial news from a region mostly untouched by war, Parker discovered that his two older brothers, along with the cavalry to which they were assigned, had passed that way late last summer after doing battle up in the densely wooded area below the Rapidan River, appropriately called "the Wilderness". Parker already knew about this battle, and that General Lee had dealt a severe blow to the combined armies of Grant and Meade. It was also the first time Parker had heard the name "Grant" referred to as being a formidable opponent on the battlefield, unlike the many other weak-kneed Northern generals with whom he was accustomed.

As youngest siblings often do, Parker's younger brother Caleb went off and joined the Confederate Navy, instead of following in the footsteps of the older, supposedly wiser brothers. In spite of this blatant heresy among horsemen, his precocious younger brother had become a first-rate seaman and was, in fact, made helmsman on the massive new ironclad *CSS Tennessee* under the command of Admiral Franklin Buchanan. The last Parker heard, Caleb's ship was stationed down in Mobile Bay, Alabama—a vital supply route for the Confederacy. Parker had not seen any of his brothers since the war began and had not heard of their fates for close to a year. The actual sighting of his two older brothers was welcomed news, and it boosted his spirits considerably.

This extended respite also allowed him to keep a watchful eye on his former commander a few more days before making his trip homeward. He wanted to be certain that a latent melancholy did not creep back into the mind of his younger friend and retake his joy.

*Isn't that what friends do?* Parker reminded himself properly.

On the other hand, Turner's days were kept busy helping the North's Corps of Engineers' attempt to untangle personal property from government property, and then determine what of the United States government's newly acquired property was still useful. It appeared these Yanks were as eager to get back home as his boys were and appreciated any assistance they could get, especially when that help came from a fellow West Pointer who knew as much about their business as they did. Turner would, of course, document all of his conversations and findings, and add them to his mounting inventory of notebooks and journals, which now filled two large tack boxes.

It did not go unnoticed by Turner that his former lieutenant had yet to take advantage of his honorable discharge and return home. In fact, not only was Parker still there, in the four days since saying their good-byes (the same night Lincoln was shot), a great many chance encounters had occurred between them. So frequent were these incidental run-ins that Turner felt much like a rabbit and Parker the hound. There was little doubt about it—he was being spied upon.

This conspicuous subterfuge went on long enough, and Turner decided the table needed to be turned on his crafty friend. On the following day, he made himself so scarce that when Parker came prowling around, he was nowhere to be found. Like clockwork, Parker arrived in the afternoon. From a safe distance, Turner watched as Parker went from place to place, in a vain attempt to run into his missing friend once again; this included three visits to his sleeping quarters. He then noticed Parker's stride become longer and his purpose more determined. Parker's inquiries as to his whereabouts were becoming abrupt and less pleasant with soldiers from both the South and the North. Finally, when Turner thought Parker might start another war, he popped out from behind a covered wagon unexpectedly, thereby startling his anxious friend.

"Lose something, Joseph?" Turner quipped with a wry smile.

"Not sure of your meaning," Parker replied hastily, as if he were a child caught with his hand in the cookie jar.

"I can't help but notice that you are still here... and dismayed that we have not been able to talk for any suitable length of time," Turner said earnestly. "You must have many questions for me, and I look forward to answering all of them during my stay at your farm."

"I am glad to hear you say that, Philip," Parker replied in obvious relief. "I must admit to you that I have had a concern for your health, and a fear that you may be wavering on your promise of a visit, in a sense of devotion to your brother." Parker paused a moment and then continued.

"But I can see that a proper diet has put a bounce back into your step, and a clean shave has given you back the appearance of a much younger man. What you decide to do with your brother laid to rest in Pennsylvania is none of my business."

*So, that's it*, Turner thought. *He thinks I am capable of doing something I have not given a second thought to since our pledge of friendship... and the discovery of the name Margaret Jane.*

"Well, then, I think I have an idea that will put both our minds at ease," Turner began. "If you would be kind enough to take as many of my journals as you wish back home with you, I would be most grateful. As you know, I have accumulated a large body of work over time, and every remembrance is of great importance to me. But for the life of me, I have not come to any workable solution on how to transport all of it—short of a horse and buggy."

"And quite a large buggy and hearty steed it would take, too!" Parker stated, tongue-in-cheek. Parker thought about this request for a moment and then spoke.

"As you know, I have many friends within a stone's throw from here, and every one of them has offered to me whatever I need from whatever they have left. I shall have a horse and buggy by tomorrow and will carry with me the two trunks that I know of, and anything else that may lighten your load."

"Then it is agreed," Turner pronounced. "You will leave for home tomorrow, to the long-awaited relief of your family, I am sure, and I shall follow within a fortnight." Comfortable with this resolution, they separated, each to their own commitments.

"Wait!" Turner snapped. "I don't believe I have adequate directions."

"You need not worry about that," Parker said reassuringly. "Stay on the Richmond Stage Road going east, and on the second day, begin asking the local folk where the Parker farm is located. I will let people know along the way you are coming."

The following day, Parker was at Turner's makeshift cabin by sunrise with horse and wagon, his own horse tied behind it. Turner almost didn't recognize him because he, too, was now clean-shaven and came wearing well-cut, civilian clothes, from head to toe.

"Morning, Philip. These are yours," Parker greeted Turner, while handing him a set of civilian clothing, complete with hat and shoes, no less. "They are compliments from a grateful citizenry."

Turner was so taken aback with such generosity that he could only stand by and wait for the right words to express his gratitude. After several long seconds, he spoke.

"I will not depreciate their kindness with an offer of repayment, nor will I ask their names should they wish to remain anonymous, but you must send word promptly of my deepest gratitude."

"I will do so, even though I believe they already know this because I have told them of your character," Parker promised. "For now, however, I would like to transfer your papers out of those antagonizing military tack boxes and into these less offensive travel chests, if you don't mind, in case I should pass our friends from the North on the road home.

"Again, you cause me to wonder which peril would have plunged me into ruin, if not for you pulling me back to safety," Turner declared. Parker smiled but said nothing.

When all was made ready, Parker climbed back up onto the wagon and took hold of the reins. Before giving his horse the brisk command to start off, he reached out his hand and spoke.

"Stay well until our reunion in a fortnight, Philip."

Turner grasped Parker's hand firmly.

"And may the Lord make straight your path home, Joseph."

With that, Parker was gone. Now that the problem of how to transport his large cache of documents was solved (and his well-meaning friend no longer shadowed him), all of Turner's concentration turned to what was to be done once his obligation here was complete.

"Lord, you have spared my life, and I am thankful," Turner prayed on bent knee. "How may this servant bring glory to Your name?"

There he stayed a while, kneeling as if waiting for an actual response. It would have been the first time God or one of His angels actually responded verbally, but he was commanded to be still when seeking God's will in earnest. The imperative "Be still, and know I am God" from Psalm 46:10, was a great comfort to him, and he had taken this posture many times in these last few years. Therefore, unless prompted by the Almighty to do otherwise, Turner remained committed to the monumental task of setting things right in the South.

*Where, in the whole of the South, would the federal government want to spend their time and money first?*

Turner pondered, but only for a moment because the answer came quickly. *Richmond, of course!*

*The city had been the target of bombardment and seizure during war, and it will become the target of investment and renewal now that it's over*, Turner reasoned. *If the North can repatriate the city that stood alone as the symbol of rebellion, they can repatriate any city in the South.*

Turner had visited the vibrant Virginia State Capitol many times before the war, with his last visit coming soon after his promotion to major general a little over a year ago. It was actually an invitation to one of the town's "Starvation Balls", at which he was introduced to some of Richmond's highest-ranking officials and a few of the area's most powerful property owners. He quickly discovered the title of these social events to be a misnomer, and the only one's starving were the town's citizenry and the soldiers defending them—certainly not anyone in attendance that night. Nevertheless, in the grand scheme of things, he knew these charades were important to the war effort, and at this particular gala, he had even caught a glimpse of President Jefferson Davis making his way around the room.

Turner also remembered early in the evening that the city's political figures were intrigued with his understanding on the North's utilization of their railroad and telegraph systems, whereas the landowners and local businessmen were more captivated with his updates on the status of surrounding roads and bridges. In fact, Turner noticed he was quickly becoming a bit of a celebrity, due to his undeniably accurate and plain-spoken assessment of how the war was proceeding. When he began to draw a crowd with his fascinating talk of life after war, he felt it best to restrain himself from divulging too much information with too many people too soon. He left the bountiful Starvation Ball that night feeling confident in his ability to gain support for his ideas—and a notebook full of names, titles, and addresses of those hoping for a little more individual conversation with him.

Much had happened since then, and he had now committed himself to delay when immediacy was necessary. Promises and deals would be made quickly. The flow of Northern cash into the South (and into Richmond) would soon follow. He must not linger at the Parker farm, no matter how comfortable the setting—or how attractive the girl.

When the time came for Turner to leave, there was little left to carry, giving him the impression that he must be forgetting something. He finally tried on the civilian clothing given to him by Parker and found everything to be a perfect fit. Tucked deep into the pocket of the britches, he even found a small fold of Northern greenbacks totaling fifty dollars and a note with his name on it. This last gift set him to wondering what could possibly fall into his lap next.

*Be careful not to think more of yourself than what you truly are, Mister Turner,* he reminded himself. *You are nothing more, in deed, than an unworthy beneficiary of the appreciation good folk had for the many that fought and died serving their country.*

For no particular reason, Turner had an urge to stop by the general store on his way out of town. He had not been in there since the day of the surrender, when they had stopped taking Confederate money as an acceptable means of commerce. A tiny bell attached to the top of the door jingled excitedly as he entered the shop. A cheerful voice from a back room invited him to have a look around, after cleaning his boots at the door, and that it would take a moment longer if he needed assistance. Turner looked down at his muddied boots and quickly reached for the stiff, bristled brush and waste pan provided at the doorway to clean them.

*Now, how did he know that?* Turner thought.

Once inside, the store seemed much smaller than the exterior of the building suggested. This was due, in large part, to the difficulty the sunlight was having in circumventing the many obstacles in its path. Whatever light that was allowed to enter the room from the storefront windows was almost immediately absorbed into the dark, unfinished wood floors, walls, and ceiling: and then only if the floor, wall, or ceiling were not already occupied by a sign, shelf, box, barrel, crate, table, chair, counter, or the large cast iron stove. As his eyes grew accustomed to the dimness, Turner noticed that it was indeed cluttered but clean. He also noticed that there appeared to be more display furniture than merchandise, but whatever was for sale was neatly arranged and clearly priced. As promised, the proprietor showed up momentarily and gave Turner a good look before saying anything more.

"Good day, sir," the short, stout, gray-haired man began. "It is with deep regrets that I must inform you that we no longer accept Southern currency and, as you can see from my display case here, I have more side arms than I can sell in a lifetime."

Again, Turner looked down at himself. He was dressed in civilian clothes, carried no weapon of any kind, and had not spoken a word that might suggest he was of southern descent. How would this man know to say these things?

"Good day to you as well," Turner replied. "If I may inquire, what gave me away?"

"I must beg your pardon, sir," the old gentleman said sincerely. "I hope my comments did not offend you, but I do not recognize you and assumed you to be here with one of the two visiting armies. And even though you have put aside the battle dress of our countrymen, you are not so fat as those damn Yankees. Please correct me if I am mistaken so far."

"You are not mistaken... and please continue if there is more," Turner asked.

"As such..." the man hesitated. "You most likely have little to offer as payment for what remains of my once well-stocked store, other than currency that has no value and a service revolver, if only I could accept another as trade."

"And, out of curiosity, how did you know to remind me to clean my boots at the door?" Turner asked politely.

This caused the kindly old man to let out a hearty laugh.

"Oh my, my, you must think I am more clever than I truly am," the old man admitted. "You see, my regular customers know my door bell and my preference for cleanliness. They will enter without hardly disturbing my bell at all and with clean shoes. You, on the other hand, nearly took my bell off its pinnings and would therefore, in all likelihood, not know how much of my time is spent trying to keep the dirt on the outside of these walls."

This caused Turner to laugh with delight. He then looked more closely at the display case full of pistols, and his laughter slowly faded to a reverent hush. He knew these guns. In saving the life of their owners, these guns more than likely took the life of another. He wondered what the owners must have received in return. An elixir, perhaps, to help ease the memory of having to kill one or more of those "fat" Yankees, whose dreadfully frightened eyes stared back at them as they lay dying at their feet. Even now their eyes haunted him, blaming him, always blaming him. When an unexpected tear hit the display glass, it released him from his own tortured memory, and he quickly turned away.

"It is obvious that you have been very generous to our countrymen in your bartering," Turner acknowledged. "Should I find something of interest, do you accept Northern currency, then?"

"I do, sir. Indeed, I do," the shopkeeper said excitedly.

"Well then, let me have a look around," Turner continued. "I'm quite sure I will find something, although I am not so sure what it is I came in for."

If one were looking for something in particular, finding it was made easier because the shopkeeper had everything grouped in sections of like-kind items. The food and consumable section had its spices, flour, sugar, molasses, and actual coffee beans, not the mashed hard corn or ground Hickory he drank, but never could get used to. This was a section that only a month ago would have convinced him he had died and gone to heaven. The apothecary section still had some medicines, soaps, and toiletries. Items for the home—such as lamps and lanterns, pots and pans, dishes and utensils—had their sections, as well as a dry-goods section, which included bolts of cloth, pins and needles, thread and ribbon, and buttons and clasps. These were all things Turner could do without, or would have been able to acquire from his Northern counterparts if he wished. In fact, he was quite certain that much, if not most, of the foodstuff was being procured from the supply trains before they ever reached the Yankee storehouses, and then repackaged for sale. In any event, Turner was determined not to leave without purchasing something from this kindly old patriot.

*You can never have too many blankets, and mine is a bit worn*, he thought.

Turner crossed the room to where he saw a small assortment of neatly stacked blankets, lying in four rows across another glass-topped display case. As they all looked about the same, he grabbed the top one as he approached, and was about to turn and leave, when he caught a glimpse of a brightly colored object inside the display case beneath the blankets. When he separated the blankets to get a better look, he discovered the object to be a women's parasol. There was only one, and it alone occupied the protected space under glass. It was the last thing Turner expected to see because it was so out of place here, like a rose trapped within the thickets of a briar patch. Maybe that was why it lay hidden and perhaps forgotten.

*Who would purchase such a winsome item in these troubled times?* he thought.

Even so, the delicate instrument under the glass slowly refocused his brooding thoughts about side arms and worn blankets to more pleasing reflections, such as the most wondrous gift Almighty God gave man when He created woman. Women were then made all the more appealing in their summer dresses and fancy parasols.

*This would do well to shade such a lovely face as that which Miss Margaret Jane possesses from the harsh summer sun, no doubt*, he thought twice. Without lifting his head or taking his eyes off this buried treasure, he spoke.

"May I inquire as to the cost of this parasol? It does not appear to be priced."

No response came immediately, but neither did Turner take notice immediately. He was still being held captive in a semi-lucid daydream of a life without war. In fact, he was about to ask this very same question again, as if the initial question had never been asked or had not been asked for such a long time that a fresh inquiry was necessary. The intention to speak again, however, was enough to cause him to pivot his head slightly, so as to direct his hearing toward the shopkeeper's last known whereabouts. When this maneuver failed to produce a better result or a sound of any kind, he continued turning his head until it could turn no more, then his shoulders, then his waist, and then his feet until he had finally performed a full rotation of his body, only to find he was once again alone in the room.

"Hello?" he called out, as he made his way back across the room to the cash register.

"Yes, yes, I am still at your service and beg your pardon another moment," the now-familiar voice came from the back room.

"Please, do not feel rushed on my account," Turner replied.

*What are you thinking asking about a parasol, when the whole South has been laid to waste?* Turner rebuked himself as the shopkeeper reappeared.

"Ah, I see you have found yourself a blanket," the gentleman said. "And a fine blanket it is, too. Made from the finest cotton the South ever produced. It will take Miss Strauss a week on her loom to manufacture one blanket, if you must know. Will there be anything else?"

"No... I mean yes," Turner replied nervously, but did not say anything more.

"And that would be?" the gentleman asked, as he looked on the counter and again at Turner for the item he may have missed.

"The parasol," Turner stated shyly. "What are you asking for it?"

"Parasol? Hmm," the gentleman said quizzically. "To what parasol are you referring?"

"In the glass case... under the blankets, over there," Turner replied, finding it difficult to speak other than in short, choppy statements.

"My word, I had forgotten all about that one," the gentleman said in a reminiscing tone. "I used to have quite a nice collection of them before the war. So, there is a lady back home?"

"Yes... I mean no," Turner confessed merrily, but then denied abruptly.

"Well, which is it, young man?" the gentleman asked in a playful manner and smiled.

When his lighthearted inquiry did not produce the kind of joyful reaction he had expected, the kindly old man backed off. He had seen this look of uncertainty and distress a hundred times in the past month; men who had entered the war not much older than children now expected to return home unscathed by it. If he had not lost his own grandson to this detestable conflict, he may have gone on with this careless bantering but not now. Now, he would have eagerly traded that parasol for Turner's side arm, if it would bring him peace.

"Son, there is no shame in wanting to purchase something nice for someone you have affections for, regardless of how she might receive it," the kindly old man said with impassioned empathy. "In my mind, the sooner we get back to the Lord's good purpose for men and raising families, the better off we will be.

"That will be five dollars for the blanket, which I will split with Miss Strauss, and five dollars for the parasol, which is far less than was paid for it, I can assure you."

"I will take the blanket for five dollars," Turner began, encouraged by what he heard. "But I will not ask you to part with the parasol for less than ten dollars." Both men stood straight and tall gazing upon one another, astonished with the other's generosity.

"Agreed!" the sharp response came with another hearty laugh. The old man then opened and closed several drawers and cupboards beneath the register. After a minute or two of this curious behavior, he finally brought to the counter a pair of lady's gloves and continued speaking. "But only if you accept these silk gloves free of any charge. They are the only set left."

This latest act of kindness caught Turner off guard.

"You must understand that without their beautiful umbrella to hold on to, they would only languish here," the shopkeeper said in a hushed voice, as if the gloves had ears to hear.

"I accept your offer with humble gratitude," Turner said in disbelief and handed the storekeeper three five-dollar bills. He was taken aback when he was presented the parasol in its own tailor-made carrying case.

*This thing must have sold for ten times what this man had asked and five times what I paid*, Turner thought, as he surrendered to the gentle man's goodwill and walked toward the door with his purchases.

"I don't believe I got your name, young man," the shop-keeper called out to Turner, as he was about to exit.

"Philip Turner, sir," Turner replied.

"Well, good day, Mr. Turner," the old gentleman said.

"Good day to you, as well," Turner replied and left.

*Major General Philip Turner*, the storekeeper thought with a grin. *I should have guessed. Joseph was exactly right about him... exactly right. And won't Miss Margaret be surprised, too*?

# 4

# Turner's Journey

M iss Strauss's new blanket immediately became the winsome parasol's protective shroud, and the precious cargo would not leave Turner's side. Without his papers to occupy his mind, the gift and how it was to be presented consumed nearly all his thoughts as he traveled. He passed several Union patrols, but only one asked to see his parole pass. The request was cordial, however, and a genuinely respectful salute was shared upon its completion. It seemed strange to him that at the end of the second day, he was told by one of the locals that it would still take another full day to reach the Parker farm. This was especially strange for someone who was considered to be an expert at making good time.

For the life of him, he could not think of one good reason why this trip was taking longer than expected. The weather could not have been more suitable for making haste; his burden was light, thanks to Joseph's generous offer to carry his trunks; and for the most part, the Yanks were letting him be. Turner began to wonder if there was something that had become more important than getting to Richmond and initiating one of his many ideas of rebuilding the South.

*Could it be that he might be dragging his feet?*

*But why?*

*Could the reason be that, despite all the time and effort, he had not produced a single satisfactory explanation for the gift?*

That would be considered crazy in anyone's book, except that at one point his frustration in this regard had him considering giving up the gift to the first little girl he passed along the way.

*Or could it be that, regardless of the explanation, Joseph's little sister might reject the gift... and him?*

Then he remembered what the kindly old shopkeeper had said about being reluctant to bestow a gift, simply because of what the person might think of it... or you. This was especially true if there might be some new affection involved. If confusion and sweaty palms were signs of affection, then it was true, and he must remain vigilant.

As in battle, uncertainty and negative thoughts must not be allowed to cloud his resolve. The success of this mission was to make a good first impression, and that was dependent on the presentation of this gift. Battlefield analogies might not be the most appropriate theme for expressing affection, but he felt he needed to stick with his strengths at the moment.

The following morning, Turner rose early. This had been his custom the previous two days, so any significant acceleration beyond his recent sluggishness was highly unlikely. Only this morning he noticed a lone horseman off in the distance, traveling in his direction at a great speed. Though he would lose eye contact from time to time, because of the peaks and valleys in the road, there was something familiar about this horse and its rider. It did not take long to realize the identity of this swift horseman.

"Joseph!" He called out loud, and only then did he find himself picking up his pace. When the two finally did meet, Joseph spoke first.

"Well, well, if it's not the great cavalry general, Philip Turner," Joseph boasted mockingly. "So swift is he that some refer to him as 'Little Jeb', but I think I shall rename him 'Little Mac' instead!"

Joseph created the moniker "Little Jeb" for this moment and in jest. It called to mind Major General J. E. B. Stuart, the ubiquitous West Point cavalryman for the Confederacy who seemed to appear everywhere at once. If, however, you were to use the nickname "Little Mac!" in public, whether it be in the North or the South, everyone would know you were referring to George B. McClellan, the short-statured general for the Yankees. So persistently slothful was "Little Mac" that Lincoln would eventually relieve him as commander of the Union's Army of the Potomac, shortly after the Battle of Antietam, for allowing General Lee's decimated army to escape back into Virginia and prolong the war.

Unwilling to admit the truth and unable to come up with a suitable white lie, Turner tactfully changed the subject.

"How did you know to find me here, my dear friend?"

Joseph had started off early himself and rode as if he were being pursued by an enemy intent on his demise. He was in no mood for his friend's art of redirecting the conversation away from himself, but was immediately disarmed by Turner's meekness. All Joseph could do was take a deep, cleansing breath and answer the question.

"Little goes unnoticed and uncirculated in these parts," Joseph replied. "To be frank, when I did not see you yesterday, I feared something had gone wrong."

"You mean that I may have veered northward... towards Pennsylvania, maybe?" Turner offered in a somewhat disappointed tone.

"You are a man of your word, Philip; that thought did not cross my mind," Joseph replied. "But as a commanding officer of some acclaim, I was concerned that one of these Yankee patrols may have revenge on their minds."

"Then please forgive me my sluggishness," Turner apologized. "Of those many patrols that crossed my path, only one asked to see my pass, and that experience was as polite as could be expected. I am sorry if my delay has caused you any distress, Joseph."

"You are all right, and that is all that matters," Joseph replied. "All this talk of delay, and now we must delay a little longer to allow Spirit to catch his breath. He is a strong horse, but I'm quite sure he thought the days of riding that hard were behind him."

"At least his master was not being shot at," Turner said, and they both laughed heartily.

They spent the next hour reminiscing on some of the more comical aspects of soldiering between narrow escapes. Then Joseph described how his two older brothers made it home with assorted wounds, but both had full use of their arms and legs. His younger brother, however, lost his life honorably as helmsman on the *CSS Tennessee* in the naval battle of Mobile Bay, Alabama. His mom and sister were grieving his loss terribly. His father attempted to hide his feelings, but Joseph noticed tears well up in his father's eyes without explanation or warning.

"And you, Joseph?" Turner asked with utmost compassion. "How are you doing, knowing this thankless war has taken the life of your brother?"

"I was not as close to Caleb as my sister was," Joseph admitted. "But of all the brothers, myself included, he was the closest to God. We all thought he might follow Father into the ministry. So, I reckon he is where he most wanted to be." After a short, reflective pause, Joseph continued. "We were told that after the explosion, there was not much left of my brother to bury, but some personal items were recovered. His Bible was given to my sister."

When Turner felt sure that his friend had said all he was going to say about the matter, he spoke.

"In life and in death, our brothers have presented us with a valuable lesson," Turner began. "You and I may never match up to their faithfulness, but we all must be ever ready to kneel before our Maker and give an account of our words and deeds."

"You are right, of course, Philip," Joseph said solemnly, "Just as I must give an account to my family of why I have kept you so long once I found you. They are all waiting to see the man that delivered their son and brother from the chilling clutches of a heartless war."

"Well, let's be off then," Turner exclaimed, "so that I may correct that lopsided idea of deliverance and share with them the many times my valiant lieutenant saved me from an early grave."

"We shall see whose side of the story they believe," Joseph replied, and they were off.

The trip back still took longer than Joseph wished. Once they were observed close to a neighboring town, many of the people there would come out and request an introduction to the war hero they had heard so much about; and they were not going to take no for an answer. Joseph only had himself to blame for this. His extensive writing back home detailed how his commander's bold, prophetic decision-making on the battlefield would time and again allow his cavalry to win impressive victories against insurmountable odds. In fact, a few of these townsfolk asked for a more complete description of a specific battle that had been left out of Joseph's letters. This request was too much, however, and was flatly rebuffed. When they were able to move on, the children would run, skip, and jump beside their horses until they came to the end of town.

"I am beginning to think my coming out to retrieve you was a big mistake," Joseph lamented. "All of this lollygagging could have been avoided if these people thought you were simply another stranger passing through town."

"Have patience with them, Joseph," Turner said, somewhat embarrassed by the attention. "It has been a long, bitter war. I am certain they have all lost someone dear to them. For my part, I will oblige them as long as they understand that I cannot, and will not, harbor any ill feelings toward our fellow countrymen up north."

It was late into the afternoon when they turned onto a long, tree-lined road that would soon lead them to the Parker home. It did not take long for the trees lining the road to become absorbed into a dense forest of Virginia pines. After some time, this canopy of trees opened up into a wide, grassy vale, filled with every kind of spring wildflower. It was contained by high rolling hills of pines, mixed with red oaks and maples, and, standing above them all, the American chestnut as tall as a hundred feet. The sun was still high in the western sky, and everything took on extraordinary illumination through eyes not yet adjusted to the brilliant light. The flowered field was divided in half by a long, well-traveled road that led directly to a large, wooden gateway. It was hard for Turner to tell if that gateway was a mile away from where they stood or two, because there were few obstacles in the vast, flat openness to help judge distance. Split-rail fencing in a zigzag pattern extended from each side of the gateway for a mile or so, and then took a turn away from them and down a slope. The field and its flowers followed the fence line until they, too, disappeared beyond the rolling hillside.

There were several stone and wooden buildings located inside and outside the fence, but the most prominent structure was an architecturally astonishing two-story home, constructed entirely of the most perfectly hewn chestnut logs. As they began their canter toward the house, Turner could see the silhouette of a man and two women standing on the ground-level porch, and two large men sitting on horses up front. He presumed that was father, mother, and daughter on the porch and the two brothers on horseback. As they slowed their pace through the gateway, he could see that whole sections of fencing were missing, and the years of neglect on the remainder had taken a heavy toll.

Joseph was now saying something about it taking years to repair so much neglect and ruin, but once Jane came into view, all Turner could do was to mumble something banal in response.

"Are you listening to anything I am saying, Philip?" Joseph finally asked.

"I see no fault in that, Joseph," Turner replied, without looking away from the porch.

"My God, man, you are doomed," Joseph remarked and shook his head. "I must warn you, she will not be as easy to win over as anything you have encountered on the battlefield."

"As you wish, Joseph," Turner replied blindly.

"Do you at least remember her name, Philip?" Joseph asked.

"You couldn't be more right, Joseph," Turner replied without altering his gaze.

"Jane, her name is Jane. Can you say that for me, Philip?" Joseph asked.

"Jane." Turner sighed. "A rose by any other name would smell as sweet."

"Well, that's all I can do for you now," Joseph offered. "The rest is up to you, Philip."

"If you think it best, Joseph," Turner replied blindly.

Joseph and Turner dismounted simultaneously and tied their horses to the same post. As soon as Turner made eye contact with Joseph's brothers, each gave him a respectful salute. Turner returned their salutes and continued his walk toward them, with Joseph following a few paces behind him. As Turner approached the first brother, he stroked and inspected the face, neck, and front quarter of his horse, as if it were the night before battle. Upon reaching the saddle, he turned his attention to the brother and reached out his hand for a handshake, which was so strong that it almost pulled the man out of his saddle.

"Philip Turner," he informed the brother properly.

"Joshua Parker, sir," the first brother replied in kind.

"A fine horse, Joshua," Turner stated truthfully.

"Thank you, sir," Joshua replied.

Turner went through the same routine with the second brother, whose name was Aaron. He then backed away a few feet and addressed them both.

"Gentlemen, that shall be the last time you need salute me or refer to me as 'sir'. We are all now civilian and equal in God's eyes and in station. Is that clear?"

"Yes, sir!" the brothers said in unison.

He then smiled generously, which punctuated his command to these two retired soldiers. This final act not only relieved the tension exuded by the two brothers, but that of those standing on the porch as well. Moving now to the porch, Turner respectfully removed his hat, walked up to Mr. Parker, and offered his hand. The father was initially taken aback somewhat by the youthfulness of this decorated general. He took the young general's hand gratefully and, without realizing it, nearly crushed it in his vise-like grip. Thankful to have his hand back intact, Turner spoke.

"Mr. Parker, sir, I cannot express how grateful I am that you would allow me to spend some time here while I determine how best to make a living and provide for a family of my own someday. I am at your service and expect to earn my keep."

"Hogwash!" the old man shouted, with a voice only a person who spent a lifetime behind a pulpit could produce. "You are our guest. Show me a man who would give his guest a chore, and I will show you a scoundrel."

"It is certainly not my intention to insult you, sir," Turner began, "but if honest and healthy labor helped bring clarity to my thoughts and add strength to my muscles, would my finding a chore of my own choosing be well with you?"

"Well, I suppose if it was good enough for Paul, the apostle and tent maker, to continue his craft while he spread the love of Christ to the known world, I suppose it would be good for you to find a use for your talents," the old man mused. "But only as it pleases you or benefits the Lord God."

"Thank you, sir," Turner replied, as he turned to Mrs. Parker.

He again offered his hand but with palm up, in order to receive her hand to be brought up to his lips and kissed modestly. This he did and then spoke.

"Madam, you must be proud of the way in which each of your sons chose to serve their country and bring honor to your family."

Mrs. Parker stood quiet and motionless for several seconds, but soon started to tremble as tears formed in the corners of her eyes. It appeared as though she might say something, but instead she lunged forward and captured Turner in a bear hug. After some time, she spoke softly through her joyful tears.

"You gave me back my son. How shall I ever repay you?" she whispered softly. "How shall I repay you, dear sir?"

She slowly released her grip and rocked backward as if to faint. Turner immediately had his left arm behind her back and his right arm under both legs. He picked her up and moved her swiftly to the closest porch bench. Mr. Parker was on one knee before his dazed wife in an instant and called for his daughter to bring some water.

"I'm all right, really I am," she said, as she wiped a lingering tear away from her eye with her finger.

"And a clean handkerchief or cloth, Margaret!" Mr. Parker cried out to his daughter.

All three brothers were now standing anxiously behind their father. Margaret Jane arrived with both water and hankie in hand. The mother took both items, thanked her daughter tenderly, and then addressed the family.

"Please, my children, I am not finished with Mr. Turner," she said with more self-control.

Turner had by now moved away from the gathering, but his ears perked up when he heard his name from beyond the wall of adult children surrounding their mother. The children slowly moved backward so that Turner had a clear view of the woman he rescued seated comfortably on the bench.

"God the Father felt it necessary to send His only begotten Son to bear the sins of the world. So it says in the Good Book," Mrs. Parker began and glanced down at her husband, who gave her a nod of agreement.

"Those of us who have accepted this Son of God as our Savior can only be grateful," she continued, as another tear escaped the corner of her eye, "for there is no other means to repay the Father other than with gratitude and obedience."

"On behalf of all the families whose sons' lives you saved throughout this long, torturous war, I am grateful to you," she said, as she looked side to side. "Although I would gladly give you any earthly thing I call my own."

This caught Turner off-guard; this kind of lavish praise always caught him off-guard. Not that it was corrupting him or his humility, but he felt it was misdirected. He always believed that his men were the true heroes and the ones deserving of this praise. Turner suddenly felt great compassion for this woman, whose grief from the loss of a son birthed a much richer appreciation for the lives of three others that did survive.

"I accept your gratitude, Mrs. Parker, and you may keep all your earthly things," Turner replied courteously. "I hope you will accept my gratitude for your son. I assure you that without him by my side, I would not be standing here before you."

"I accept, Mr. Turner," the mother said, while looking over to her son lovingly.

"And please call me Philip," Turner said in response to Mrs. Parker's acceptance, but he was actually gazing in the direction of her daughter.

"Of course I will, Philip," Mrs. Parker said, noticing Turner's new focus of attention. "I am sorry. You have not yet been properly introduced to my daughter, have you?"

"Yes, ma'am... I mean, no, ma'am," Turner answered, without taking his eyes off Jane.

"I mean, I've only seen you in your brother's picture," he was now talking simultaneously to both the mother and the daughter.

"And so it begins," Joseph mumbled to himself.

Turner offered his hand to Jane in the same gentle-manly manner he did to the mother. Jane did not move, but neither did Turner retract his hand. Jane glanced over at her mother as if to ask, "Must I?"

In response, Jane's mother gave a slight movement of her head toward Philip, as if to say, "Yes, you must!"

This brought an immediate scowl to Jane's face, which she maintained as she turned to face Philip again. Instead of placing her hand gently into his, however, she thrust it inches away from his head. Undaunted by either the scowl or the jab, Turner reached up, took her hand in his and kissed it... or, almost kissed it. As soon as his lip barely touched her hand, she jerked it back to her side.

"Wait right here, please," Turner said, as he rushed back to his horse without waiting for a reply.

Jane looked to her mom for answers, but all she got in return was a shrug of the shoulders. Her father gave her an equally uncertain gesture. Joseph, on the other hand, could hardly wait to see what Turner was up to and tried, unsuccessfully, to hide his amusement. Jane, noticing her brother's failing efforts to contain his pleasure in all this, gave him a scowl that said, "If you have anything to do with this, I will kill you in your sleep!"

Turner returned with a blanket, which intrigued everyone. When he was once again standing in front of Jane, he slid the case out from within the blanket and pre-sented it to her.

"It's for you," he said shyly. "I am hoping you like it."

Jane took the case in one hand, but it was heavier than expected and not so evenly balanced, so she had to catch it with her other hand. Turner also reacted as if the gift were going to crash to the ground, and caught both the box and Jane's hand at the same time. They gave each other a brief smile as a compliment to the other's agility.

Turner released his hand and backed away. Jane continued to hold the case out in front of her. The two latches were prominently attached and facing in her direction, yet she made no effort to undo them.

This unusual behavior had the two older brothers shuffling their feet, indicating that if something didn't happen soon, they had a hundred more important things to do. Joseph stood by, anxiously waiting for his sister to do something only an ungrateful lunatic would do. The family patriarch stood patiently and allowed the girl's mother to break the silence in her own time.

"I believe it is meant to be opened, darling," Mrs. Parker stated the obvious sweetly.

Jane undid the latches and opened the case quickly, and then hesitated again. Turner moved in gently and took control of the case, giving Jane the freedom to use both her hands if she wished. Jane reached inside the case, but it was Turner slowly moving the case down and away that produced the gift for all to see. This was no cheap imitation, and everyone knew it. All her life, Jane had watched the haughty ladies from the large plantations prance about with lesser instruments for showing off. Still, she knew how it was to be used, because she had practiced it with a broom handle or a short branch when she was younger and no one was looking. So, with all the gentility of a proper southern debutante, she opened it, placed it on her shoulder, and with some coordinated pressure between thumb and finger, had the thing spinning at a slow, continuous speed. She even did a perfect pirouette with one hand: holding the parasol with the tips of her fingers only, and the other hand holding out the side of the dress her mother had forced her to wear. It made no difference who was watching her now.

"It's beautiful," her mother gushed. "Where did you find such a thing?"

"The general store in Appomattox," Turner answered, without looking away from Jane. "It was the only one left."

Suddenly, Jane stopped her motion. The joyful smile on her face evaporated, she closed the parasol, and looked suspiciously at Turner.

"You march in here like King David, who slayed his ten thousand, and have my whole family worshipping at your feet," Jane began in a low, acidic tone. "But my beautiful and tender-hearted brother died a horrible death in your stinking, filthy war. Do you think a fancy umbrella will earn you some special treatment from me, Mister General?"

"You foolish little child!" Joseph barked loudly. "You have no idea—"

"That's enough, Joseph," his father interrupted calmly. "Margaret Jane, you may accept or decline Mr. Turner's gift, but I will not permit you to disparage his good name and discredit his service to this country and to our family. Do you understand me, daughter?"

"I am sorry, Father," Jane said with some sincerity. "Please forgive me, Mr. Turner." She continued with somewhat less sincerity.

"Of course I do," Turner replied with a hopeful smile.

"Very well, then. The box, please," she stated without returning his smile.

Turner held the case out in front of him and opened the lid. Jane put the parasol back into its housing roughly, but not so roughly as to do it any harm. She then shut the lid with a loud thwack, barely allowing Turner to move his fingers out of the way, and took possession of case and all.

"Thank you, Mr. Turner, and good day, sir," she said and, without waiting for a response, turned and disappeared into the house.

Mrs. Parker excused herself politely and followed her daughter inside. The two older brothers also felt it was time to quit this greeting and, having been given permission by their military superior to treat him as any other citizen, left without a salute.

"She took it," Turner said to himself under his breath and smiled broadly.

"You must excuse my daughter, Mr. Turner," Mr. Parker said, though clearly moved by what his daughter said. "She is taking Caleb's death badly... as we all are. She was right in this: he was a tender-hearted, young man."

"Caleb joined the navy of his own free will, Father!" Joseph protested boldly, still seething from his sister's comments. "There is no excuse for Jane's confused ideas about this war, and you both diminish my brother's bravery and his honor by talking about him in this way."

"You are a soldier, Joseph, and a good one. Your sister and I are not," Mr. Parker answered soberly. "We simply see Caleb's life and death differently, yet we all can say we loved him the same. Be patient with us, son."

"You have my deepest sympathies, sir," Turner offered, in hopes of mitigating the trouble caused by his actions. "If you don't mind me saying it, Caleb sounds much like a young Union soldier I met on the battlefield in Pennsylvania. I find myself praying for this young man's good health often."

"It would appear that you have a kindness of the heart yourself, praying for your enemy, Mr. Turner," his friend's father said respectfully.

"He did me a great service," Turner answered truthfully. "Unfortunately, it appears that my presence here is having a negative effect on your family, sir, for which I am truly sorry. It might be best for me to leave as soon as I can acquire a means of transporting my belongings to Richmond."

"The hell you will!" Joseph shouted, with the same fierce passion he had expressed when Turner stated that he was going to stay on that Pennsylvania battlefield to bury his brother.

"Mr. Turner," Mr. Parker said in the same calm voice. "The decision to stay or to go I leave with you, but do understand this: my wife and I consider it a privilege to have you here with us for as long as you wish to stay. The trials the Sovereign Lord has placed before our family did not begin with your arrival and will not end with your departure.

"Joseph will show you to your room, and a light supper is planned for later," Mr. Parker continued, turned, and took the same path into the house, as had done his wife and daughter.

"She actually took it," Turner again, whispered happily to himself. His satisfaction and smile did not last long when, turning to face Joseph, found him staring back ominously with his massive arms folded out in front of his equally massive chest.

"Don't say another word, Philip," his friend commanded. "After we tend to the horses, I will take you to your room where a hot bath will be drawn for you. You will put on the set of clean clothes that was to be laid out for you this morning, and then we will eat. We can talk later... after you have scrubbed, eaten, and come to your damned senses."

\* \* \*

Mrs. Parker did not follow her daughter into the house to confront her or to offer advice unless it was requested; there was simply too much to do. Margaret Jane went directly to her room and closed the door softly behind her. She did not expect a visitor, but she was expected back downstairs shortly to help her mother in the kitchen. She laid the gift on the bed and, after stepping out of her dress, she plopped down beside it.

*He is much more handsome than I expected,* she thought.

Since only a few of his laborers had returned from war, and they were out in the fields all day, it was Mr. Parker who prepared the hot water for Turner's bath. The guest room where Turner would reside was located on the opposite side of the house on the first floor and had its own washroom, equipped with a porcelain-footed tub. This room was rarely used except for the most honored guests. It was well known that it had been occupied by at least two United States presidents, one Confederate president, and almost every Virginia State governor since Patrick Henry. Soon after delivering Turner to his new living quarters, it was Joseph who delivered the two pails of hot water to be added to the tub's tepid water in whatever proportion Turner desired. Before leaving, he informed his friend that supper would be ready in an hour.

Supper was prepared and served cheerfully by mother and dutifully by daughter. Neither woman found a meal eaten so late to be either healthy or enjoyable, so they did not join the men. Turner noticed that Jane was now wearing a different dress than before, and her hair was styled in a different fashion. He did his best not to stare at her too long, but on several occasions their eyes would meet, and he would apologize with a, "You caught me again," half-smile. Only once did she respond to this eye contact, and that was to give him her patent scowl. For whatever reason, Turner took encouragement from this gesture.

*She does notice me, at least,* Turner thought. *But now you must use all the self-control you have, Turner, so not to appear rude or overplay your intentions.*

The conversation at the table soon turned to talk of war and alternated between the battles out west, where the older brothers spent most of the war, and the battles in Virginia, Maryland, and Pennsylvania. Whenever possible, Turner was determined to redirect the success of a battle away from himself and back to his men, and especially to Joseph, when it was appropriate to do so. When asked about his plans to go to Richmond, Turner had everyone at the table leaning on his every word. His bold ideas for using the North's technology and innovation to rebuild and reinvigorate the South captivated his hosts, just as he had captivated the rich landowners and politicians at the Starvation Ball the previous year. Most of this information was even new to Joseph, who, then and there, gave thanks to the Lord for saving this man. This did not go unnoticed by either mother or daughter, who gave the appearance of disinterest. Nevertheless, both were present the entire meal—just not seated at the table.

Mother and daughter went about their business serving, cleaning, and going back and forth between rooms for some purpose or another. Whenever the two met in the kitchen or elsewhere, they would talk freely, but it was made abundantly clear by the daughter there was going to be no discussion concerning the events that occurred earlier on the porch. From time to time, however, the mother would inject a comment regarding their guest, such as, "A most charming and humble man young Mr. Turner is," or, "It seems Mr. Turner is filled to the brim with ideas," or, "My word, what beautiful eyes Mr. Turner has." Margaret Jane chose not to respond to these observations.

When supper was over, Turner politely offered to help clear the table but was rebuffed. When all was put away, the two women said their good-nights and retired to their rooms upstairs. Now furnished with some good Virginia whiskey and tobacco, the men retired to a large, comfortable sitting parlor and continued their conversations late into the evening. Turner declined the alcohol, as did Mr. Parker, but received with great delight real coffee and a pipe. By midnight, the only two left, were Joseph and Philip.

"Now that the others have gone, may I be candid with you?" Joseph asked.

"I would have it no other way," Turner spoke.

This sounded too much like the absentminded responses he was getting this morning once Turner set eyes on his sister. Joseph spoke again.

"Philip, does the rain in Spain fall mainly on the plain?"

"Pardon me?" Turner began, somewhat bewildered by the rhyme in the form of a question. "I'm quite sure I have no idea about the rain in Spain."

"Good, I have your attention!" Joseph continued without explanation. "I believe you know where I stand on your leaving the sanctuary of our home too soon, and especially for the reason you gave my father earlier this day. If you truly believe what you say and that my counsel has been of value to you and that, on occasion, perhaps even saved your life, then I beseech you to listen to me now."

"Next to the truth of the Holy Bible, I value your wisdom most," Turner said. "Please continue, and I will heed your words, both easy and uneasy to hear, knowing they are for my good."

"I believe leaving now to be a mistake for reasons of which you have not yet been made aware," Joseph began. "First, I have received correspondence from several sources close to Richmond that tell me most of the city has been burned to the ground. There are conflicting stories as to why this is so. Some say it was our own General Ewell, in an effort to leave nothing for the Yankees to use against them in their retreat, while others say it was the inhumanity of General Weitzel and his Fourth Massachusetts Cavalry."

"Their desperation provides me less reason for delay, not more," Turner interrupted.

"You miss my point, good friend," Joseph responded. "Where chaos reigns, no one will want to listen to your ideas of restoration and unity with the North. There was even a rumor that while the women and children of Richmond have been under constant bombardment and nearly starved, there were huge stores of smoked meats, sugar, coffee, shoes, and clothing in the abandoned government buildings. In this state of confusion, you are more likely to be caught up in who was right and who was wrong than in putting any of your plans into effect; for now, anyway."

"Those are, without doubt, uneasy words to listen to," Turner said sadly.

"So, my question to you is this," Joseph paused. "Will you be going to Richmond to become a damnable politician or remain true to your calling?"

There was much in Joseph's question to consider, and since there was no enemy bent on his destruction sitting a mile away waiting for the sun to rise, Turner had time to think about it. He thought for a moment longer and then spoke.

"You said 'first'. Was there something else you felt I should know?"

"There is," Joseph replied more gently. "Although my baby sister and I do not see eye to eye on many things, she is dear to me, and I wish her life to be safe and happy. It might not appear so at this moment, but I believe the two of you have much in common and much to offer the other... if you are willing to be patient with her."

"Tell me what to do, and I will do it," Turner asked without hesitation.

"Be yourself... that is all," Joseph said, as he stood up and stretched. "It is late, and I am guessing it is not just I who has a busy day tomorrow.

"Oh, there is one more thing," Joseph continued. "You may want to stick around. Any return of your affections could take a while. Good-night."

"Good-night," Turner said, as his friend turned and started toward the stairway.

"Joseph!" Turner called out. "Thank you."

Joseph turned, smiled, and then continued on his way. Turner rose and started off in the opposite direction, slow and measured, but his mind was racing. He knew sleep would still be a long way off that night.

The following morning, Turner woke to the cock's crow and with surprising energy. Unless something different was requested of him today, his intention was to ride the fence line to determine what materials and labor were going to be necessary to restore it and the gateway. The other question was, would this project be something he could complete on his own by his departure date, which also remained in question. From the craftsmanship of the home and the miles of fencing, he guessed there was some kind of woodworking shed on the property for cutting to length and then splitting large quantities of wood. Without a few modern tools in good condition, however, he might need to find some other project less daunting.

He made his way down the long hall in the direction of the kitchen, where he might be able to grab a bite left over from supper before heading out. As he rounded the corner, he saw light peeking out from under the kitchen door and heard his first sound of the morning, a feminine voice humming a song or hymn. He coughed loud enough so that the person on the other side of the door would not be startled when he entered. The voice was that of Joseph's sister, and she was busy opening and closing cupboards, pulling this out of one, and putting that into another.

"Good morning, Miss Parker," Turner said politely. "You have amazing pitch for one up so early!"

"That is because I go to sleep at a reasonable hour, Mr. Turner," Jane stated with minimal inflection in her voice. "You may call me Jane, if you like."

"Thank you; that would be wonderful," Turner said, trying to contain his joy. "But I must insist you call me Philip, please."

A slight smile escaped Jane's mouth, but she said nothing. Turner could not help but notice this ever-so-slight change of conduct toward him. Not wishing this uncontentious dialogue to stop, he spoke again.

"I wasn't sure which name you preferred, since you can go by several names, and that depends on the day of the month, according to Joseph."

Jane scowled and slammed the cupboard door she had just opened. Somehow retaining her composure, she did not turn to face Turner to dispense another taste of her medicine. After a few seconds of thought, she wasn't exactly sure which one of these two fools she was angrier with—her brother for his tasteless suggestion, or his friend for the careless repetition of the tasteless suggestion. This did raise a few questions, however.

*Could this young general be so strong and competent, and yet be so naïve... so benevolent... so sweet... as he appeared to be? How could this man be so successful at war and not be transformed into something hardened and cruel? Did he actually have the hand of God on him, as Joseph suggested in his letters?*

Turner flinched at the sudden interruption of tranquility in the room and was thankful his fingers were nowhere near that cupboard door. Not having a clear view of the expression on Jane's face this time, he continued speaking in hopes of saying something that might begin a conversation.

"Will the others be getting up soon?" he asked politely.

"The others have been up and have already gone off to their duties. You are the last," Jane said, equally as polite. "I have a few minutes before I must see to the hen house. May I boil you an egg, or will coffee do until breakfast? The breakfast bell will not sound for another hour or two."

Feeling rather shamed for oversleeping, and then slightly embarrassed for his obtuse comment about the others, Turner sat quietly for a moment before responding.

"Jane, I must admit to you that I feel a little like the man standing on the edge of the station platform, watching as his train pulls away without him on it, except that this laxity on my part provided me an opportunity to see you once again."

Turner could not believe his courage in openly sharing what was on his heart, but his telling remark did not answer Jane's question and, indeed, seemed to throw her off balance. He quickly realized there was no way for Jane to respond to his remark, other than to approve of their meeting or not. Not liking those odds, Turner spoke again.

"I have imposed upon you long enough, Jane, and believe I can make it until breakfast."

Turner stole another look at her. *Yes, her beauty would sustain me until breakfast*, he thought. He smiled pleasantly and left. Jane remained stationary a moment longer, while several incomplete thoughts unraveled themselves until her mind settled on one.

*What beautiful eyes he has.*

# 5

# Fire!

A day turned into a week, a week turned into a month, and so on. Turner's decision to go ahead with his plans to repair the fencing and rebuild the gateway was an immense project that was still nowhere near completion, but Joseph was right as usual. Richmond was in turmoil, and if he could not begin his reconstruction of the South there, then he would begin it here, and he was happy to do so. The first thing he had to do was resurrect the steam-powered circular saw, which had not been used since the war began. It took several trips into town, among other places, for suitable replacement parts. Turner was as surprised as anyone when it started spinning. Once this amazing feat was accomplished, he built a set of short wagons that could be readily attached to each end of a downed tree, allowing a single horse to pull, rather than drag, it back to the workshop. This had the added benefit of allowing a horse of medium stature to carry greater lengths in half the time. Turner had to modify the cutting table in order to accommodate a larger log, and then he singlehandedly designed an elaborate set of pulleys suspended from the rafters above and a weighted pendulum to help move a log through the saw blade. There were other useful inventions (he was an engineer, after all), but it still came down to him laboring alone from forest to fence rail.

Turner had several fantastic ideas on how to double the size of the gateway and, at the same time, replace the old Virginia pine with American chestnut to match the house and the stable, but the necessity to close the gaps in the fencing and regain the grazing pastures for livestock took precedence. In fact, it gave him great satisfaction to see the cattle, goats, and sheep roaming the fields he enclosed days before, but nothing matched the beauty of a Parker horse, as it glided effortlessly across the open field. The war had diminished their number, but not their strength and majesty.

They were all thoroughbred chestnuts and buckskin horses, except for Jane's dappled, gray-on-white pinto named Topsy. She had intentionally named her pony after the young slave girl in *Uncle Tom's Cabin*—not a particularly popular book in the South. This was not done so much in protest to slavery, although her entire family despised its inhumanity, but rather Jane felt that when her pony was younger she was as stubborn as a mule, like young Topsy. Only by loving her pony, like Eva St. Clare loved Topsy, did she convince her rebellious pony to change, like young Topsy.

From Monday to Saturday, Turner's day rarely varied much. For one, he never again allowed any of the Parker men to beat him to the kitchen in the morning before heading out. From time to time, Mr. Parker would take notice and comment on the fact that no matter how early he rose, Turner always beat him to the kitchen. This innocent observation always put a smile on Joseph's face. Of course, the story of Turner arriving in the kitchen and asking when the others would be getting out of bed—only to discover he was the last one up—was a great source of amusement in the Parker home for quite some time. Nevertheless, Joseph knew that this embarrassment was not the only reason for his friend's early-morning diligence. It also happened to be the perfect excuse for Turner to meet with the one he had affections for without anyone asking questions, including the object of those affections.

Joseph was not the only Parker to come to this conclusion, nor was he the first one to notice. It had always been the habit of Mrs. Parker to assist her daughter in the kitchen on most mornings. Mrs. Parker recalled that when Turner first started arriving earlier and earlier, he talked little but would always ask in the most courteous fashion if there was anything with which he could be of help. Without ever being given anything to do, the undeterred young man began inquiring of her as to what life was like on the Parker farm before the war. This opportunity to recount her fondest memories provided Mrs. Parker with a much-needed outlet, as Turner was patient with her many stories.

Jane hesitated to join in the conversation, even though every bone in her body had something to say. As time went on, however, perhaps she finally came to the realization that Turner was not going away, for she began to express herself more often. It wasn't long after her daughter's decision to begin speaking freely that Mrs. Parker found herself less and less noticed.

Oh, Turner was sure to offer her a pleasant, "Good morning," with genuine sincerity, but then he and Jane would go off on some wild, uninterruptable dialogue, as if they were the only two in the room. They would only stop talking when one of her sons or her husband appeared, but then they would pick up where they left off the following day. On occasion, Mrs. Parker would see Jane ride out on Topsy with some type of refreshment in Turner's direction and not return for hours. Not wishing to inhibit this behavior, of which she approved, Mrs. Parker began coming downstairs later and later, until one day she walked in on a vibrant discussion on who could beat whom in a horse race and found Turner had taken over her kitchen chores.

* * *

Another daily routine on which Turner had placed a high value was to review and prioritize his vast collection of papers. Like the miles of fencing ahead of him, this process seemed to be a task without end. His mind was as sharp as ever, but the sheer volume of names, places, dates, and pictorial diagrams of equipment he had amassed over the years was staggering. He would be utterly lost without these manuscripts. Knowing how valuable these documents were, Joseph had hidden the trunks in the hayloft above the horse stalls in the stable behind the house. Turner had decided to leave them there for protection, but he also discovered the hay in the loft to be a comfortable place to study and take refuge from the afternoon sun for an hour or so.

Sundays were a day of rest and always began with church. Turner would ride alongside the family wagon to listen to Mr. Parker preach God's Word in a small church house outside of town. Attendance there doubled when it was discovered that the famously successful young general had made it his place of worship. The number of families with single daughters in their early twenties quadrupled when it was learned how handsome the young general was. Even a few black families started showing up after their emancipation to hear Mr. Parker preach, and they were most welcomed. In fact, this new integration caused little commotion in the congregation, since Mr. Parker had been professing the sin of slavery since before the war anyway. What trouble it did cause was handled quickly and easily by the Parker boys' more direct brand of persuasion.

Jane was sure to wear her silk gloves and carry her new parasol over her shoulder, but only if it promised to be a perfectly sunny day so not to do any harm to her enviable gift. It did not take long for the church's new young female arrivals to discover who the giver of the gift was, as well as where and when it was acquired. Even its extravagant cost was thoroughly researched, but the price paid was never disclosed. What was still left to the imagination was the "Why?" Jane found the whole preoccupation with her parasol funny, but did nothing to diminish the gossip. Turner was always the gentleman, but only added to the intrigue with his silence on discussing personal matters. On occasion, he even had to gently remind a few somewhat immodest young ladies that this was the day set aside to worship the Lord and, if it was within him to do so, not to distract him from that purpose.

The only exception to this distraction rule would be to engage family members of one of Turner's regiment if they were to discover his whereabouts. By far, most of this correspondence was handled by mail, but every so often someone would travel a distance of a hundred miles or more to hear their beloved's story in person. Therefore, it did not matter where or when he was approached, he would stop everything and take as much time as was needed to fill in the missing years for those who lost their loved ones in battle. Fortunately, the first time this happened, he was able to recall from memory the name and the particulars of how the inquirer's son served and died. From then on, Turner was never without the journals containing the names and biographies of every man with whom he had the honor to serve. Many of those who wrote to him, or took the extra effort to visit him, were family members of men who had actually survived the war. The fact that they were alive filled Turner's heart with great joy.

It was only a few weeks before that Jane secretly overheard one of these heartbreaking testimonials taking place outside the church house during service. She was close by when the couple introduced themselves to Turner before service began and asked to speak to him about their son. Jane could not resist standing breathlessly around the corner of the building from where Turner would share with the older couple what he had written in his journal shortly after their son was killed. This he read:

There was none like young Thomas. He showed up when I took command after the second Battle of Manassas and fought bravely at Sharpsburg. I, myself, witnessed young Thomas take his pistol from its holster, shoot twice while riding at full gallop, and kill two Yankees while I was looking straight down the barrels of their rifles. I promised myself that if we both were to survive this bloody battle, I must, in good conscience, personally extend my hand for saving my life. He received my gratefulness kindly but didn't recall the event; that was young Thomas. He died from a gunshot wound outside of Chancellorsville on May 3, 1863. His body was found and was buried.

"Mr. and Mrs. Miller, your son was one of the best marksmen from a horse I have ever seen," Turner added extemporaneously. "I recall a man say he would miss young Thomas's joke-telling most of all." Turner sat quietly, giving the couple time to absorb what he had told them. The father broke the silence.

"Thank you, Mr. Turner," the father said, in a losing effort to remain poised. "He was our only..." This was all that the man could say before sadness took away his ability to speak. After a brief pause, the mother spoke.

"Did he suffer, Mr. Turner?" she asked tearfully.

*The night of the third*, Turner thought carefully. *Thomas was missing at camp, and so I asked Parker if he had seen him. Parker told me that earlier in the day he watched as Thomas had his killer in his sights, but his pistol jammed. He was then shot himself at point blank range and died instantly. Parker then said some time later that he shot and killed this Yankee.*

"No, ma'am, he did not," Turner responded, in hopes of easing a mother's grief. "I was told by my lieutenant he was shot and was received by our Heavenly Father the next moment."

This news brought tears to Jane's eyes, as she looked around to find something to dry her tears and runny nose. When she turned, she was so startled to see Joseph standing behind her that she let out a hushed cry. Jane had no idea how long her brother had been standing there, but he said nothing. After a second or two, he reached into his back pocket and then extended his crumpled, but clean, handkerchief to her. She could do nothing but hand him her parasol and take the handkerchief, wipe her eyes and blow her nose, fold the handkerchief neatly, and return it to him. From that point, she took possession of her parasol and walked silently back into church.

Having come out of church to find out why his sister and friend had not yet made it inside for service, Joseph stood silently for a second more and then heard Turner's soothing voice come from around the corner of the church.

"Mr. and Mrs. Miller, may I pray for you?"

Joseph did not hear a reply, but he knew immediately what was happening.

*Miller? Miller?* Joseph thought hard. *Thomas... young Thomas Miller!*

"Father, You have brought young Thomas back to Your Self, and yet, in so many ways, we wish we could have him back with us," Turner spoke, as if it were he and God. "When we think this way, we ask Your forgiveness, Lord. Open our eyes, Father. Instead of asking that Thomas come back to us, we should look forward to the day we will all be together again in Your house... for eternity.

"Until that glorious day, Father, I ask in the precious name of Your Son, Jesus, that You will comfort Thomas's folks down here. They suffer right now. Dearest God and Father, we come before You humbly. Fill that brokenness in their hearts and minds with Your love and Your peace and Your joy. We ask this with thanksgiving. Amen."

Joseph pulled the slightly used handkerchief from his back pocket and dabbed his eyes.

*I do miss you, Caleb... but we shall meet again, my dear brother*, he thought and walked slowly back into church.

It was several more minutes before Turner could return to the church service himself, but he would have stayed in that place until the cows came home if that was what the Millers needed. When Turner quietly entered the back of the church, Mr. Parker casually paused in his sermon and glanced in his direction. This was accomplished with great discretion, so as not to concern anyone sitting in the pews. It was also done with great admiration, because he knew of Turner's exception to the rule. His assumption was confirmed when he witnessed the look on his daughter's face and then again on his son's face, as they returned to their seats.

When Turner returned to his seat and saw the distraught faces of Jane and Joseph sitting next to him, he was sorry he had missed such a moving sermon, except that everyone else in the room was quite at ease.

The following day, Turner was out working on the fence. It was before noon, but it was getting darker. The clouds had turned from white to dark gray imperceptibly, and the wind was now bending the tops of the trees in waves. He figured he had about an hour before the storm hit. He stopped what he was doing and headed back toward the house to help secure anything that might want to fly away and to stable the horses. The storm, however, was approaching much faster, and with greater intensity than he first expected. Within a few miles of the house, he saw the first lightning strike hit no more than ten miles from him. The race was on. With a mile to go, sunlight had given up all attempts to penetrate the dense cloud cover, but he could still see the men furiously trying to get as many horses into the stables as they could. Turner's horse, Courage, never accepted a stable for any reason and was, therefore, turned loose as soon as Turner reached the closest building, where he could store his saddle, pad, and bridle. The storm's front was now on top of them, and it was useless to try to do any more outside due to the force of the wind and pounding rain. As soon as the flash of lightning was seen through the shuttered windows, the two-foot thick American chestnut walls shook from their foundation.

It wasn't long after the Parkers and Turner were all safely inside the house when a loud cry could be heard from outside. It was one of the Parker's laborers.

"Fire... fire!" he was hollering over and over.

Joseph was the first to the back door.

"The stables on fire!" he yelled back to the others and exploded out the door, only to be knocked backward by the wind and rain.

Leaning sharply into the wind was the only way Joseph was able to make any progress. His father and brothers followed in a rush and were, likewise, forced backward initially. Turner was the next person to the back door. Through the curtain of rain, he could see the difficulty the Parkers were having, as they made their way slowly toward the burning building.

"My papers!" he said to himself and exited the house a little more prepared for what was to hit him.

The slow pace to the stables gave Turner time to assess the situation before him. The hundred-year-old oak tree standing beside the stables had taken a lightning bolt and split in two. Both halves of the oak were on fire, with the wind fanning the flames faster than the rain could extinguish them. One half of the giant tree fell to the ground harmlessly, but the other half fell onto the roof of the stable, virtually cutting the top of the building in half and then setting it on fire. As he got closer, Turner could see four of Parker's men desperately trying to open the two large doors without success. Apparently, when the fiery tree hit, it also collapsed the building enough to jam the doors tightly. He knew that as soon as those doors were opened, it would become a funeral pyre for the horses, and his precious papers would be gone forever. He had seen this happen to burning buildings many times in battle. His only chance of saving both was to find some small way inside, bring his trunks down from the loft, release the horses from their stalls, and then break the hinges off the doors—all before the structure collapsed on top of him. He had no time to discuss this plan with the others and headed straight for the blacksmith shed.

Jane and her mother, who had been upstairs shuttering windows when the alarm was sounded, were now at the back door.

"Topsy!" Jane screamed. She bolted recklessly out the door and was immediately slammed back into the side of the house.

"Margaret Jane, where are you going?" Mrs. Parker cried out.

"I can't stand here doing nothing, Mother!" Jane called back, as she began clinging to anything stationary that would get her closer to the stables.

Turner returned to the stable with a large blacksmithing hammer. He quickly found a small opening close to where the tree hit and squirmed inside. He could hear the others on the other side of the stable now. The heat inside the building was almost unbearable. Fortunately, the main fire was still contained to the fallen tree and roof line with only small fires on the floor, where pieces of burning wood were falling all about him. It was a miracle these embers had not yet ignited the hay in which his trunks were hidden, but he knew it was only a matter of minutes before this luck would run out. The smoke, however, was hovering perilously close to the heads of the horses, and they were all in a panic—except for one.

In stark contrast to the others, Topsy stood motionless in her stall watching Turner's every move, content with her fate. Turner could hardly take in the hot, humid air and had trouble seeing clearly from the salty sweat that started to sting his eyes. He looked to the loft where his entire future sat in two large trunks, then to the ceiling where fire rained down on top of him, and then to Topsy. He had a feeling that time would not allow him to accomplish all he wanted to do here, and a battle decision needed to be made. Without reservation Turner ran to the doors, and with all his strength he began pounding on the hinges. His original plan was to release the horses first and then work on the hinges. In their frantic states of mind, however, these 1,000-pound horses could easily crush him like a bug before he had a chance to remove just one pin. His only hope was that the door would remain standing at least until he opened the gates to all the stalls.

When the last pin fell to the ground and the door held, Turner began freeing the horses, starting with Topsy. The horses knew where the two stable doors where and, as they were released, began to gather close to them, even bumping into them with their huge bodies. When the final stall was opened and the last horse was free, Turner looked to the door he detached from its hinges. It was still standing, and the only way of escape was now surrounded by a dozen powerful horses. His only recourse was to get one of those horses to finish the job—but how?

The unrelenting heat, humidity, and smoke that were robbing his body of precious fluids by the second, and causing his body to weaken, were now muddling his mind. All he could think to do was pick up several burning branches that littered the floor around him and begin waving them and shouting like a drunkard. Thankfully, it did not take long for one of the largest of these great animals to rear up on his hind legs and kick down the disabled door. Within seconds the horses were outside, but a minute after that, the whole top half of the stable erupted in flames.

The horses were safe, and that gave Turner some satisfaction. For a brief moment, he felt an overwhelming desire to follow them to safety. The heat and smoke had intensified when the door came down, and the driving rain outside was undeniably alluring. There was still a chance to save his own life, he thought, but what good would life be without the contents of those trunks? Turner tried desperately to assess the risk of making it up to the hayloft, but the salty sweat and smoke that made his eyes burn persistently would not wipe away. The best he could do was to find something that appeared like the bottom portion of a ladder in the general direction of the loft. If he had been able to see clearly, he would have noticed that the hay, as well as the upper part of the ladder, was now on fire. The short journey across the room was made painfully slow by the constant bombardment of fiery debris from above. By the time Turner reached the bottom rung of the ladder, he was on his knees and gasping at the thin, unsatisfying air. It was only by sheer willpower that he advanced up the ladder a few feet. He stopped briefly when he thought he heard a voice.

That was the last thing he remembered.

* * *

"Philip... no!" Joseph yelled from the open doorway, as he watched his friend attempt to climb the burning ladder and then drop, as if life itself had suddenly abandoned him. He ran over to Turner's bruised and burned body and, with one fluid motion, pulled him up and over his shoulders and headed back toward the door where his men now gathered.

"Quick! Grab as many saddles and harnesses as you can," Joseph shouted without stopping. "Let everything else burn."

Joseph ran past them toward the house. Fortunately, the wind was with him now, and it allowed him to carry Turner as fast as he wanted to go. On his way he passed his sister, who was holding onto a small tree tightly. She had witnessed the stable door fall all by itself and the horses come streaming out, including Topsy. Then, a few minutes later, she watched as Joseph came running from around the building, followed soon after by the rest of the men.

"What happened?" Jane cried out to her brother.

"He saved the horses by himself!" Joseph answered loudly without slowing. "I don't know if he is alive or dead!"

"Who?" she shouted.

"Philip!" he shouted back to her.

* * *

Turner regained consciousness in the comfort of his bed, but he knew things weren't going to be normal. First, his eyes burned slightly, even though they were closed, and it hurt even more to try and open them. They were also covered with a loose bandage or cloth. Second, when he tried to remove these bandages, a sharp pain ripped across his chest, causing him to cry out in agony. This initiated a succession of painful coughs mixed with agonizing cries that lasted a minute or more. When he was finally able to suppress this miserable combination, he heard a pleasing voice speak to him.

"Philip, you are hurt badly. Please don't do that again," Jane said softly, as she gently wiped the sweat from his forehead with a cool, damp cloth. "I will try to explain to you what happened to relieve your mind, but you must not try to speak, for you have inhaled a lot of smoke, and that will start you coughing again.

"First, I have been instructed by the doctor to get as much water into you as I can now that you are awake. I must also keep your wounds clean and free of infection, and do this without aggravating your injuries or causing you any unnecessary discomfort."

Turner thought he heard her begin to weep, as she carefully positioned his body with pillows so that he could drink from a glass. As best he could, he tried not to show

how painful this whole process was to him, so not to cause her any unnecessary discomfort.

"This is water mixed with a little whiskey, by doctor's orders. It will satisfy your body's need for water and help you sleep. I am warning you, brave young general," she said tenderly, "I will not begin storytelling until you drink this entire glass."

Turner struggled with the first few sips, but was more than willing to finish the first glass and was agreeable to another. This seemed to him to have pleased Jane, and so she began to recount what she knew of the events of the day before.

"You have been unconscious since Joseph carried you out of the stables yesterday. He immediately saddled his horse and rode into town to retrieve the doctor, who without a moment's hesitation, rode back with him in the storm. You were examined and bathed, then given morphine by needle, I believe, and then brought here to rest."

Jane stopped suddenly. Without being able to see her face, Turner thought he heard her begin to weep again. After a brief pause, and after the water glass was brought to his lips, she started speaking with unfeigned emotion.

"I was told you had many bruised and broken ribs, and not to move you unless it was absolutely necessary. Then I was given instructions to keep your bandages fresh, and all your many wounds and burns clean and covered in this aloe ointment, or infection would set in and do you worse harm.

"You were so fragile and so close to death," Jane was now speaking through her tears. "I did not want that responsibility. I could not live with myself if I failed to restore you.

"I was told you found some way inside the burning stable, knocked the pins from the door, and set the horses free while the others toiled futilely outside. Joseph picked you up off the floor after you fell from the ladder. He then went for the doctor, fearing you might not make it through the night."

After another long pause and another offer of drink, Jane was ready to share what she had felt deep in her heart for a long while—maybe even as long as the first day they met.

"Oh, Philip... from your first words to me, you have been so kind and gentle and forbearing." There was no reservation in her words now. "My brother was right. I have been a foolish child, and everything he has said about you has been proven many times. In my stubborn vanity, I have ignored your goodness for too long. Please forgive me.

"I promise to return your kindness," she continued affectionately, "and love... if that is your intention... if only you will get well again."

"Jane..." was all Turner could manage before the coughing and pain took control over his body. Jane waited patiently for this latest episode to subside, wiped his brow, and then started removing the pillows so that Turner could rest.

"Please don't do that again," Jane said lightheartedly. "I will give you time to think about what I have said. Sleep now. The doctor promised to see you again sometime today."

Before leaving, Jane leaned in close to Turner's ear and whispered, "Thank you for saving Topsy, my brave young general." She kissed him softly on the cheek and left the room. The whiskey had its intended effect, and Turner eased into a deep sleep. When he woke again, he could hear several masculine voices talking.

"Ah, ha! It appears that our hero is alive!" Turner overheard a stranger's voice say above the others. "Do not try to speak or move yourself unnecessarily, if you please, Mr. Turner. I am told you have already experienced what this might bring upon yourself, heh?

"Miss Jane—ah, what a lovely, young lady—has performed her duties admirably, and I have no doubt that you will make a full recovery, if you continue to do as she commands.

"You do understand a command, don't you, General?

"Yes, yes... it reminds me of the time I had to order General Lee to two days' bed rest. Ah, ha! You should have seen his face, but there he lay for two days.

"I am leaving now, but I am glad we had this little chat. You will be provided more water to drink and a pot to piss in. Drink all of it, Mr. Turner. I have already given you another shot of morphine to help you with your cough and your pain.

"If, however, you should awaken during the night in some degree of discomfort, there will be a tall glass of diluted whiskey by your bed. Drink it before disturbing someone else's sleep, heh?

"By the way, Mr. Turner, you should know that treating you has brought with it some notable popularity. That is, instead of asking my health, everyone asks me about yours. Ah, ha! Can you imagine that, Mr. Turner?

"I am a busy man these days, but I will return in two days to check on your progress and procure more news to tell your many admirers. You should be able to speak, see, and move about much better by then.

"Before I leave, however, please let me acknowledge that I consider your actions of yesterday to be quite magnificent... magnificent indeed. Have a peaceful rest, Mr. Turner."

"Thank you, Doctor," Turner heard Mr. Parker say. "Will you consider dining with the missus and I tonight?"

"No, no... can't tonight, Randall," the doctor replied. "But please give Miss Susan my fondest regrets, and do let me know when she bakes another sweet potato pie. I'll come running then, heh?"

"I will do that," Mr. Parker replied, and with that the voices disappeared, except for one. It was Joseph.

"So, my friend... you perform yet another miracle and, in the process, add significantly to your reputation."

Turner smiled and motioned with his pointing finger for Joseph to come closer. Joseph noticed the gesture and responded.

"You heard Doc. No talking!"

Turner grimaced and motioned again for his friend to come closer. Joseph could only shake his head and exhale loudly, knowing that if he didn't comply, Turner was more than willing to injure himself further to be heard. Joseph moved in as close as he could to allow his friend to speak in the lowest possible voice.

"I'm listening."

"Papers," Turner whispered softly enough to cause only minimal coughing and pain.

"I'm sorry, Philip," Joseph said apologetically. "Everything is gone.

"I know those papers meant a lot to you. I also know you spent a lot of time working on those door hinges and saving the horses before attempting to save your papers. It makes me wonder why you chose that particular order," Joseph pondered rhetorically. "I'll be back with your pot to piss in."

It did not take long for the bandages covering Turner's eyes to become soaked with tears. It hurt to cry, but it hurt him even more to realize that his plans, his dreams, his calling were nothing more than a wet pile of ash.

# 6

# An Angel's Kiss

Two weeks under Nurse Jane's tender love and uncompromising care, and Turner's health improved rapidly. It was during this time together that the lovers were able to talk about the many changes that had come about since the fire. So as not to inflame his smoke-impaired throat and lungs, Turner did most of his talking by writing down longer responses, which also provided a perfect opportunity to use his pitiful condition to subtly maneuver in for his first real kiss. This time of recuperation was not spent simply sharing their true feelings for each other: Turner would also confide in Jane his concerns about going to Richmond with nothing to back up his ideas and his promise to retrieve the body of his friend that had been buried hastily in Pennsylvania. Jane would confide in him her concerns about leaving her father and mother, as they must start over while growing older and then over what kind of wife and mother she would be. This willingness to discuss anything—and being gentle with their words—only deepened their affections for each other.

In the third week of his recuperation, Turner was showing the others how to use his woodworking inventions to help rebuild the stable, but only in half-day increments (by Nurse Jane's orders). In four weeks, he was in the saddle once again. By week five, there was little evidence he was ever hurt, much less near death, and Joseph caught him moving his belongings out of the house.

"And what do you think you're doing?" he demanded to know.

"As you can plainly see, my dear friend, I'm moving out," Turner said calmly.

"And where do you think you're going?" Joseph inquired straightaway.

"If you must know," Turner began in the same relaxed tone of voice, "I do not believe it is suitable for a man to share the same house with the one he intends to marry until after they have married."

"And why do you think—" Joseph stopped midsentence. "Hey, wait a minute. What did you say?"

"I have just informed your father that I am madly in love with his daughter," Turner said with a stifled smile. "I then asked for his permission to begin a courtship with the intentions of asking her to marry me... if she will have me."

"You rascal, I knew it!" Joseph exclaimed wildly. "I knew it all along, didn't I?"

"Yes, I believe you did," Turner replied calmly.

"'I must go to Richmond immediately,' you said. Didn't you?"

"Yes, Joseph, I believe I did say that."

"'Much too chaotic right now,' I said. Didn't I?"

"Yes, you did."

"'A negative effect on your family I am,' you said. Didn't you?"

"Yes, I believe those were my words."

"'The hell you will,' I said. Didn't I?"

"Yes, you did."

"'She won't ever talk to me… woe is me,' you said. Didn't you?"

"Yes, Joseph, I…" Turner stopped to think about that quote. "I don't recall saying those words, actually."

"Maybe you did, maybe you didn't. Still true!" Joseph barked.

Joseph had him there.

"So, where do you think you're going?" Joseph asked again, jovially.

"I'll be moving into the bunkhouse with your men," Turner stated unequivocally. "I have already spoken to your foreman, and you won't talk me out of it either!"

"Philip, Philip, Philip, why would I want to talk you out of such a commendable plan?" Joseph asked deviously. "Of course, you will be eating with the men, and bathing out of a pail like them, and will be using their outhouse, which isn't too far down the path. I suspect you'll be using that quite a bit.

"By the way, did good ol' Pete tell you about their flea problem? Yup, I reckon, when you let your mangy dog sleep with you, they come with the territory. Oh, I almost forgot. I suppose those early morning rendezvous in the kitchen with that girl of yours will have to stop.

"Here, let me give you a hand." Joseph offered his help, as if Turner had already thought through these things, which he had not.

Stunned into silence, Turner thought to himself that if it got too bad, he would simply move outdoors. He hadn't become so domesticated that he couldn't find a nice shady tree to camp under until winter. This got him to thinking that a nice, quiet fall wedding would be fine with him.

Without the ability to command his bunkmates to shut up and go to sleep instead of playing cards all night, it took less than a week to make the decision to part ways. This actually worked out well, in that he could pitch his tent wherever he was working and get a little more done each day. Although he did miss the kitchen ritual in the mornings with Jane, she would come out to see him almost every day with a basket of food and drink for lunch. Since Turner was under no obligation to work, and since Jane's mother knew these two had much to talk about, this new ritual was viewed in a positive light and encouraged. A few times, Jane arrived with lunch riding in a buggy, wearing a pretty dress, and in possession of her parasol. Turner looked forward to these days because he knew that the stay would last longer and she would bring with her a book of some sort, which they would take turns reading to each other.

Since it was never the parents' idea for Turner to leave the comforts of their home, Turner found himself being invited to join them for supper almost every night. On most nights, he could not resist having a home-cooked meal with his sweetheart by his side. On other nights, Joseph would join him out at his campsite for a smoke and conversation, like old times.

On one particular evening, Turner had once again accepted the invitation to dinner and was enjoying both food and family when there was a knock on the front door. Joseph was the first to react to the unexpected interruption and returned a short time later holding a telegram in his hand.

"It's for you," he said, as he handed the envelope to Turner. "The messenger said he was being paid an incentive for this to come into your possession today. I reassured the young man that he may collect his payment in good faith."

Turner looked at the letter and then at Joseph, who had nothing else to offer but a shrug of his shoulders. He had received regular mail before, but never telegrams delivered by personal messenger.

"May I?" Turner looked to Mr. Parker for permission to look at the telegram at the table.

"Of course you may, Philip," the father responded. "It apparently has some urgency attached to it. And please do not feel obligated to share its contents with us."

"Thank you," Turner replied, as he began reading the message to himself. It did not take long to read, but it left him puzzled. Because of his acknowledged love for Jane and how it might affect her and her family, Turner thought it would be best for all to hear.

"May I again interrupt?" Turner asked politely. "I do not believe I should keep this to myself."

"Please do... if you feel led to do so," Mr. Parker responded.

"It begins thus," he said and read:

Philadelphia, Pennsylvania, August 10, 1865. Major General John Philip Turner, CSA, now retired.

Dear Sir, you have been named sole legatee in Benjamin Franklin Hillary's Last Will and Testament, belated due to war. This document has been determined authentic and reliable. Therefore, you are hereby summoned to appear before a probate court held in Gettysburg City Courthouse, located in the Town of Gettysburg, being located in the south-central portion of the Commonwealth State of Pennsylvania.

We ask that you respond without delay, as the State of Pennsylvania would be more than willing to receive the testator's property if you are unable or unwilling to accept it.

We have been informed of your circumstances and that traveling may be a hardship for you. If this is still the case, funds will be made available for transporting you safely to Washington. You will then be provided railroad boarding passes from there to Gettysburg. These expenses have been paid for by a third party and will not diminish the decedent's estate. Please advise immediately.

Yours truly, and with profound sympathy to your loss,
Simon Stanton Fitzgerald, Esquire.

Turner immediately looked to Jane, who remained uncharacteristically quiet and on the verge of tears. The telegram made perfect sense to the two older brothers, and they said so. Joseph agreed the telegram was quite clear and Turner must go. His only regret was that he could not reasonably leave the farm at this time to accompany him. He also made the point that from Gettysburg, and with a good horse, Turner could make the battlefield where Benjamin was buried in half a day. Mrs. Parker was similarly silent, which caused Turner to conclude there was something the men were missing—including himself.

Then Mr. Parker spoke.

"You should be honored that your friend entrusted you, above all others, to inherit his worldly possessions... even if it turns out to be an old pipe and spectacles.

"I have not had time to consult with Mrs. Parker, but I believe she would be in favor with what I am about to say," he continued. "I am not so old as to have forgotten love. I thank Almighty God every day for the everlasting love He has given me for my wife. And I would have to be blind not to see love increasing daily between you and my beloved daughter.

"In that respect, I already consider you my son. Since you consider Benjamin to be like a brother, I must also consider him to be like a son. Therefore, should you be able to exhume his body, he will have a final resting place here in our family cemetery."

Turner was speechless. Mrs. Parker beamed and, without a word, got up from her chair, walked over to where her husband was seated, wrapped her arms tightly around his upper body, kissed his cheek, and then rested her head lovingly next to his. Jane was moved to unrestrained, but joyful, tears and gave her shaking hand to Turner under the table. The three Parker boys toasted the evening's resolutions the best way they knew how—with a shot of their best Virginia whiskey.

The next day, a response was sent to the Philadelphia law firm. The following week, Turner received another telegram stating $100 was wired to the First National Bank of Richmond (now in Northern hands) located in the Custom House (previously President Davis' office). It urged him to begin his journey to Washington at once, with the understanding that sections of the RF&P (Richmond, Fredericksburg & Potomac) Railroad may be unusable, and alternative modes of transportation may need to be arranged. It also noted that once he began the trip from the B&O (Baltimore & Ohio) Railroad Depot in Washington to Gettysburg, his time of arrival could be predicted with more certainty and a court date scheduled within a day or two. A post script was added to let him know that there was no need to account for money being spent and, if additional funds were necessary, he should make his request known at the B&O Station, where his boarding passes awaited him.

\* \* \*

Before receiving this second telegram, Turner and Jane spent much of each day together, uncertain which day would call him back to Gettysburg. Other than the young fellow who delivered both telegrams, there was much to be uncertain about—wills and testaments, law firms, boarding passes, expense money from unspecified third parties, and probate court in the town that brought back such haunting memories. As much as he tried, Turner could think of no other person—besides Joseph—who would know or have reason to care just how close he and Benjamin had become.

*Unless it was someone on that battlefield*, Turner thought carefully. *Oh, well, what better excuse than this to spend more time in the arms of my true love.*

He had this and many other thoughts, as he laid his head comfortably on Jane's lap. Jane had many thoughts of her own, as she leaned back against the trunk of a large shade tree and played with her sweet general's hair.

"Phillip?" Jane asked softly, while still fiddling with his hair.

"Yes, my love," Turner replied without opening his eyes.

"What was he like?"

"What was who like?"

"Benjamin," Jane said, as she tried to understand how a man would think to draft a will leaving all to a person he had met at school.

"You would have fallen in love with him immediately," Turner stated automatically. "He was... irresistible."

After giving his answer more thought, Turner continued.

"I wanted to hate him. We were both extremely competitive and, by all accounts, shared the same degree of competency. But I had to work twice as hard to keep up with him in this regard. Knowing this, he would still attempt to help me at every turn, as if he wanted me to better him. At first, I rejected this help and thought of it nothing more than pity for the poor, orphan boy. But he rejected my bitterness and kept giving and giving and giving until hating him was like hating myself. He withheld nothing."

"Like a caring professor might do," Jane added.

"Like a caring professor might do," Turner agreed. "Only the subject matter being taught was selflessness."

"At what point did you stop being classmates and begin life as brothers?" Jane asked, knowing her question was put in a fashion that Turner could properly answer.

"Soon after my discovery that he, too, was orphaned," Turner replied sorrowfully. "And I was ashamed."

"What do you mean, my darling?" Jane asked sweetly.

"He never once used his dire straits to gain an advantage over another or seek some misbegotten sympathy, as I found myself doing on a shamefully regular basis. In that moment I asked his forgiveness, and henceforth, we walked as brothers.

"Even though I saw little evidence to his confessions, he would freely admit to being a rotten sinner and capable of terrible misconduct. He warned me not to look to him for goodness but to Jesus and God's Holy Word. But there was no burden or confession too great that we could not entrust to each other, which drew us closer still.

"Does that ease your mind, my love?" Turner asked tenderly.

"I confess that my mind was in turmoil over you returning to what, only months ago, was enemy territory," Jane responded softly. "I want you to know the depth of my love and how I could not bear losing you now.

"But the war is over, and your explanation has sufficed to calm my fears. So, I will watch you go with reservation, realizing this is what you must do. I will pray for your safe return daily."

Jane then leaned forward slightly, as she lifted Turner's head from her lap and kissed his lips in a fashion so soft and pleasing that he believed himself being awoken by an angel.

* * *

When it was time to leave, Turner was given a perfumed, lace handkerchief, and Jane was given a lock of his hair to help remind them of their undying love. Joseph would accompany him to Richmond and see to it that all was as it was supposed to be. It was; Turner was soon on a locomotive headed north in a manner, and for a purpose, he could not imagine.

Before boarding the train, Turner thought it best to turn his wartime journals, that were thankfully spared from the fire (as he had kept them apart from his other writings), over to Joseph in the event some misfortune occurred while in Northern territory. Along with the journals, Joseph was given permission to open his mail and respond to the requests of soldiers' family members in any way he wished and, preferably, addressed as quickly as possible.

The contrast between winner and loser could not have been made more apparent during the trip from Richmond, in the south, to Gettysburg, in the north. Turner figured he lost at least two days' traveling time between Richmond and Washington by having to alternate from locomotive to stagecoach, and back again as a consequence of war. Finally, a steamboat up the Potomac had to bring him into Washington. The locomotive from B&O Railroad Depot to Gettysburg, on the other hand, ran virtually uninterrupted and practically deposited him on the steps of the courthouse. As soon as Turner stepped off the passenger car and onto the platform, he was approached by a black hotel porter, who introduced himself and asked if he was the gentleman from the South named Turner. When Turner confirmed this, the man picked up his bag and politely asked him to follow.

"May I ask where you are taking me, sir?" Turner asked politely.

"Da Duke suh, o' course, suh!" the porter replied in a strong, southern accent.

"Am I to meet the person who is responsible for showing me such great hospitality there, sir?" Turner inquired.

"Dat's all I knows 'bout it, suh," the porter said.

The Duke and Duchess Hotel, named after Gabriel Duchene and his wife, Sophia, was a short walk, and Turner was delivered to the hotel's front desk in short order. Without any mention of payment, he was given a key and told that Samuel, the porter, would show him to his room on the second floor. Samuel entered the room first, through the opened door, and laid Turner's bag on the bed. He wished Turner a nice stay and headed back toward the door.

"Pardon me, Samuel, but please accept this token of my appreciation for your labor," Turner said, as he handed his escort two dollars.

"Why, I do thanks yo, suh," Samuel replied, somewhat astonished by such a large sum of money for such an easy task. "Mighty kine of yo, suh, mighty kine."

"You're not from around here, are you, Samuel?" Turner asked in a humorous reference to his accent.

"Al'bama, suh," Samuel replied with a smile.

"You're a long way from home then?" Turner added jokingly.

"I done 'scaped, suh," Samuel's smile vanished. "Mean'n to makes it aw da way ta Can'da but I only done makes it dis fah when da woh come to a stop."

"Are you planning on going back home then, Samuel?" Turner asked with much more empathy.

This question affected Samuel more than Turner had anticipated. Something in Samuel's silence told him he had gone too far, and he quickly tried to make amends.

"I am truly sorry if I offended you, Samuel," Turner said earnestly. "There is no need for you to tell me more."

Samuel had no intentions of sharing his personal story with anyone, especially a southern man, but the words that had been packed down so hard welled up inside of him like a gusher. As much as he tried, the words could not be contained any longer.

"When I done saves me up some money…" Samuel began slowly. "I's gonna go back down an' fine my wife an' my chi'dren."

Turner stood motionless, silently giving this heart-broken black man standing before him the opportunity to speak freely if he wished.

"Dey was sold jus' befoh I runs away like I done," Samuel continued through his tears. "I prays to God dey aw still live. I do.

"Every day I prays to da Lawd. I says, 'Jesus… you take good care o' my wife an' my boy an' my li'l angel girl now, hear?

"'You let'm know I'm a-com'n foh'm, yo hear dat, Lawd? I'm a-com'n. You done makes me dat promise, Lawd Jesus. Please, Lawd, keep 'em alive. Please… yo is God. Keep 'em alive… let 'em…"

Without a word, Turner walked slowly over to where Samuel stood hunched over, quietly weeping, and gently wrapped his strong arms around him. In his grief, it took several seconds for Samuel to realize he was being com-forted in this fashion, but comforted he was. When they separated, Turner left his hand on Samuel's shoulders and echoed his prayer that the Lord would protect the man's family until they were united once again.

With that, he gestured for Samuel not to leave yet and walked over to the bed where his bag had been laid. Reaching into a side pocket, he pulled out the bank envelope containing what was left of the $100 given to him in Richmond. With everything having been provided for him since leaving Washington, and since he had every intention of paying this money back, there was still over $70 left.

"I want you to have this," Turner said, as he handed the envelope to Samuel. "We will both go downstairs this instant and I will explain to your employer that I have freely given this sum of money to you. This is so you are not accused of stealing. If asked the purpose of this transaction, I will tell him that is none of his concern."

Samuel peeked inside the envelope and nearly fainted. Turner had to help ease him over to the chair in the corner of the room.

"If you are not comfortable carrying with you that amount of money," Turner continued, "I recommend we go to the nearest bank and set up an account in your name."

"Why is you doin' dis, suh?" Samuel asked skeptically.

"First, my name is Philip," Turner replied, "and I give you permission to call me by that name... when not on duty, of course.

"Secondly, I believe the Lord intended for you to have this money all along, Samuel," Turner smiled. "Come, now. Let us find a bank and start making some interest on your money."

After delivering this unexpected news to the hotel's proprietor, Turner asked if he might take Samuel over to the bank before it closed for the day. Gabriel Duchene, affectionately known as Duke, was a kindhearted man; he agreed that was the safest option for that amount of money. Before the two reached the front door, Duke called for them to wait a minute. He came out from behind the counter and handed Turner a note written on high quality paper.

"I almost forgot; this arrived prior to you coming downstairs," he stated. "Also, supper is provided and will be served at six. If you plan to join us, please be prompt, Mr. Turner."

Turner was happy to hear of this invitation to supper, because he had forgotten all about the day's expenses and was now down to whatever was left in his pockets. He thanked the kindly old gentleman and opened the note. It requested his presence at the city courthouse tomorrow morning at nine sharp. That was all it said.

The bank was several blocks away, which gave each man time to tell one more story about themselves. When they arrived at the bank and Samuel appeared at the window requesting to open an account, the cashier didn't know what to do. He quickly summoned the manager, who was equally astonished by the deposit and the depositor, but was more than happy to receive both. When all was said and done, and as the two headed back to the hotel, each gave thanks to God; not for the giving or the receiving of money, but for His great love for them. Before going up to his room, Turner requested and received two sheets of writing paper, a fountain pen, and some ink. His intention was to write a letter to Jane before supper, and this he did. When it was done, he took it downstairs to be stamped and sent out with the hotel's mail. Supper was delightful, and after a long walk to settle the stomach and quiet the mind, Turner retired for the evening. It had been a long day.

Turner awoke early the following morning, washed, dressed, and went downstairs in hopes that breakfast would also be complimentary. It was, but it would not be ready for another hour according to Mr. Duchene, who was also an early riser. Turner was offered coffee, and they talked, but not about the war or the battle that raged here. He was told where he could lease a good horse, but learned nothing more about who was paying his expenses or why a Philadelphia law firm was representing him in a probate case in Gettysburg.

At 8:00 AM, Turner went and stood in front of the courthouse in hopes that someone would want to make contact with him prior to the hearing. No one did, and so he walked inside at ten minutes before nine and took a seat on the bench in the lobby. At nine o'clock sharp, two richly dressed men walked into the building and greeted Turner formally. He was told that their law firm, one of the largest in the Commonwealth of Pennsylvania, had been working on this case for years and today should be "cut and dry". Turner was given no time to ask a single question before his case, and several others were called to enter the courtroom. This caused a large number of people to begin shuffling into the room at the same time, and for a second, he thought he might have recognized a younger man several strangers ahead of him. As Turner cleared the doorway, he quickly glanced in the direction the young fellow turned, but again all he could see was the back of a head among many.

Turner was ushered to the front, as if his case was going to be the first heard and took a seat in between the two lawyers. Once seated, he was then told by the one on his right that, other than answering a few yes-and-no questions by the judge, there would be little for him to do or say. This presumptuous remark, delivered with a touch of arrogance, was the last straw. Turner reached over and, with minimal effort, spun the man's body around to face him.

"I want answers, and I want them now," Turner stated in a low but powerful voice, which stunned the lawyer. "I have come two hundred miles, and I want to know: Why the secrecy?"

After his initial shock, the lawyer attempted to remove Turner's single-handed grip from his tailor-made suit, even using both hands to do so. He gave up trying when it became apparent that the only way of escape, and of preventing damage to his expensive garment, was if Turner released him voluntarily. The lawyer stopped all efforts to free himself and simply returned Turner's unwavering gaze. This stalemate caused Turner to slowly release his grip. The man straightened his jacket and spoke in a whisper.

"You have no idea what you're looking at, do you?"

"I have been told to come and go—that is all," Turner replied.

"Mr. Hillary's estate is worth over a hundred and twenty-five thousand dollars in cash," the lawyer whispered again.

Turner froze; this was a sum unimaginable. The room suddenly became quiet, and all were asked to rise while Judge Douglas entered the room, and then they were asked to be seated again. After some activity at the bench, Turner was asked to stand, place his hand on the Bible, and promise to tell the truth, "So help you God". Before sitting back down, he turned to look toward the back of the room for a familiar face, but the one he thought might be known had his face pointed downward at some papers. Several motions were made, and Turner was asked a few yes-and-no questions, as the lawyers predicted. The judge asked Turner to stand.

"I see you are from the South and a decorated Confederate general," the judge said, barely hiding his contempt. "Perhaps you were even in this town with your band of cutthroats a few years back, huh, Mr. Turner?

"If it were up to me, I would hold you personally and financially liable for all the damage that has been perpetrated on our peaceful, little town, sir," the judge seethed and then relaxed. "But you have good representation, I must admit.

"So, it appears I have no choice but to name you the benefactor of Mr. Hillary's estate," the judge stated and then added his own quirky requirement. "All that is needed now is for you to produce a citizen in good standing with the State of Pennsylvania to corroborate your testimony in this courtroom today."

The judge was right when he said Turner had good representation. The lawyers had come to know this judge's infamous eccentricities, and with this much at stake, they had two years to anticipate them all.

"I am that citizen in good standing, Your Honor," a voice came from the back of the room.

"And who are you?" the judge demanded in obvious irritation.

"Nathanael Dylan Walker, Your Honor," the young man responded politely.

"Nathan!" Turner called out.

# 7

# Nathan's Journey

There was nothing left to do but sign the papers, making this filthy rebel a rich man. The judge knew he was out-maneuvered and outgunned. How could he have known this young general from the South had ever heard of the most prestigious law firm in Philadelphia—much less be able to retain their services? If that wasn't enough, as soon as the young man in the back of his courtroom used the surname of Walker, all efforts to prevent this settlement from occurring were rendered useless. The Walkers were a rich, powerful, and influential family from Philadelphia. Their generational wealth came from the buying and selling of real estate in Pennsylvania and New York. In fact, soon after the battle of Gettysburg, various entities representing the Walker dynasty came in and bought up farms for pennies on the dollar. Nathan's father had a knack for discovering advantages in tragedies, and he expected to make huge profits exploiting the North's most costly tragedy (in terms of lives lost). This was nothing new; the Walker patriarchs were well known for their ruthless ambitions, going back several generations until now. Nathan did not appear to have inherited the coldhearted gene.

In spite of all of this, Turner only knew that he now possessed more money than he could spend in a lifetime. He wasted no time in giving the brave young private he left with the responsibility of burying his dearest friend a crushing embrace outside the courthouse.

"Private Nathan Walker!" Turner said cheerfully, after releasing his captive. "You are alive and as fit as a fiddle I see; thanks be to God."

"It is good to see you again, General—on friendlier terms, thankfully," Nathan replied with deep emotion. "When I first saw you yesterday, it felt like Colonel Hillary was back... as best I can put it, sir."

"Please, Nathan, let that be the last time you call me 'sir'. Philip will do fine," Turner ordered unofficially. "And, once I am given enough time to explain myself, you will find that I am but a shadow of your colonel."

"I do think of him many times," was all Nathan could manage to say.

"I understand the depths of your affection and your sorrow," Turner acknowledged. "Since I was without a brother of my own and you without a father, he more than fulfilled our greatest needs."

"I did learn some time ago that you were not true brothers," Nathan pointed out. "But I am not without a father, just without a good one, in my eyes. It is why I enlisted at the age of sixteen without his knowing."

"Well, now, perhaps we both need time to explain ourselves," Turner said in surprise. "If you have the time to talk, may I ask that our conversation include a meal of some kind? I have had nothing to eat since supper last night."

"I am at your service, sir... pardon me, Philip," Nathan answered. "So, let us eat and talk. I haven't had an appetite the last couple of days, and now, all of a sudden, I could eat a horse."

They found a tavern that served food, and after ordering, Turner began the storytelling with his life at West Point—the reputation, the isolation, the studies, the love of country, the comradeship between cadets that remained unshakeable even when on opposing sides of war, and of course, his admiration and brotherly love for Benjamin.

Little was said about the war, but for an instant Turner recalled to mind those three days of hell that raged in every direction from where they were now seated. The unspeakable horrors bundled into one great, violent wave of painful thought that caused his entire body to tremble and then to go numb; this did not go unnoticed by Nathan.

"Are you ill?" Nathan asked with concern.

"No, I believe it is the flesh attempting to cling tightly to dark things, but the spirit won't have it," Turner theorized. "Perhaps it would be best for you to tell me a little about yourself, if that is all right with you?"

"Of course it is!" Nathan agreed anxiously. "I think you will find much of this story interesting, if not so improbable as to be believed, so to speak."

Turner did, in fact, find himself mesmerized by the young man's journey to fulfill his beloved commander's final wishes. Nathan described it this way. After the battle in which his cavalry regiment was routed, he buried his commander as instructed. When this was done, he assisted his fellow survivors in the gathering of the dead and, with great care, placing them in neat columns, so that they could be readily loaded onto the wagons that were sure to be arriving in the morning. As soon as this was accomplished, they lit fires and ate. A few horses returned of their own accord, but there was no need to flee—the battle was over, and the enemy was gone. They took turns overnight guarding the remains of their fellow soldiers from wolves.

At the first opportunity, Nathan relaxed against a stack of orphaned knapsacks and opened the Bible that was given to him by the man seated across from him now, only to have a single sheet of paper fall out of it and onto his lap. It had the appearance of being a legal document, and within the first paragraph, it stated, "I, Benjamin Franklin Hillary, declare this Instrument, written in my own hand, to be my Last Will and Testament, revoking all others." It was dated August 21, 1861, and one month to the day after the first Battle at Bull Run; the paper was witnessed by none other than the superintendent of West Point. What struck Nathan that night as being the most peculiar about the document was that it left all to the colonel whose army had just left the battlefield. (Turner noted that Nathan was careful not to mention whose army it was that caused Benjamin's death.) The will listed two Pennsylvania banks and the accounts in each, but not their value. No other property was mentioned.

This was the document probated in court that day.

Nathan continued his recollections and said he was given the opportunity to visit the superintendent at West Point, while traveling home to Philadelphia from Harvard University (another unlikely story yet to be told). He showed the document to the superintendent and explained how it fell into his possession (again without mentioning Turner's regiment).

The superintendent remembered signing the document and the conversation with Benjamin. He said that Benjamin paid him a visit soon after participating in the first Battle of Bull Run and, from that experience, feared the war would not be the short, political kind for which he had hoped. This set in him a desire to arrange for the proper distribution of his estate that he characterized as being "significant", and that it should all go to his "fellow classmate and dear friend, Philip Turner," for he had no other living relative. Nathan then asked the man if it would be possible to have the names of Benjamin's parents and their last known address to help verify the statement that he had no living relative. To Nathan's surprise, he was given this information and more. He was told both parents had made two successful trips into the jungles of South America as Christian missionaries. It was on their third mission that they disappeared sometime after arriving in Brazil and were presumed dead. This sad event preceded Benjamin's arrival at West Point by four years. Of course, Turner knew that Benjamin was orphaned, but had not known how it came to pass.

"Then, before leaving his office, the superintendent asked of me this favor," Nathan continued. "Should I be fortunate to cross paths with you someday, I was to wish you well. He thought kindly of you and stated his belief that both you and Colonel Benjamin were on the brilliant side of knowledge and skill, those being the words he used."

"Thank you for sharing that with me, Nathan," Turner responded humbly. "Now, excuse me for interrupting your story here, but did I hear you mention Harvard University?"

"Yes, in fact, that would be the true beginning to the story of how we have come together here today," Nathan began. "And this tale could have easily ended as soon as it began if my desire to remain a soldier was satisfied, one could say."

This was Nathan's account immediately following the battle that took Benjamin's life. When his father discovered what had happened to his regiment, it was the last straw. By this time, he knew his son had enlisted without his permission and, yet, still expected Nathan to beg to

come home once life in the army failed at becoming a sub-
stitute for being a "Walker". However, now the tables were
turned. The details of the battle were too much for a father
to bear. It only took days for the father's influence to reach
the War Department and Nathan found himself discharged
for lying about his age on his enlistment forms, a crime for
which only the wealthy need be concerned.

Nathan made it absolutely clear to Turner that he
protested vehemently to this dismissal with anyone who
would listen. Finally, his sergeant, who knew of Nathan's
bravery and commitment to his commanding officer, took
him aside and explained what really happened, even
though this honesty could have cost the sergeant his rank.
After the explanation, his sergeant assured Nathan that
nothing but Lincoln's signature could keep him in the army
and suggested that he "take these setbacks like a man".
This Nathan did and, without complaint or retaliation, went
home. Within weeks, he would take his father's advice and
enroll at Harvard.

"Had my life continued as a soldier, instead of as a student, there remained enough war to cause me to follow
my colonel's footsteps into eternity," Nathan admitted.
"But I was prepared to die for my country."

"I have no doubt you mean what you say when you say
it," Turner acknowledged.

Nathan continued with his story this way. He found that
Benjamin's family was not particularly wealthy before the
war, but did own one piece of real estate near Pittsburgh.
This parcel became increasingly more valuable, as that
town became more important as a producer of wartime
steel. Just after resigning from West Point to fight in the
war, Benjamin put it up for sale. With determination, some
ingenuity, and a lot of dumb luck, Nathan soon discovered
from settlement papers that one of his father's enterprises

purchased the property and paid less than half the fair market value. Within a year's time, his father would personally turn around and resell the property for five times what was paid to another shrewd businessman by the name of Andrew Carnegie.

Enraged by this blatant inequity, Nathan justified paying all of Turner's expenses to Gettysburg, as well as the expenses incurred from the best law firm in Pennsylvania, from out of his father's coffers. Nathan told his father that if he didn't agree to this remedy, he would leave and never come back. His father, who would still make an enormous profit on the deal after these expenses, simply shrugged and complied.

"So, it was you and you alone?" Turner whispered softly, introspectively. "Nathan, I would have never known."

"That was quite obvious when you thought nothing of reaching into Colonel Hillary's coat and handing me his Bible containing this valuable document," Nathan replied. "You would have buried a fortune, you might say."

"How am I to repay you?" Turner asked with a deep sense of indebtedness. "You have made countless discoveries and performed so many insurmountable deeds on my behalf that, I believe, no other person could have hoped to accomplish as much. So please, consider any part of Benjamin's estate to be yours."

"Heaven forbid it, sir!" Nathan protested forcefully. "It pleases me only to accomplish what Colonel Hillary clearly stated as his last command while on this earth. You may do what you wish with it, but not a penny shall come back to me!"

"Of course. I beg your pardon, Nathan," Turner pleaded innocence. "My intention was not to impugn your integrity but, in some way, to make good use of it. I can't help but sense there was more to Benjamin's legacy than to make me rich."

"I don't understand," Nathan replied.

"Well, in your discoveries, were there any other papers that could shed some light on what Benjamin's intentions might have been after the war?" Turner pondered. "He obviously had no intention of going into the ironworks business."

"No, sir... Philip," Nathan corrected himself. "There were no other papers, unless you consider every margin in his Bible being taken up with his writings the same as having written another paper. I have not even begun to read all these notations, I must confess."

"We shall have to start there, I reckon," Turner mused. "Now then, could there possibly be more to your story, Nathan?"

"Oh, quite a bit more!" Nathan exclaimed. "I have not yet told you about the rock!"

"The rock?" Turner asked curiously.

"Yes, the rock... and more," Nathan responded without further explanation. "But let us pay for our meal and head out to the battlefield before it gets too late in the day. I have taken the liberty to lease three hearty workhorses to get us there and about quickly."

"Three horses?" Turner repeated curiously.

"Yes. I have asked Samuel to join us as cook and quarter-master. He has been given instructions to ready our horses and purchase three day's provisions," Nathan responded briefly. "Without having to worry about running a camp, it should give us plenty of time to explore the property."

"Samuel?" Turner asked joyfully.

"Yes, Samuel," Nathan responded bluntly, hoping to prevent the telling of a story with every new detail that escaped from his mouth.

From Turner's body language, however, it was evident there would be no movement until a better explanation was forthcoming. Nathan had no choice but to provide another quick story, and it went like this. With the aid of a few of his father's business associates, he learned quickly that Turner's cavalry was at Appomattox the day of the surrender. From there, it was fairly easy to follow his progress across Virginia due to all the commotion surrounding a Southern general and war hero in Southern territory. Since the discovery of Turner's whereabouts, Nathan had spent many days in Gettysburg sitting in the courtroom simply observing Judge Douglas' rulings. That surveillance was done to help the law firm prepare for this day in court. Each time he would come to Gettysburg, he would stay at the Duke and Duchess Hotel. He found Samuel to be a hospitable attendant, with many tall tales to tell when encouraged (though Samuel never shared the story of how he lost his family with Nathan). Nathan also enjoyed the challenge of understanding the words and their meaning when spoken in that deep, southern accent.

This morning, as Nathan came to the railroad station to greet the two lawyers from Philadelphia, he had an opportunity to meet with Samuel, who was already there waiting for the train to arrive. This was not the first time he had met Samuel on the train platform. Samuel knew the train schedule as well as any conductor and, with an acute sense of timing (though he owned no timepiece), never failed to be on the platform moments before the train appeared in the distance or could be heard sounding its whistle. This gave Nathan the idea that there may have been an incentive paid to him for directing well-to-do travelers to the Duke and Duchess.

In fact, this was how he first met Samuel; as soon as he stepped off the passenger car, Samuel approached him with an air of confidence, introduced himself in that slow, inviting southern drawl, took possession of his bags, and politely asked Nathan to follow him to, "Da Duke, suh," even though he had made no advanced reservation at that hotel.

It was at this chance meeting on the railroad station platform this very morning that Nathan came up with the idea to have Samuel join them in their excursion for the reasons stated earlier. He made, what he believed to be, a fair offer to pay Samuel twice his wages for up to a week's worth of service and also pay his employer the cost of Turner's room for a week, whether he needed it for that length of time or not. Samuel wavered at first—that is, until Nathan offhandedly mentioned Turner's name.

"That is when Samuel became absolutely frantic and said he would come along for nothing at all," Nathan said in amazement. "I do not believe I have ever seen a person go from ice cold to piping hot so quickly before, if you get my meaning.

"So, I must ask you, Philip, is there a story for you to tell?" Nathan asked, in hopes of getting a clear picture of why Samuel would react in such a manner.

"There is," Turner replied reticently, "but I have not been given permission to tell it, I'm afraid. Now, I must ask your indulgence to allow me time to get off another letter before we leave. My first letter would not have addressed the outcome of the events of this day. I believe an additional week or more without any communication back home may cause further distress to those who might still believe this to be a ploy for my undoing."

"Very well, I shall find Samuel and meet you back at the Duke in one hour," Nathan agreed. "No need to have the letter stamped. When you have finished, give the letter to me, and it will be in Virginia in three days."

Turner would again address this new letter to Jane. This allowed him to communicate to everyone that he was safe and would be spending the next three days visiting Benjamin's gravesite before returning home, while also permitting a short passage to state his eagerness to be back with the one he loved, in expressions that she might keep to herself.

After grabbing another set of clothes, Turner headed out the door of the hotel and was immediately greeted by Nathan, Samuel, and a stranger on horseback. Another horse, saddled but unmanned, was tied to the hotel's hitching post. Turner handed the letter to Nathan, who immediately handed it to the stranger, who then took off.

"The letter will be on the next train to Washington and then Richmond, and then hand-delivered as your other letters have been," Nathan promised. "Now let us make haste, gentlemen. There is much to do and little time, as you will see."

# 8

# The Rock Won't Move

All three men were excellent horseman, and they made good time. Nathan had made this trip three times, including each of the two anniversaries since the battle. He had ridden the same horse all three times and knew its capabilities. He had brought the other two horses along once before and found them to be as reliable. This allowed him to plan only one stop to rest them.

Nathan took advantage of this rest stop to tell another short story. After their fateful battle in May, his involuntary discharge, and the great battle at Gettysburg in July, Nathan wanted to get back as quickly as possible to see that nothing had disturbed his commander's grave. Those attempts, however, had been prevented for one reason or another. There was a war still waging, after all—although the fighting was now contained in the South. The earliest he was able to make it back was the battle's first anniversary the previous year.

At first, he wasn't sure that he had found the right hillside. The open field he was looking at had apparently been abandoned by its owner and was overgrown. It was only after making his way into the tall grass and weed that he stumbled upon the broken carriages for the Howitzers and other equipment that was left behind in their defeat. The orientation of the battlefield was made easier now that the battery of cannon was found, but still something didn't look right. He remembered standing with his commander maybe a hundred paces behind the line of cannon when the attack began. Colonel Hillary was struck immediately and fell to the ground. Nathan drew his pistol and began screaming for help, but men were falling all around him. He could only think of protecting his wounded commander from further harm by shielding him with his own body.

That was the spot where Turner found them when the hostilities ended.

Once Nathan found that spot, he felt confident in finding the location of the dead oak tree and the mound of stone covering Colonel Hillary's grave. There was indeed a large dead oak in that direction, but now lying in between him and the oak was a rock as big as a coal tender and white as snow.

"A rock the size of a locomotive's tender!" Turner cried out. "How is it possible for a rock that size to roll itself through a forest of pines and hardwoods and come to rest on Benjamin's grave? Even if I did recall a rock that impressive... which I did not."

"It's quite square, actually," Nathan stated calmly, while ignoring the other chain of events Turner mentioned.

"Square!" Turner cried out again in disbelief.

"Rectangular, to be more precise," Nathan added matter-of-factly. "Since its length is longer than its height and width, I was informed by my Harvard classmates we must refer to it as a rectangular cube."

"Nathan, you must realize what you are telling me is impossible," Turner concluded.

"Hard as a diamond, I might add," Nathan said, without acknowledging the question put to him. "I ruined two miner's pickaxes without causing a scratch."

"Po'haps dat rock o yo's is a sign," Samuel spoke effortlessly, and to no one in particular.

"I'm sorry; what did you say, Samuel?" Turner inquired.

"Po'haps da Lawd done put da rock on dat spot," Samuel completed his thoughts, instead of directly answering the question.

"Samuel, I'm not saying the Lord couldn't put a rock anywhere He wants to, but why?" Nathan asked curiously. "It only prevents us from giving Colonel Hillary a proper burial."

"I don't see's it mak'n no never mine to da Lawd where ya'll bury yo dead, Mista Nath'n, suh," Samuel responded respectfully. "Po'haps da Lawd thinks yo colonel is buried proper 'nuf where he lay."

Samuel could sense that his companions were still having trouble with the idea that this could all be for the Lord's purpose. He didn't intend to get mixed up in their conversation, and he certainly didn't want to share another painful memory of the day they took his family away, but he felt led to speak. Perhaps his testimony would do some good for these two men who had been so kind to him. He slowly began talking.

"After dey done takes away ma fam'ly like dey done, da other slaves come up an' prayed over me aw day long. But dat night, I be lay'n aw 'lone, an aw I wants ta do is kill. I was terrible angry, an' woulda killed me da first person from da masta's house if'n I had a chance to. It made no matter to me if'n it was da masta his self, o his wife... o his chi'dren."

Samuel's jaw set and his hands clinched ever tighter on the knife and stick he had been whittling, as he put himself face-to-face with the depth of his hatred once again. He hated himself even more for ever thinking he could relieve his pain or serve justice by taking revenge on another, especially an innocent woman and child.

"Samuel, it's all right—" Turner was about to suggest to Samuel that his feelings were quite understandable, given the circumstances, but was interrupted.

"I got's mo' to tell, Mista Phil'p," Samuel continued, as he was unconcerned right now with self-pity.

"It were dat same night da Lawd spoke to me."

"The Lord spoke to you, Samuel?" Turner asked, not in disbelief, but for clarity.

"He says 'Samuel, git up and go...' jus' like dat He says to me," Samuel recalled vividly. "I says, 'Is dat yo, Lawd?'"

"He says, 'I am da Lawd yo God, Samuel. Yo must leave dis night,' He says to me.

"I says, 'Where's I suppose ta go, Lawd?'"

"He says, 'Go up no'th!'"

"I says back to Him, 'I ain't goin no'th, Lawd, when my fam'ly bin taken so'th!'"

"He says, 'No'th, Samuel!' Real angry like dat.

"Den I says, 'But da masta is watch'n fo' me to 'scape ta night. I knows he is 'cause I hears da hounds. Dems good hounds, Lawd.'

"Den He says, 'No harm will befaw yo o yo fam'ly fo' I will bind up Satan's hands.'

"Den I pleads wid Him, 'Lawd, gives me revenge on da masta.'

"Den He says, 'Has yo not heard, I haves mercy on dem I wants to haves mercy?'

"Mista Phil'p, Mista Nath'n, dem hounds had me dade ta rights... dat's jus' a fact," Samuel stated bluntly. "But the Lawd done put someth'n up dem dogs nose 'cause here I

134

is. Po'haps, the Lawd dun put dat rock on top of yo colonel 'cause He got a plan dat ain't y'all's plan."

Samuel went back to quietly whittling on his stick. Nathan and Turner looked at one another and smiled; for a brief moment, they took great pleasure in themselves for having played some role in bringing Samuel along with them. There was no denying that much of what had happened up to this point would be hard to explain or believe other than by Providence. Both men had a strong urge to allow Samuel more time to talk if he wished to do so, but after another moment or two of silence, Nathan suggested they press on. So, on they rode, making the tranquil battlefield before sunset.

It was not difficult for Turner to orient himself to the battlefield once the large, white rock came into view. It was no less than what had been described to him, and there was no other rock formation like it in any direction as far as the eye could see. Samuel began to set up camp just off the battlefield grounds, while Nathan and Turner walked over to examine this unlikely tombstone that only God could have delivered. Even though the night would soon fall, the rock still reflected a soft glow off its unblemished, white surface. Its shape was not perfectly uniform; it was narrower on one end than the other, but it had six distinct sides. Everywhere, the surface was smooth and cool to the touch. Leaning against the dead oak were two broken pickaxes.

"The rock won't move," Nathan said. "I used all three of these powerful horses to try and move it, but they could do nothing. I don't suppose ten horses would fare any better."

"I'm beginning to think Samuel was right," Turner responded, as he circled the rock and surveyed the undisturbed landscape that surrounded it. "It does appear to be

God's plan for Benjamin to stay at rest here, but what are we to do with that?"

"Well, that reminds me of another story that I have yet to share," Nathan stated. "But I think I shall save it for tonight when Samuel is within earshot. We might benefit from his thoughts a second time, if truth be told."

The two spent the remainder of what sunlight was left walking the pasture, picking at relics, and talking about family. Speaking of family was a new concept for Turner, now that he was able to add something to the conversation; it felt good. When they arrived back at camp, Samuel had a salted pork-and-potato stew, sourdough bread, and coffee waiting. As best they could make out, he was apologizing for having to serve something less than his best, since he had only a little over an hour to cook the ingredients combined. The normal time would have been three times that, at the least. Apparently, he was able to compensate for this culinary transgression by cutting the meat and potatoes thinner and browning them on a skillet, and then adding a little flour to thicken the stock. Both Nathan and Turner agreed it was superb, and said so with each ravenous bite. When everything that was intended to be eaten was eaten, and the pots and pans cleaned, Samuel produced three pipes and some Maryland tobacco to the amazement and overwhelming gratitude of both Nathan and Turner.

This last act of thoughtfulness, along with a three-quarter moon, a chill in the air, and a decent fire, set the stage for good conversation. Samuel was immediately given the honor of going first, if he wished. Without a hint of hatred or malice in his voice, he spent the next half-hour tenderly describing how smart and lovely his wife was, and how far more intelligent his son and daughter were than himself.

"I cain't read a lick, but every night befo' supper, dem chi'dren o' mine would take a turn read'n from da Good Book," Samuel said with pride, and ended his time with Psalm 46:1: "God be our refuge, our stren'th, our help in d'ese troubled times."

With that, all three stood up simultaneously, stretched their legs, relieved themselves over the same small embankment, replenished coffee, or leaf, as it suited them, and took their seats back around the fire. Turner was given the opportunity to speak next and spent his time talking about how his love grew for that little girl in the faded picture. He had to pause in his reflections only once when both Nathan and Samuel could not stifle their laughter at the thought of Turner surviving a war without as much as a scratch, but then almost having to explain the loss of several fingers in the abrupt closing of a parasol case by an unimpressed love interest. Turner did not find it quite as amusing.

"While I was recuperating from the fire, Jane would come sit beside me and read. Her beauty, which I could not behold because of my temporary blindness, was in her voice, for when she spoke, it was the sound of an angel speaking," Turner said and ended his time reciting from Shakespeare's *Romeo and Juliet:* "See how she leans her cheek upon her hand! O, that I were a glove on that hand, that I might touch that cheek!"

"You two shall not trick me into talking about the beauty of a woman... or of love," Nathan countered quickly, as it was now his turn to speak. "And, if you must know the reason for my reluctance, there are two: as soon as I cast one eye on a beautiful woman, the other eye has picked out another. And the other reason is my belief that love comes and goes like the waxing and waning of that moon up in the night sky.

"But I do have a story to tell, if you still wish to hear it," Nathan offered.

"Spoken like man who has had his heart broken a time or two," Turner answered with playful suspicion. "What do you say, Samuel?"

"I reck'n he be tell'n da truth, Mista Phil'p," Samuel replied, picking up on Turner's good-natured banter. "But see here... dat ain't noth'n a good suth'n woman couldn't set straight."

"How right you are, Samuel!" Turner agreed heartily. "Once you have tasted the best, nothing else will satisfy a man of refinement. That's how it is with the women of the South."

"It be say'd da wo'm suth'n air done ripen dem up thru an' thru... so's dey aw sweet inside," Samuel continued to fabricate his story as earnestly as he was able. "It git too co'd up here ta ripen dem up like dat."

"The warm southern air does what?" Nathan took exception vigorously, with the full understanding that he was being poked fun of.

"The claim is true, Nathan," Turner said confidently, while trying desperately to keep a straight face. "I am surprised you have not noticed how pale are the faces of your women folk up North, compared to those of the South. They simply have not had time to ripen."

"If you gentlemen are finished having your fun," Nathan chided, "I would like to begin my story before daybreak."

"Please do so then, but remember we have not yet finished this discussion," Turner added with mock sincerity.

Nathan hastily agreed to this meaningless resolution and began his story; it was in May of that year (1865). General Lee's army had surrendered the month before, and Nathan told his father that he was once again going to visit the property where half his regiment had been seriously wounded or had perished. This was the second anniversary and Nathan's second visit back to the place of his own, personal battle of Gettysburg. His father appreciated his son's dedication to the memory of his fallen buddies and asked if he might join him in his pilgrimage. Nathan would discover a few months later that this goodwill was all a ruse. Even while there, Nathan could sense indifference toward his recollections of battle and that his father's interests leaned more toward who owned the property. This nagging feeling of insincerity on his father's part caused Nathan to make an unscheduled trip back to Gettysburg to determine the name of the owner himself.

Upon this third visit, Nathan found the homestead abandoned. The modest country home itself was empty of all furnishings and in acute disrepair. When he returned to town, Nathan was told by several of the locals that after the bloody skirmish that occurred on the property, the owner, a retired doctor, and his wife sold their livestock and much of their personal belongings at a great discount, and moved farther north just before the great battle of Gettysburg had begun. On the final day of departure, the doctor was reported to have said, "The blood shed upon my land is unbearable, and I will not be returning."

"To make this long story short, my father is now the owner of this property," Nathan said in disgust. "And he paid one thousand dollars for the ten thousand acres."

"I don't suppose he is willing to sell it?" Turner asked after some thought.

"I proposed that very question before coming here," Nathan responded. "My father's reply was, 'Of course, for the reasonable price of one dollar per acre.'"

"Ten thousand dollars!" Turner gasped.

"The complete conversation with my father went like this," Nathan began.

"'That is larceny,' I proclaimed.

"'No, that's business, son,' my father replied calmly. 'How do you think I got to where I am? I am not stupid. I have known of your plans with this rebel for some time,' my father said shrewdly. 'I even allowed it to occur. I bought the property knowing you and your friend, who is an enemy of this country, would purchase it back from me at any price I should come up with. I have come up with that price. What is ten thousand dollars to a man who will inherit over a hundred thousand dollars, but did nothing to earn it? Be thankful I don't ask for more.'

"'You do not understand their relationship, Father,' I pleaded. 'They were like brothers... they considered themselves family. I was only helping my commanding officer fulfill his desire to see his family receive his inheritance.'

"'Your commanding officer's brother is a criminal!' my father's voice flared.

"'Let this be a lesson to you, son,' my father's voice was now even-tempered again. 'Your tender nature is a weakness and will be your downfall. I will not allow it to be the downfall of this family's fortune.'

"'And please do not try to blackmail me with your leaving the family again.' My father continued his punishing words. 'It would not have succeeded the first time if I did not already know how I could profit from it, and it will not work now. But before you go and do something rash, think carefully how your actions will affect your mother's health.'

"'Nathan, you are my only son and I love you like no other.' I believe my father said earnestly. 'You have been a soldier. You have seen what men are capable of doing to one another. You need to understand that it is no different in the ways of business. Learn from this; with another person's money, learn from this, my son.'

"I believe my father is the criminal. I do love him, yet I pity him," Nathan stated sadly. "He is right about leaving, though. It would break my mother's heart, so I dare not use that approach again."

"Nathan, I would never ask you to do anything that would cause harm to your family," Turner replied.

"Yo done learn't yo'self a lesson, Mista Nath'n... dat's true 'nuf," Samuel spoke in the same effortless manner as when he spoke earlier about the rock. "Just ain't the one yo daddy thinks it be."

"What do you mean, Samuel?" Nathan asked.

"Ya'll 'tended evil a'gain me, but God done used it fo' good, ta bring ta pass dis day, da sav'n of many lives." Samuel quoted Joseph's rebuke and forgiveness of his brothers (Genesis 50:20).

"Yes, that verse from Scripture came to my mind, as well," Turner pointed out. "I think we can all agree that what Nathan's father did was wrong, but what is done is done."

"Beg'n yo pardon, Mista Phil'p, but y'all may be see'n only half what da good Lawd wants ya'll ta be see'n."

"Please go on then, Samuel," Turner responded graciously. "What have we missed?"

"Well now, Ol' Jacob, he love dat boy Joseph da best... done made him dat coat with aw dem colors. Dis an' dat made his brothers so mad dey want noth'n mo' than ta see Joseph dade and gone. So, when dem boys was out in da wild an' Joseph come up wear'n dat fancy coat, dey done picked him up an' throws him in a pit ta die.

"What dem boys was think'n a do'n to po' Joseph was wrong," Samuel said. "Mista Nath'n, what yo daddy done to yo was wrong—not so bad as kill'n, but ain't so good as grace an' mercy."

"I know that, Samuel," Nathan sighed.

"Good... but dat ain't da whole story, no suh," Samuel continued with more exuberance. "Joseph don't stay in dat pit long. He done hauled off to Egyp' a slave. He gits sold to Pot'fer an' den gits throw'd into Pharaoh's dungeon fo' someth'n he ain't done. But Joseph don't stay in dat dungeon, neth'a. He come out afta making sense o Pharaoh's dream an' gits put in charge of stow'n up food for da com'n famine.

"See it now? Y'all see it?" Samuel inquired fiercely. "Aw dat bad, goin' back to dat coat of aw dem colors, was ta bring ta pass dat day... dat day... da sav'n of many lives from dat fam'n. Dat story ain't 'bout Joseph, no suh! An' it ain't 'about dem no-good brothers neth'a." Samuel hesitated momentarily to catch a breath. "Dat story 'bout God sav'n dem folk from starv'n!

"Now listen ta me, an' listen good." Samuel was not to be denied saying his piece now. "Aw dat good an' aw dat bad, goin' back to when y'all first met Mista Benj'min, was ta git dis here land... dis day. Dis ain't 'bout yo friend. An' it ain't 'bout yo two neth'a."

Samuel took another deep breath of air. "Dis is 'bout God sav'n some folk!"

When Samuel finished speaking, he appeared tired and old, as if he had aged a decade in the course of this powerful lecture. He struggled to his feet, but before taking his first step, he turned and looked Nathan straight in the eyes.

"Now, Mista Nath'n," Samuel spoke softly and with great compassion. "He don't knows it yet, but yo' daddy... well, he bin used by God His Self. So, don't yo go bein' so haw'd on him, ya hear me now?"

"Yes, sir," Nathan responded appreciatively. "Samuel?"

"Yes, Mista Nath'n?"

"Thank you."

Samuel smiled, said good-night, and went off to sleep next to the horses. Turner and Nathan sat motionless, each to their own thoughts. Finally, Turner broke out of the trance of watching the constant activity of hot coals in what was left of a waning fire and spoke.

"Nathan, please listen to me carefully."

The unveiling of his thoughts took on the manner of a battlefield commander who had mapped out his strategy, and was now detailing the sequence of events he wanted to see in battle.

"When you get back to Philadelphia, I would like for you to tell your father that I accept his offer for this property. I will not be going with you. Before leaving Gettysburg, I will make arrangements giving you powers to access monies and make purchases in my name. Once the transaction is complete, I would like you to begin the process of putting the ownership of this property in trust—one that even your father could not prevail against.

"And I want you to repay your father every penny spent on my behalf," Turner added as an afterthought. "That would include the expense of those two fine Philadelphia lawyers that were here this morning."

After a brief pause, Turner changed battlefronts.

"I will be going south with Samuel, if he is willing. After stopping briefly in Virginia to see my family, he and I will go in search of his family. Once they have been found, I will bring them all back to Virginia until *we* have decided what it is the Lord has planned for *us*."

"We? Us?" Nathan interrupted.

"Yes, you," Turner responded affectionately. "I certainly would not be sitting here without you. And Samuel... well, although I'm not yet prepared to call him a prophet, I believe he did hear the voice of the Lord, and his path was directed to be here with us. I suspect Samuel will keep our course firmly planted in God's perfect will; and besides that, he reminds me a great deal of Benjamin.

"I do not foresee any great commission 'to save some folk,' as Samuel put it, prospering without you both," Turner continued. "Once this land is in trust, the decisions on its usefulness to the Lord shall be shared equally amongst the three of us, with the majority having their way. And, unless God is in a rush, I believe you should finish with your schooling."

After another brief pause, Turner continued his strategy.

"It is also true that I hope to marry soon. My darling bride-to-be has already made it known to me that she wishes to remain in Virginia to help her aging parents rebuild their family farm. That is a worthy and selfless act. It also coincides with my belief that the Lord brought me through this war to help rebuild the South. I do not see those purposes changing with the events of this day. I can see myself being used here only whenever an incorrigible engineer might be needed or whenever it pleases the Lord."

Turner could sense Nathan's excitement, but the young man remained quiet. It was late, and tomorrow promised to be a busy day. Turner opened his bed-roll and scooted down into a prone position, using his knapsack as a pillow. Nathan did the same without a word. After a time, Turner spoke again as if speaking to the stars above him.

"I have also been thinking about that rock over there and how you have fit into all of this. I mean to say, besides fulfilling your commanding officer's final wishes admirably, of course."

Turner's voice was now gentle and paternal.

"In between thoughts of what the Lord's intentions might be for this land, I can't help thinking about what Samuel said about your daddy being used by Him. In that story of Joseph, it was Judah's idea to sell his brother into slavery in the first place. When that famine finally did come, it forced Judah and his other brothers to Egypt in search for food. The only brother not making that trip was Benjamin, the youngest. While in Egypt, Joseph put Judah and his brothers to the test. If you recall, it was none other than Judah who offered himself up to become a slave in Benjamin's place.

"A very selfless thing for a scoundrel to do, don't you think?" Turner asked rhetorically. "Then it occurred to me, if the Lord did use your father to help gain this property by way of selfish means then maybe, just maybe, your father may still have an unselfish role to play before all is said and done."

The prospect of turning his father's heart around gave Nathan much needed comfort.

"Well, I have kept us from enjoying a good night's sleep long enough, but if there is one last thing to confess, it is this," Turner continued. "Benjamin would have been awful damned proud of what you have done; awful proud, indeed.

"Good night, Nathan," Turner said and turned on his side.

"Good night," Nathan replied gratefully.

# 9

# Hallowed Ground

The sun had not yet appeared above the horizon, but the eastern skies were already preparing its arrival with soft, warm colors. It seemed as though their heads had finally found comfortable spots on their knapsacks when Philip and Nathan were both awakened by Samuel.

"Git up! Mista Phil'p, Mista Nath'n, git up!" Samuel was hollering excitedly, as he danced back and forth around the cold fire pit. "It's gone... sho' 'nuf, it is!"

"Samuel, what's gone?" Turner asked sluggishly.

"Dat rock of y'all's!" Samuel responded even more excitedly. "Da Lawd done took it back, hallelujah!"

Both Turner and Nathan sprang to their feet and gazed in the direction of the rock—or where the rock should have been. They put on their boots in haste, and all three men ran as fast as they could through the tall grass until they were standing in front of a wide clearing with a large pile of rock that could have only been stacked by hand. There was no trace of the giant white rock, not even a rectangular impression in the ground to show it had ever rested there.

"Well, I'll be damned," Turner uttered in amazement.

"No, suh, yo be blessed. Yo sho' is," Samuel corrected him.

"That is the way I left it two years ago, Philip," Nathan added in stunned disbelief, "if you understand me."

"I am certain it is, Nathan," Turner said with a broad smile.

Turner was as awestruck as the other two, but after a slow look around and a brief moment to reflect, he became blissfully content with this resolution. He was even more grateful for being able to give his dear friend the proper burial he deserved... and right where he lay.

"So, what do we do now?" Nathan asked.

"Well, I don't know about you, but I sure could go for some coffee," Turner stated casually. "Samuel, if you have brought with you eggs and bacon, I shall be inclined to dance all the way back to camp."

"Well, Mista Phil'p, yo can start kick'n up dem boots," Samuel said, finding it hard to contain his joy. "An' I be a-danc'n too. Oh yes, I will!"

"That's it?" Nathan said, as if he were the only sane person remaining. "Coffee, eggs, dancing... what about the rock?"

"What about it, Nathan?" Turner asked sincerely. "What will you have us do?"

"Da Lawd done giveth an' da Lawd done taketh away, Mista Nath'n, suh," Samuel concluded.

With little left to be said, Turner and Samuel looked at each other, clasped arms, and began hopping and skipping, hooting and hollering, spinning, and kicking back toward camp.

"Now I guess I've seen everything," Nathan said to himself and started running to catch up with the two dancing loons he considered his friends.

During breakfast, Turner's battle strategy from the night before was repeated and adopted by all. It took a good deal of time to console Samuel, once it was suggested that he and Turner would begin a search for his family after a brief stop in Virginia. It was also decided that all three men should survey the property together, now that Samuel was invited into the decision-making process—which took even more explanation and consoling. It was a long breakfast.

Their first quest of the day would be to inspect the abandoned house to see if it could be made livable again. If so, that would become Samuel's new home while things got sorted out; if it were to meet with his wife's approval, of course.

"It do git mighty co'd in d'ese hills, an' my sweet Rosetta is a li'l thing," Samuel admitted. "I'm a guess'n I need to whoop me a bear fo' his hide jus' ta keep her wo'm."

Fortunately, the house was well built with the absolute comfort of a retired doctor in mind. Although empty and in some disarray, its complete restoration was certainly achievable and could begin as early as the following spring. This would allow Samuel's family to stay at the Parker farm over the winter. Without some explicit purpose for the property, there was no rush to make any other improvements. The only real hurry was to get back home and take care of personal matters. So, for the time being, the property remained a 10,000-acre memorial devoted to his dear friend and the others who died there.

The remainder of the day was spent galloping around in the woods, and it was unanimous: if you have seen ten acres of Pennsylvania hillside, you have seen all ten thousand. Therefore, it was decided at supper they would return to town in the morning. There was plenty left to do in Gettysburg before leaving for home. Since it was the most convenient town with a train stop, it seemed reasonable to spend a day or two developing a few useful relationships there. The banker, for one, and the authorities for another; that is, those charged with protecting the holdings of the bank.

The accusing words spoken by Judge Douglas in the previous day's hearing did not go unfelt or forgotten by Turner. The battle that raged here did take a terrible toll on the quiet, unsuspecting village and brought to mind a remedy; not so big as to undo all the damage incurred but a good start at least. As soon as it could be arranged between banks, Turner planned to transfer a significant sum of money (large for a little town bank, yet a rather small portion of the total inheritance, say $5,000) to the bank in Gettysburg. It would come with the understanding that if these funds were used to make small loans to local residents on generous terms, there would be no attempt to withdraw this principle for a period of one year. If discoveries were made to the contrary, the money would be withdrawn expeditiously and no further business with the bank would be entertained.

Thoughts and conversations like this lasted late into the night until all three men woke the following morning, not knowing who fell asleep first or when. Not wishing to waste a single minute getting back to town, or Alabama more specifically, Samuel was up before the sun and started working on coffee and breakfast. Turner and Nathan slowly came to life, but only after daylight began pushing the starlight off the eastern horizon. Rather than rising with an appetite, however, Turner awoke with a strong urge to walk out to Benjamin's gravesite. As he began moving in that direction, he asked if anyone would like to join him. It took but a second for Nathan to fall in behind Turner; it would be spring at the earliest before his next return. Samuel continued his preparations but spoke kindly.

"Y'all go say good-bye to yo' friend. I be right here when yo done."

As they walked solemnly across the overgrown field of battle, it suddenly occurred to Nathan that his last three visits had been more focused on how to get the giant rock to move off his beloved colonel, than to show his appreciation and deep affection for the man below it. Turner's thoughts had also been on the rock. He, too, suddenly came to the realization that Benjamin had become secondary to the rock since Nathan first mentioned it. It was time for them to pay their overdue respects without a big, white stone staring back at them.

After twenty minutes, Nathan was finished saying what he had come out to say (without speaking a word) and let Turner know he was headed back to camp. Turner begged his pardon and asked for just a little more time. He promised not to be much longer.

"You need not beg for anything from me," Nathan replied compassionately. "You take as much time as you need. It would make sense that a farewell between brothers should take longer."

Now that it was just Benjamin and himself, Turner spoke aloud. Until there was Jane, he had kept his emotions in the realm of thoughts and dreams. He now preferred these expositions of the heart to be conveyed in an audible fashion.

"Well, here we are again my dear, dear friend," he began. "It has been a long road back to you. I hope you understand the reasons for my delay.

"And then there was this matter of a large and formidable rock that came to rest upon your grave like a faithful hound protecting its sleeping master, refusing to leave even by force. Then it decides to walk off on its own accord in the middle of night."

This lighthearted banter did not last long, however, as a mist began to form in Turner's eyes.

"I'm sorry, Benjamin... I'm terribly sorry. Who am I that I should argue with God, but there isn't a day that goes by that I do not believe the wrong man was taken from this earth.

"I have no doubt you have already forgiven me, dear brother," he softly confessed. "Now all that is needed to remove this perpetual ache inside me is to forgive myself—a much greater stumbling block than I expected."

Anticipating that this block, over which he kept stumbling, would not be pushed aside in the few minutes he had left, Turner changed topics.

"You did well with Nathan. You most likely knew who this young, confused boy being delivered into your care was by the Walker surname. I have no doubt the father's wealth and power meant little to you. Perhaps you even prayed for this tyrant," Turner stated with some irritation. "Now I suppose you want me to take over the hopeless responsibility of praying for this selfish bully's salvation?"

The idea caused a momentary pause.

"You need not look at me that way," Turner said sternly, as he imagined seeing the sadness in Benjamin's eyes. This scenario was not uncommon between them: the casual dismissal of something that Turner deemed unworthy or objectionable when all that was being asked of him was a little grace. He believed his reactions were always quite justifiable, reasonable, and not intended to hurt anyone, but it did hurt someone; it went straight to the heart of God, and Benjamin would let him know it. This lesson was accomplished without arguing. The look of disappointment on Benjamin's face never failed to cause Turner to look inside his own heart. The slow, brooding process would cause Turner to turn away momentarily, as he turned away now.

"Very well, I shall add his name to my petitions," Turner huffed, after turning his attention back to the neatly stacked pile of rocks. "In all fairness, Nathan deserves a good father."

After some more introspection, Turner continued.

"Now that I have acquiesced to your will once again, would it be asking too much of you to fill my mind with your desires for this property and the wealth you have entrusted to me?" Turner asked in earnest. "You must give me some purpose, Benjamin, or I shall have no choice but to obey my own conscience and use whatever resources I have to fulfill my purpose, which is to help rebuild the South."

*Or is it that I am asking the wrong person?* Turner thought. *The massive rock that has been sitting here for two years most certainly came from God Himself.*

"Is it He I should be asking and not you?" Turner asked with a sigh. "Ugh... sometimes the two of you can be so infuriating."

There he stayed for a moment in pensive ambiguity. With reluctance, he looked over his shoulder toward campsite and then back to the pile of rocks.

"I must be going now," Turner said tenderly.

The words made him shudder. How could he have even entertained the idea of leaving so quickly? How could he be going when there was so much left unsaid? He hadn't even told Benjamin about Jane yet. Suddenly, he felt a hand press on his shoulder and heard Joseph's voice.

"Sir, we must be going, or we shall all die."

"Yes, you are right, Sergeant," Turner replied, unconcerned with the game being played on his mind. He turned to have a look anyway, but saw no one.

As much as it distressed him, *he knew* he must be going. *He knew* Nathan and Samuel were waiting on him to leave. *He knew* he could not turn back time; *he knew* what was done could not be undone. *He knew* somewhere in this tragedy, God had a plan. *He knew... he knew...*

He knew all the right answers, except for the one to his great guilt and despair. For this, he would have to wait for solace or judgment; he would accept either. In an attempt to bring this heart-wrenching farewell to a close, Turner spoke boldly. It was a futile attempt.

"I will return in the spring to help tidy up the place and..."

In a wave of unfettered emotion, he collapsed on the pile of rocks, caressed them as if they were no less than Benjamin's broken body, and grieved uncontrollably. No more was said.

In time, Turner returned to camp and gratefully accepted a hot cup of coffee, but kindly refused anything to eat. Little was spoken, as they broke camp and mounted up for the return ride back to town. Once he was on top of his steed, Turner hesitated. For a moment longer, he could see himself looking out over the smoky, early morning battlefield, littered with the dead and wounded. He saw Benjamin's lifeless body lying peacefully on the ground with Nathan's darkened, yet youthful, face looking up at him and, in the distance, the large dead oak.

Nathan and Samuel waited patiently... as did Joseph on that fateful day.

"Damn this cruel war," Turner said with utter disdain, and was off.

There is nothing like a vigorous ride on horseback to restore a jovial spirit, and by the time they took their first rest, Turner was himself again. It was early afternoon when the men arrived back in the quiet, welcoming existence of Gettysburg. They returned the horses to the livery at the end of town and began the short walk back to their temporary lodgings. Although Turner had not eaten all day and was famished, he expressed to Nathan and Samuel his desire for solitude and an early bedtime rather than an evening meal and said would meet them both for breakfast, if that was agreeable to them; it was. The three then bid each other good night and went their separate ways.

It was a long and fitful night's sleep for Turner. The unimaginable events of the last two days could hardly be explained, much less believed. If asked, "And how was your trip, Mr. Turner?" there would be no retelling the finer points of this story. It was still more than an hour before breakfast would be served. He washed up, dressed, and went downstairs in hopes of being offered coffee and quiet conversation from the owner before things got too busy. My, how things changed.

"Good morning, Mr. Turner," Duke said with unexpected enthusiasm. "May I offer you coffee and a bite to eat?"

"And good morning to you, kind sir," Turner responded curiously. He looked again at his pocket watch and confirmed its accuracy using the grandfather clock standing in the corner. "I thought breakfast was not for an hour yet."

"It is our pleasure to make every accommodation for you, Mr. Turner. I have also taken the liberty to find you the most current edition of the *Philadelphia Inquirer* and our own *Gettysburg Compiler* for your reading pleasure."

"Coffee and conversation will be fine," Turner replied gratefully, "if you have the time."

"The two things I enjoy most at this hour. I will be right back with your coffee."

The kindly old gentleman returned with coffee and a plate topped with a generous assortment of breads, pastries, and jams—compliments of Mrs. Duchene. This quickly prompted Turner's stomach to growl noisily, due to his self-imposed fasting the night before. Using the excuse that he did not wish to offend his host's generous nature, Turner began to help himself to several cakes and muffins before initiating any type of serious conversation. Duke accepted this explanation, but had to smile at the ravenous quality with which Turner set upon the baked goods.

Turner did not recognize the scope of his hunger until half the plate was devoured and he finally looked up to see the pleased expression on the face of his host. Somewhat embarrassed by his unwitting behavior, Turner wiped the crumbs from his face and lap, and spoke.

"You must share with your lovely wife my... um... enthusiasm for her ability to bake some of the most delightful pastries I have ever had the opportunity to make a pig of myself over."

"I will most certainly do that," Duke said and chuckled. "Now, was there anything specific you wished to have a conversation about?"

"Yes, thank you," Turner said politely. "But first, if possible, could you explain this change in disposition toward me?"

"I believe I can do that."

He stood and walked over to the reception desk. There, on the counter, was a neatly stacked pile of mail. He picked it up and returned to his seat. Once seated, he handed this stack of cards and letters to Turner.

"These are yours... and I have a feeling this is just the beginning," the gentleman stated. "I suppose they are from those who wish to make bygones be bygones."

"Would this have anything to do with my court hearing the other day, Mr. Duchene?"

"It would have everything to do with your court hearing, Mr. Turner."

"Could you please be more specific?" Turner asked, not wishing to give away the answer.

"You are a rich man now," Duke replied unceremoniously. "You would have had to live under a rock not to have heard the news and drawn an opinion about it. In fact, every room in my hotel is now occupied—by those who hope to have a conference with you is my guess."

This was a course of events that Turner never contemplated and was unsure how it should be handled. There was so much he needed to accomplish before leaving and little time for anything else. Noticing the effect this news was having on his guest, Mr. Duchene spoke.

"I have been giving this some thought. If you wish, I can have Mrs. Duchene fix you something to eat that can be carried with you, thereby avoiding any intrusion on your breakfast here. I also recommend leaving anything of value with me. I will see to it that it is kept safe. Your room cannot be watched at all times; therefore, I ask that you leave the door open when you are out. I am afraid that closing it and locking it will not stop a thief, and only cost me a door."

He then pulled out of his pocket a small double-barreled Derringer with five extra rounds and handed it to Turner.

"Take this. Your reputation as a West Point cadet and decorated soldier are now as well known as your wealth, so I doubt you will find much trouble here. But since the end of war, our small town has seen many strangers come and go. You may return the weapon to me when you can find yourself a suitable replacement, or just before your departure.

"Is there anything else I can do for you, Mr. Turner?"

"Even before this great transfer of wealth, which is still shocking to me, you have shown me nothing but kindness," Turner replied graciously. "Yet, you must harbor some resentment towards me. Why, then, would you do this for me?"

"As I have said, opinions have been drawn. So have mine."

"Yes... and?" Turner asked, hoping for more.

"I detect no moral shortcoming in your character—only generosity and goodwill. That appears to be the same reaction from all who have come to know you, regardless of their affiliation in this God-forsaken war. Most surprisingly, that would include young Mr. Walker, whom I have known for many years, and the Union colonel whose wealth you inherited.

"The war is over," the old gentleman concluded. "Let us begin there."

"Your words are comforting to me, and I thank you for them," Turner said gratefully. "As far as breakfast, I will be sharing what little appetite I have left with Nathan and Samuel. That reminds me, about Samuel..."

"No need to explain. Samuel and I spoke last night while you slept," Duke interrupted politely. "And as I have said, it seems all who know you hold you in the highest regard. That would include Samuel."

"Then, to return to your question as to whether there was anything else you could do. There is," Turner said with some reservation. "But it would be to ask the most gruesome thing."

"Ask it, Mr. Turner, and I will let you know if it can be done."

With this response, Turner described what he knew of Gettysburg shortly after the blood bath that raged on for the first three days of July two years before (1863). It was his understanding that sometime in late November of that same year, Mr. Lincoln arrived in Gettysburg and addressed a crowd there. Turner was not shown a copy of the Union president's remarks, but he had heard that, although brief, it was quite eloquent. The ceremony was to dedicate a cemetery on a hill to bury the thousands of dead from the three-day battle, even though many of these men were citizens from states other than Pennsylvania.

*That same hill is where Major General Pickett lost most of his division on the 3rd of July—with most of these men coming from Virginia. My orders were to attack the Union rear and not stop until my cavalry reached the copse of trees*, Turner recalled in his own mind.

After this brief internal reflection, Turner finished the extent of what he knew. He was able to learn during his interaction with the Union soldiers at Appomattox earlier that year that this cemetery in Gettysburg was made available to Union soldiers only—not his Confederate countrymen. This meant that the remains of thousands of fallen brothers, sons, and fathers were still out there. Granted, when he left Virginia, it was not his intention to see a wrong and make it right, but he did confide this anguish to Mr. Duchene.

*My only concern was for one body... not a thousand*, Turner thought.

"I have since been put in a position to do something about this injustice, Mr. Duchene." Turner concluded. "But how, I do not know."

The old gentleman listened attentively and patiently. This was not unlike some of the stories coming out of the South concerning his countrymen, whose lives were lost in battle and left to rot in a field or pecked apart as it lay against a rock. But the war was over.

*Let us begin there*, Duke thought.

"That is gruesome work," the kind, old man agreed. "But not so gruesome as it was two years ago when the summer sun bloated bodies to twice their size and turned men's skin black as coal."

This was not a rebuke of Turner's request. The old man was simply reminiscing a horror that no civilized society should have to go through.

"I will find you a trustworthy contractor who will show reverence for those lost—and then found—on Gettysburg's hallowed grounds," Duke offered. "If you wish to have the discovery location recorded for each soldier and then have them placed in small coffins for transportation down South, that would add to the expense. Or will you be burying them on Dr. Peterson's abandoned property west of here?"

"You know about the property as well?" Turner asked in disbelief.

"I am a hotel proprietor and an excellent listener when spoken to."

"I don't rightly know what will be done with the land," Turner admitted. "But I do not get the sense that this property was for the receiving of these poor souls."

"If you are considering the purchase of this land, but do not know what for—who *would* know its purpose, Mr. Turner?"

"The Lord is my hope, Mr. Duchene."

As if on cue, in walked Nathan and Samuel; as Turner reached out his hand of greeting in Samuel's direction, Samuel reached out his hand, but in the direction of the half-empty plate of pastries.

"Dat ain't Miss Duchene's bak'n, is it, Mista Duke?" Samuel asked with all sincerity.

"Yes is it, Samuel," the old gentleman stated with a smile.

"Den yo mus' tell me, suh, who in dey right mine would let go a plate half full o yo wife's bak'n?"

Without a word, Duke looked accusingly at Turner, which immediately caused everyone to do the same.

"What?" Turner barked defensively. "I ate half the plate!"

"Please help yourself to the remainder, Samuel," Duke offered.

"Oh, I will, suh," Samuel said joyfully.

Samuel picked up the plate and walked it over to Nathan. He then suggested that Nathan take as many as he could handle, because it would be the last offer he would receive. Samuel then turned to his former boss, who would lighten the plate by one blueberry muffin. Turner, however, was ignored completely until the plate was empty.

"I ate half the plate!" Turner said, still trying to defend his actions.

"Mr. Duke, please inform Miss Sophia that, had I been given the same opportunity as my friend, not a crumb would have been spared," Nathan said politely, bowed, and made his way out the door. "No more truth than that, sir."

"I ate half the plate!" Turner snapped in Nathan's direction.

"Mista Duke, it gonna be yo wife's bak'n I's gonna miss da most," Samuel said earnestly, bowed, and began his walk out the door. "Sho' 'nuf is."

"I ate half the plate," Turner said softly in Mr. Duchene's direction.

"Indeed you did," Duke replied gladly, knowing it was all just a charade to needle a friend. "What my curious mind would like to know, however, is what exactly happened out there that would cause the three of you to become so close when, by all rights, you should be enemies?"

"A rock, I suppose," Turner said earnestly.

"A rock?" the gentleman replied, somewhat confused.

As intended, Turner shied away from any notion to explain the last two days—or the last two years. Allowing his comment to remain as clear as mud, Turner excused himself.

"I shall pray about our conversation of this morning and look forward to some workable solution by our next meeting. At your convenience, of course," Turner stated politely. "Good day, Mr. Duchene, and thank you for all you are willing to do." With that, Turner followed the path of his two conniving friends.

*A rock?* the old man thought. *Must have meaning only to them, I suppose.*

It was quite a sight to see two white men and a black man sit down for breakfast together, but soon the inquisitive eyes stopped staring, and the meal proceeded without incident. Nathan mentioned receiving a telegram from the law firm confirming both of Benjamin's bank accounts being changed to reflect Turner as new owner. It was agreed that Nathan would be given authorization to access $10,000 for the acquisition of the property on Turner's behalf. It was also agreed that, once all receipts had been tallied, Nathan would have access to funds for the expeditious reimbursement of all other expenses incurred by his father to bring Benjamin's last will and testament to court. It was then agreed that each man should pray diligently for God's long-term plan for this property.

"Nathan, did you happen to bring with you Benjamin's Bible?" Turner asked.

"Yes, I have it."

"May I borrow it until next we meet?"

"Of course," Nathan replied. "For what purpose, may I ask?"

"As you have already observed, Benjamin fancied himself an essayist in the margins of his Bible. I am hoping to find a clue for the use of this property somewhere in those margins." Turner began. "I do not see my life slowing down anytime soon, but neither do I see it being more harried than that of a student at Harvard. I recommend you concentrate on your studies; I will concentrate on Benjamin's essays for now."

"Mista Phil'p, suh," Samuel said quietly. "I still don't gits it."

"What don't you get, Samuel?"

"I ain't got noth'n. An' I ain't nev'a gonna have noth'n. What ya'll need me fo'?"

"My dear Samuel," Turner began thoughtfully. "Do not allow the devil to fool you, not now. The Lord put you here for a reason. I believe that. Nathan believes that. You are a warrior, Samuel... God's warrior. We need your strength, your courage, your wisdom, your friendship."

"I reckon if dat's good 'nuf fo' yo, it sho' be good 'nuf fo' me."

"Samuel, you may correct me if I am wrong, but I believe there is a train going east due here tomorrow," Turner said. "Let us make every effort to be on that train. I have much to do before then, as I am sure you do. So, I will see you both tonight for dinner, if that is agreeable."

Once Turner was back outside, there was not a street that he could walk where someone did not stop him and introduce himself—or give him a bone-chilling glare.

*Opinions have been drawn*, Turner thought, as he fingered the tiny pistol in his vest pocket.

His morning began in the telegraph office, where he sent a short message to Jane with his departure date from Gettysburg and his longing to be with her once again. After that, considerable time was spent with the banker and Mr. Duchene's associate, who agreed to exhume Confederate soldiers for $1 each. This included documentation of where the body was found and its placement inside a small coffin (along with buckles, buttons, and other articles close to the body), with the coffins being purchased separately. An account with an initial deposit of $2,000 was established at the bank for the purpose of making payments for this work. Mr. Duchene was given authority to access these funds and agreed to twenty-five cents per soldier for his time and oversight of the project. Turner would telegram Duke with the address where these coffins could be transported, once he reached Richmond and had spoken to Virginia's provisional governor, a West Virginian.

An account with an initial deposit of $5,000 was also established for purposes of making small, affordable loans to locals. The remainder of Turner's day was spent sitting on top of Culp's Hill in deep thought. It was calm and peaceful now. It was not how he remembered it, but how he preferred it.

Dinner was pleasant, with each man declaring his readiness to hop aboard the 9:00 AM train out of Gettysburg the following day. Turner would have enjoyed spending more time with Nathan, since there were no plans to meet again before spring of the next year, but there was one more thing that needed to be done before the night was through. Excusing himself from the table, Turner walked outside and climbed onto the buggy that had been borrowed from Mr. Duchene earlier in the day. He headed west out of town, according to the instructions given to him, and, in twenty minutes' time, pulled up in front of the large stone country house.

Turner knocked on the door and was greeted a moment later by a young black man in a well-fitted servant's uniform. He was asked his name and invited inside to wait. From deep within the walls and chambers of the house came a loud, coarse voice asking, "Who, do you say?" The owner of that voice soon appeared at the other end of the long hallway and began walking in Turner's direction

"Well, now, if it isn't our rich, young rebel," the angry man declared. "Come to gloat, has he?"

"I have come to ask forgiveness, Your Honor," Turner replied calmly.

"Honor? What would you know about honor?"

"I know enough about honor to know that I fall short of it every time, yet I will never stop striving to measure up to those that do have it, Your Honor."

"You are a murderer, Mr. Turner," Judge Douglas proclaimed. "Are you telling me there is honor among murderers?"

Turner stood silent.

"If I could sentence you to hell, I would," the judge said harshly. "Go now. You will find no forgiveness here."

"I believe the One who has the power to sentence me to hell has already pardoned me, Your Honor," Turner replied meekly. "I am truly sorry for the things that I have done in the course of this terrible war. I beg your forgiveness."

"I do not know what spell you put on Mr. Hillary to cause him to leave you his money, but you will not put it on me," the judge spat. "I will never forgive you. Daniel, show this horse's ass to the door."

"I'm sorry to have disturbed you. Good evening, sir." Turner turned and followed the butler to the door. Then, just before the door shut, he heard a strong, yet gentle voice come from behind him.

"I forgive you, mister."

# 10

# Homeward

Turner was up before the two bells mounted on top of his bedside table clock could begin their harassing competition to wake him. He was going home. He was going back to his angel and the kisses that could make him forget all else. With Judge Douglas' stinging rebuke still fresh in his mind, he could benefit from the use of this love-induced amnesia. It was a much earlier start to the day than on previous mornings and would test Mr. Duchene's claim to be an early riser, but Turner was actually hoping to slip away without fanfare. Conversation, although pleasurable, would be a secondary preference to some solitary reflection on the train station platform right now. The hotel bill was settled and the unused pistol returned the night before, so there was no need for the two to meet again.

The darkened hallways and lobby below were encouraging. Turner eased down the stairs quietly and was almost out the door when he noticed a large sack on the bench where the kindly gentleman would normally sit. In the dim light, he could see there was a note attached and as he came closer, he noticed that it was addressed to him. It read:

> Mr. Turner, have a pleasant journey home. Mrs. D. sends her regards along with these pastries. There should be enough for you and two others, but we will leave that up to you.
>
> Yours Truly, Duke

The sack contained a large supply of baked goods bundled up in linen. Although he was not as ravenous as he had been on the previous day, the aroma alone caused Turner's stomach to softly growl its excitement once again. He walked silently over to the desk, where he found a single sheet of letterhead and penned this response:

> Dear Mr. Duchene, thank you. Please express my gratefulness to Mrs. D. My decision to share these treats will be based solely on the quality of the groveling I receive from my two traveling companions.
>
> Till we meet again, Philip

The walk from hotel to train station was short, and Turner arrived before the six o'clock bell. It would be a long wait, but the seating was comfortable and the interior well lit—a perfect environment for leisurely contemplation. The Gettysburg railroad station was the end of the line for locomotives going west, so it had become a popular destination with a steady stream of travelers coming and going. For this reason, the wait to be going back east again would be prolonged, while the locomotive engine was detached, placed on a turntable, spun around and reattached. Turner had just sat down in hopes of remaining hidden behind one of the two newspapers that had been given to him the day before, when he could not help but notice an attractive, young lady in fashionable dress glide effortlessly through the doors of the station.

*How is it even possible to be so perfectly adorned at six in the morning?* Turner thought.

It wasn't long before a waft of fine perfume occupied the air he breathed and a fancy women's hat appeared over the top of the newspaper he now held in front of his face. Dropping the paper and rising at the same time, Turner now stood facing perhaps the most beautiful creature he had set eyes on since Jane.

"Good morning, miss," Turner said pleasantly. "May I be of service?"

"Good morning, sir," the lady answered sweetly. "Will the next train be arriving soon?"

"Not for another two hours is my understanding," Turner replied politely, but curious why she would be asking him when there were railroad attendants present.

"Oh my, that is quite a long wait," she said and let out a soft sigh. "May I sit?"

"Of course," Turner said kindly.

Turner waited for his unanticipated guest to make herself comfortable before sitting himself. Not wishing to appear rude, he did not immediately return to his reading (or hiding) but did consider this unusual behavior. A woman this attractive, and so open to engaging strangers, may fall prey to an unsuspecting villain. If unescorted, he would keep a safe eye on her while they traveled.

"Are you travelling alone?" Turner asked with concern.

"Oh... I never travel alone sir," she replied and pulled her own pearl-handled Derringer up to the opening of her purse.

"I see," Turner replied with an agreeable smile.

*A popular little thing, this Derringer; its accuracy cannot be depended upon beyond a few feet, but it conceals well,* Turner thought.

"Have you been in Gettysburg long?" she continued.

"Several days," he replied, hoping to get through any courteous small talk quickly. "And you?"

"A few weeks now," she said. "I come to visit my uncle every summer. Perhaps you know of him... Judge Douglas?"

"Judge Douglas!" Turner answered louder than he intended.

"Yes, but he has been in such a miserable state lately," she began. "I told him if he did not cheer up, I would have to leave. Last night he was his worst, so here I am."

Turner said nothing. This young lady seemed so sincere in her demeanor, but could the story be true? He had not spoken to anyone about his experience, and as far as he knew, the only people in the room last night were himself, the judge, and his butler.

*Could this meeting be more than coincidence?* Turner thought. *One way to find out.*

"Your uncle is a good man," Turner said honestly. "You must forgive him; he is in a position that causes him to relive things that no person should be forced to relive."

This did not appear to be the response the young lady had anticipated, leading Turner to believe she knew more than she was saying. He could see the wheels turning in her mind. After reorganizing her thoughts, she spoke tenderly.

"Perhaps you know what troubles my uncle then, sir?"

"Be careful what you say," came a voice from across the room.

"Nathan!" both Turner and the lady exclaimed simultaneously. This shared greeting caused Turner and the lady to look at one another awkwardly. Nathan, however, approached them both as if this gathering were not that unpredictable.

"Hello, Emily," Nathan spoke with unmistakable affection. "You look lovelier each time I see you."

"What are you doing here?" Emily replied with less tenderness.

"You two know each other?" Turner asked in fascination.

"Oh yes, we go way back," Nathan replied, without taking his eyes off the young lady. "I believe we were both eight years old when you first expressed your love and devotion to me. Isn't that right, Emily?"

"It was ten... and I was ten years old," Emily acknowledged dismissively. "And what are you doing here?"

"First, introductions, if I may," Nathan stated. "Philip Turner, meet Emily Preston, an old family friend. Emily, I believe you know whom you are talking to, or am I mistaken?"

Emily said nothing.

At this point, Nathan began an explanation of what he had hoped to avoid—this encounter. He had arrived two days before Benjamin's probate hearing and already knew that Emily's uncle would be the judge. What Nathan didn't know of was Emily's presence in Gettysburg to see her uncle. Emily spoke truthfully when she told Turner about her visits here during the summer months, and the timing of this visit was purely coincidental. Nathan made this discovery by chance when Emily nearly bumped into him at the train station, but passed without recognizing him. Her appearance was the reason he did not seek a room at the Duke and was careful to protect his anonymity before the court hearing. If he were to be discovered by Emily, it would have brought attention to the hotel and, thereby, attention to Philip. After two years of committed preparation, he was not willing to take any unnecessary risks.

These precautions were unfortunate but necessary, Nathan explained. Despite his deep affection for Emily, he thought her to be, for lack of a better term, a gossipmonger for various newspapers. He knew that much of her early work had come with a history of inaccuracies and a propensity for sensationalism. This carelessness, or deliberate falsehood, had caused more than one of her articles to be labeled fallacious or malicious and retracted. One such column was written for the *Pittsburgh Chronicle*: it was penned under a masculine pseudonym; it had Nathan as its subject matter, and it put into question the validity of his dismissal from the army. The article left the reader with the impression that Nathan wanted out, and his wealthy father had bought this escape for him, while many more of his colleagues went on to die bravely in the great Battle of Gettysburg. When the truth finally came out in court months later, it was too late. The article neglected to mention Nathan's age, or the fact that he had been awarded the Medal of Honor for "bravery in the field of battle" just weeks earlier. Because of the weaknesses of their own minds, many people preferred to believe the worst—even to this day.

"Do I speak falsely, Emily?" Nathan asked.

"I am a journalist, Nathan. I write what I see and what I hear."

"You could have asked me. I would have told you the truth."

"You were nowhere to be found, and my sources seemed reliable."

"I was at school and wrote to you once a week."

"You were a soldier, and now you are a student of Harvard. You have a life, and so do I."

"Did you want it to be true? Did you intend to hurt me?"

"I was given an assignment and did my best, nothing more."

"Emily, you must know how I feel about you."

"Nathan, you are a Walker, and I am a Preston. We are not meant to be in business... or in love."

"I am not my father!" Nathan snapped.

"Please," Nathan said, after regaining his composure. "What our fathers do in business should not affect our feelings for one another. Can we talk about this?"

"I cannot love you, Nathan, so let us just drop this."

"Now, where were we, Mr. Turner?" Emily asked, but found her new assignment missing. "Now look what you have done!" she said angrily. "I promise you, Nathan; I will find out what you two are up to."

"I must give up, then," Nathan announced with arms outstretched. "You may take me as your prisoner. I promise not to resist."

"Oh, could you be more insufferable?" Emily replied sternly. "Good-bye!" With that, she turned and stormed out the door. Nathan waited patiently and then spoke.

"You can come out now. She is gone."

"Not a chance," came the reply. "You can come in here."

"Where?"

"Behind this drapery... and bring the large sack with you."

Nathan grabbed the sack and popped his head through a set of large curtains that provided another small waiting area. There, he saw not one, but two newspapers being held up in front of the readers' faces. Upon closer inspection, he found one set of hands to be light-skinned and the other dark-skinned.

"I am sorry, Philip," Nathan stated apologetically. "I could attempt an explanation, but it would be like shooting in the dark, as best I can put it."

"We heard everything," Turner stated without dropping the paper. "Did you bring the sack?"

"Yes."

"Good. Take what you like and pass down the rest, if you please."

"Samuel, is that you?" Nathan asked, while untying the knot on the linen covering the pastries.

"Yes, suh, Mista Nath'n," Samuel replied without dropping the paper.

"I thought you couldn't read."

"I cain't. But I cain tell things from da pi'tures."

"I can't believe I kissed a frog for her," Nathan admitted as he passed down the sack. Both Turner and Samuel dropped their papers at the same time and looked at Nathan with disgust.

"Yo done what?" Samuel asked first.

"When we were eight or nine, I asked her for a kiss. She agreed, if I first kissed a frog. This was to prove my love... or something like that. So, I kissed the frog."

"So, you are in love then, Mr. Walker?" Turner managed to say in between bites of his apple tart.

"Just when I think I am over her, she reappears in person or in thought," Nathan confessed, while taking the corner off his Danish.

"She is an attractive, young lady," Turner opined. "With a sharp mind of her own."

*Not unlike my precious love back home*, he thought.

"An' did yo' git dat kiss?" Samuel couldn't resist asking.

"No," Nathan replied. "Not that one, anyway. She told me she could never kiss someone after he had just kissed a frog. I have tasted her kiss, though, the last one coming just before joining the army... before she knew I had joined that is.

"What foolish people don't want to understand is that doing business with my father is a curse in disguise," Nathan continued. "My father has the ability to make you rich but, in the process, make you totally dependent on him. Then, on a whim and for reasons only he knows, he will cut you off. So it was with Emily's father."

"Well then, it is fortunate for us that we have nothing to hide from your enchanting sleuth," Turner replied gently. "If you are given another opportunity to speak with Emily, I see no harm in talking to her about what has happened here. Your conversation may even include entertaining her thoughts on the rock that would not move by physical means. It may be the rock can serve more than a single purpose if it were to start you two talking again. Nathan, above all, be patient with her, and try not to be someone you are not."

This sounded similar to the welcomed advice given to him by Joseph on the night he first arrived at the Parker farm. Turner smiled to himself when the memories of him standing on the front porch and his presentation of the parasol to Jane came to mind. He continued.

"Fortunately, you are both young, and have school and career to occupy your restless minds until this shadowy thing called love gets sorted out. Now, Samuel, it is also not my intention to make you into someone you are not," Turner segued to more prevailing matters. "But, as I am perusing this newspaper, I could not help noticing the clothier's advertisements. It is my suggestion that we seek out a reputable clothier either in Hanover or in Washington, this depending on the delay at each station. We do not need to begin our travels throughout the South with people believing we are not equals—or some semblance of it.

Even I must have one proper suit of clothes if I am to sway men in high places off their positions and onto mine while in Richmond.

"We must also make the effort to find a nice women's apparels store. Picking out something that our lady folk back home might want to wear may prove challenging, but it will let them know they remained continuously on our minds."

"Yo knows d'ese things best, Mista Phil'p."

The three men came out of hiding and were allowed to board their locomotive thirty minutes before departure. At Hanover, Nathan remained on the train from Gettysburg, since it was to continue on to Philadelphia. It was necessary for Turner and Samuel to disembark this train, however, and wait for their connection to Washington. This gave them an hour and a half to roam the town in search of their new clothes—and new identities. It was quite satisfying to find modest suits to their liking, have them masterfully tailored, and be back at the station just as the last whistle for "all aboard" was sounded.

The five-hour ride from Hanover Junction through Camden Station in Baltimore and then on to the Baltimore & Ohio (B&O) Station in Washington allowed Turner time to relax. He opened up Benjamin's Bible and began reading his good friend's thoughts among the scripture verses. It did not take long for him to discover a handwritten sermon on virtually every page he read. These were his thoughts:

*Did Benjamin think of himself as a pastor?*

*Planting churches was not something they had discussed, nor something Benjamin ever mentioned.*

*If a church was the purpose now, why was the rock delivered forty miles away from the nearest town?*

*Keep reading.*

Turner and Samuel arrived in Washington a little before five in the evening. The lateness of the hour was not in their favor, but luck seemed to be. They still managed to acquire two passenger tickets aboard a stagecoach headed for Hamilton's Crossing, just below Fredericksburg, and it was to leave in the morning. From there, they could catch a locomotive into Richmond. They also managed to find clean rooms for their overnight stay—even though this required separate hotels. These hotels were located in better sections of town, and the upscale addresses reflected in the cost, but they had amenities such as tubs for bathing, laundry services, and access to a barber. These were most likely necessities they could not expect again for several more days.

The following morning was cool and dry. This would provide the best possible road surface to travel on for the long, grueling coach ride into Virginia, but Fredericksburg was still a welcomed sight for the many jostled passengers. The brief stopover allowed them to stretch their legs and take refreshment in the war-ravaged town.

Many of Turner's fellow travelers focused their attention on the broken bridge piers rising from the mighty Rappahannock River, without a bridge resting upon them. Turner had viewed this scene before. It was a battle that took place in December of 1862 and was a major defeat for the North's great Army of the Potomac and its newest Commander, Major General Ambrose Burnside. The slothful George McClellan (aka Little Mac) had been discarded by Lincoln in November, never to return to military service again, but Ambrose proved himself to be even worse. In fact, General Lee's victory was so lopsided, it would come close to collapsing the Northern president and his administration. It even produced a vociferous groundswell for McClellan's return. Turner recalled his cavalrymen gallantly protecting Major General James Longstreet's flank in the defense of Marye's Heights.

The journey from Fredericksburg to Hamilton's Crossing was short and uneventful, but the stagecoach had kicked up so much dust off the dry road that, when they arrived, everything was covered in dirt. Filthy and dirty was how Turner and Samuel slept in the train station that night, and how they boarded the train the following day, and how they arrived in Richmond late that evening, except now the fine dust on their faces had turned to a thin layer of dried mud. This was hardly the look for making friends and influencing people. Before approaching the new governor with his ideas on returning the Confederate dead from Gettysburg, Turner would need to have everything cleaned, including himself. This was not so easily accomplished in Richmond as it was in Washington. The effort would take all of the next day and half of the following day to complete.

It wasn't until the morning of the third day that Turner was finally given permission to address the General Assembly and the provisional governor with his plans for returning the bodies of the fallen left in Gettysburg. When he asked for logistical support for the distribution of the dead, once they reached Richmond, but no reimbursement of his out-of-pocket expenses for their delivery, his motion was quickly approved. Turner was promised a contact person in due time. This person would be given authority to handle the remains of any soldier returning from Gettysburg until arrangements could be made with other states to receive their own. It was also proposed that any returning Virginian soldier, and any unidentifiable soldier in Butternut and Grey, be buried with full honors in Richmond's Hollywood Cemetery.

Once his overture to the politicians was delivered and accepted, Turner sent word back to Jane that he could be picked up in Richmond at the earliest possible convenience and that he was bringing back a friend. The expected two or three-day lag time for Joseph to return with a couple of horses would give him an opportunity to speak with as many railroad executives as would agree to see him. The railroad lobby remained strong in Richmond. It was his hope that, by offering to pay for the return of soldiers from Gettysburg out of his own pocket during the General Assembly meetings, his name would have already circulated among this group by now. He also referred to himself as "Major General" Philip Turner when asked his name, so that perhaps a few might even remember him and his ideas for rebuilding the South from conversations at the Starvation Ball two years ago.

This short-term prominence could serve him in two ways: first, he might be able to convince one or more of the railroad companies to assume the entire cost of transporting soldiers back from Gettysburg. If that idea was not acceptable to the Northern railroads, perhaps he could find a Southern railroad to foot the bill from Richmond to the soldier's home state. If handled properly, he could have these same railroads compete with each other for the honor of bringing these fallen heroes home.

Secondly, the idea of rebuilding the South without the use of railroads was a waste of time. He must find out more about who owned these railroads, and if they were patriots or opportunists—men like Nathan's father. His newfound wealth would not be enough, and he would never offer to buy anyone's influence, but he needed help: powerful help, inside help. If the two Northern newspapers were to be believed, support for President Andrew Johnson's hands-off reconstruction plan was eroding fast.

This could undermine tomorrow everything that was being attempted today. An extraordinary amount of patience would be required if Turner had any hope of making any lasting difference.

*Must a politician be forever the radical?* he thought. *All the way here or all the way there... never a thought to moderation!*

While Turner flitted across Richmond like a water bug skimming the surface of an unsettled pond, Samuel made his rounds trying to find information on another kind of railroad—the Underground Railroad. The abolition of slavery might have ended the need for such a system, but his interest was not in escaping. His was a search for anyone who might help him find his family. It was a long shot, but someone sympathetic to fugitive slaves may have crossed paths with a family of three heading north from Alabama. His unwavering quest led him to several riverboat captains and to the homes of a few abolitionist and Quaker families. No family fitting his description was remembered, however.

Samuel's efforts were not without peril. On several occasions, he was forced to run for his life from those wishing to avenge their own suffering. Turner offered to accompany him, but Samuel declined; this was something he needed to do alone. It was agreed that by having a white Confederate General for a companion might inhibit Samuel's access to the very people he needed to speak to most. The very next day, however, Turner presented his friend with a .41-caliber Derringer that matched his own. The weapon was to be used only when there was no way of escaping his own murder, but if it was used, it must be a shot to kill. A trial in the South (or in the North, for that matter) of a wounded white man versus a former slave would be a virtual death sentence, regardless of the facts. Since it did not have a trigger lock, it was also recommended that Samuel keep the unpredictable pistol unloaded to prevent shooting himself by accident.

Three days had passed since Turner sent his message home. On this day, he had arranged an early-morning meeting with a representative from the beleaguered Orange and Alexandria Railroad (O&A). The fact that his cavalry helped destroy two of their locomotives and rip up a mile of their track at Bristoe Station, near Manassas Junction, in the summer of 1862 would forever remain a secret as far as Turner was concerned. Instead, it turned out to be a productive discussion with a strategically important railway line that held many promising avenues for a West Point–trained civil engineer. Content with his day so far, and his stay in Richmond overall, Turner headed back to the hotel. What he saw, as he approached, made his heart swell with joy. There, tied to the hitching post, was his horse, Courage; next to his was Joseph's horse, Spirit, and next to Joseph's, another magnificent Parker buckskin.

After spending some time greeting Courage, Turner burst through the hotel door.

"Where are you?" he shouted and scanned the lobby. "I know you're in here!"

"Well, if it isn't the wandering general," a voice came from the dining room. "Back from his exploits up North and looking no worse for wear, I might add."

"What a sight for sore eyes you are, my friend," Turner said, as he hastily walked over and grabbed the man in a strong embrace. "How long have you been here?"

"An hour, I suppose," Joseph replied. "It is good to see you. And where is your friend?"

"Samuel will be along shortly," Turner said. "He is even more desperate to be leaving than I am. When do you think the horses will be ready to ride again?"

"Thinking you might want to leave at once, I did not press them yesterday, and I spent the night with a family friend not five miles from here," Joseph replied. "We can start as soon as you have settled your bill."

Turner looked past Joseph and saw Samuel standing at the hotel entrance.

"Right on time," Turner said with a smile. "There is Samuel now."

"Where?" Joseph asked.

"At the door," Turner replied.

"Where at the door?" Joseph asked again.

"At the door," Turner replied again.

"I see only a black man standing there."

"That black man is Samuel," Turner replied. "Come, let me introduce you two."

After the briefest of introductions, it was decided to leave straight away. Turner would provide a more complete account of his adventures once they were on the road... and it would take a good deal of road for a complete account.

# 11

# The Prince and Princess

It could be said that no other city changed more radically from war than Philadelphia. This was not accomplished with bombs and bullets; in fact, other than the one scare in June of 1863 that was easily repelled with the simple burning of a bridge across the Susquehanna River by a reserve group of volunteers, the city was never put in jeopardy. Antebellum, Philadelphia was definitively on the side of the South. The city's abolitionists were blamed for producing the secession movement in the first place, and their caustic rhetoric was denounced quickly and harshly.

That would all change after the attack on Fort Sumter in 1861. It was the Southern sympathizers that were on the run now. When the three-day battle in Gettysburg ended, war found few opponents in Philadelphia, and the proof was made perfectly obvious. The city alone enlisted ninety thousand soldiers (not including its black soldiers). Its Navy Yard produced nearly a dozen ironclads. Its businesses were the main sources of blankets, uniforms, munitions, and breech-loading rifles for the United States Army. It was home for the North's two largest military hospitals, with over seven thousand beds. As if to add an exclamation point to this shift in allegiances, the majority of Philadelphians voted for Abraham Lincoln over "little Mac" in the 1864 presidential elections.

The *Philadelphia Inquirer (July 1862)* put it best: "In this war there can be but two parties, patriots and traitors."

This was Nathan's home: where he grew up, where his friends lived, where he fell in love. He enjoyed living the Philadelphia lifestyle, but he was also growing increasingly fond of Gettysburg. He could feel his heart dance when Turner included him in his plans for the property. It was more than an escape from the tyranny of living the life of a Walker, where people could love you one minute and hate you the next. Life in Gettysburg was simple and unpretentious. He imagined this was the reason why a doctor would buy ten thousand acres of rolling countryside and retire close by, and what kept Emily coming back every summer.

He boarded the train in Gettysburg, hoping that Emily was speaking the truth when she told Turner her sad story about leaving. Of course, she never really did say she was going to leave right then, so the truth was muddled; that was Emily's way. She could make you think you heard something when it was only what you wanted to hear, but Nathan was getting better at catching these subtleties. That did not make her a bad person, and in many ways, Emily was a very kind and thoughtful person. It just required excellent listening skills to understand her meanings and motives. Whether he wanted it to be or not, the train ride from Hanover to Philadelphia was hopelessly devoted to thoughts of Emily.

There was no one to greet him when Nathan's train rolled into West Philadelphia Railroad Station. He preferred not to concern his mother with these kinds of matters, and although his father knew of his plans for going to Gettysburg, he showed little interest in the outcome.

"If the traitor doesn't buy the property, someone else will," his father had told him.

Nathan would stay at the Walker house located in town before heading out to the family's opulent country estate, along the Pennsylvania Railroad's mainline, outside of the city. His mother rarely stayed in town, preferring the solitude and comforts of country living. His father would stay at the city residence only when business required his immediate accessibility; otherwise, it was used mainly to accommodate family and friends passing through town. Since no one was there, Nathan assumed everyone was at the country home. He was already a week behind in his studies at Harvard Law School, but a good night's rest in a familiar bed would be all he needed. There was still much to do.

The following day, Nathan wasted no time in acquiring the services of a prestigious real estate settlement firm and an attorney with no affiliation with his father's many enterprises to process the papers for the acquisition of the Gettysburg property. He had witnessed this undertaking many times in his lifetime and knew that within a week, the property would be purchased and its deed transferred securely inside an irrevocable trust—just as Turner requested.

The fulfillment of this momentous task came with a rewarding feeling and left only the return of all travel and court costs back to Nathan's father, a voluntary act based solely on something deep inside Turner's sense of what was good and right. The amount had already been tallied, so a quick trip to the bank in the morning was all that was needed. Once the banker's check was drafted, Nathan would head out to the country home. Hopefully, he could drop off the reimbursement without confrontation, kiss his mother good-bye, and hop on the next locomotive bound for Cambridge, Massachusetts before noon.

Neither Harvard nor the practice of law was on his mind when Nathan returned home from war, but they had since become passions. Most of his schoolmates were young, energetic young men like himself, looking to make a difference in this world of greed and injustice. The law program was tough, and any lack of discipline or the slightest sign of apprehension was shown no mercy—an environment to which he was well-accustomed. He immediately gravitated toward the curriculum that would best help the small, disenfranchised members of society get equal justice before the courts. Nevertheless, as his fascination with Gettysburg turned to affection, he questioned whether this course of study would be profitable to him or his future clients.

*What good would life be as a trial lawyer if I spend it arguing most of my cases in front of a possibly vengeful Judge Douglas?* he thought.

There was only one minor irritation Nathan felt toward Harvard, and that was the necessity to travel off campus to find his spiritual nourishment. Evidently, since the appointment of Hollis President of Divinity Henry Ware back in 1805, and then a succession of liberal university presidents, the once Puritan and Congregationalist institution of its founders had turned into a solidly Unitarian institution. Unfortunately, although quite at ease when speaking of religious matters, these men (and their contemporaries) could not seem to find an appropriate pigeonhole in which to fit the Lord Jesus: Was He God? Was He the Son of God? Was He a prophet? Was He a good fellow with many confusing attributes? Who was this man of Scripture?

*As distasteful as it sounds, it won't be long before the name of Jesus will be counted as "one of many" or even a "has been" at Harvard*, he predicted sadly.

After a blissful second night's rest, Nathan was at the bank's front steps the minute they unlocked the doors. The signed documents describing the limited powers of attorney on Turner's accounts immediately produced a banker's check, and he was on his way to the train station in less than an hour. Both the train ride and coach ride were also without delay or complication, and his arrival at his own doorstep an hour before noon was most appreciated. Regardless of the tensions, it was always good to be home. Nathan blasted through the doors and dropped his bag.

"Anyone home?" Nathan's call echoed throughout the house.

"In here, darling," his mother replied.

Nathan entered the sitting room where his mother was entertaining two ladies, one being Emily's own mother. His mother was full of emotion, but not weak. She worked very hard to maintain her friendships, regardless of what the husbands did to one another. This lifted his spirits greatly, as he bowed gracefully to both ladies.

"Where is Father?" Nathan asked politely.

"I'm sorry, is my Medal of Honor recipient too high and mighty to kiss his mother hello before asking directions?"

"Of course not, my apologies," Nathan said, showing obvious signs of embarrassment.

He walked over to his mother, with as much dignity as he had left, wrapped her in his strong arms from behind, and kissed her gently on the cheek. This tender treatment of an adult son to his oft-forgotten mother brought a smile to the faces of her two guests, and they gave each other a glance of approval.

"Now may I have those directions?"

"Your father is in the study with a gentleman from the Union League."

"Thank you, Mother. Please enjoy your conversations," Nathan replied, while exiting the room expeditiously. Nathan strode down the long hallway toward the rear of the house and turned the corner. Once at the door of the study, he gave it a few sharp raps and waited to be invited to enter.

"Come in," he heard his father say.

"Good day, Father," Nathan said pleasantly and waited to be introduced to the man seated opposite his father.

"It is a good day, Nathan," his father replied. "May I introduce you to the honorable Mr. Eugene Briarwood, a sitting judge on Pennsylvania's Supreme Court."

"Yes, I have heard your name mentioned on several occasions with high esteem," Nathan responded respectfully. "It is indeed a pleasure to meet you, Your Honor." Nathan moved closer to shake the judge's hand, which was strong and friendly.

"Your father tells me you are studying law in Massachusetts rather than right here in your own backyard," the judge chided. "Tell me, young man, what does Harvard offer that the University of Pennsylvania's Law Department does not?"

"Separation!" the father interrupted. "My son would do anything or go anywhere to get away from his father, I'm afraid." For better or worse, Nathan's father was brutally honest, and it did not matter to him who heard what his mind was thinking.

"I began my studies at Harvard simply by being obedient to my father's wishes, Your Honor," Nathan replied truthfully. "However, I remain at Harvard because of men like Adams, Emerson, Meade, and Abbott."

"I am familiar with the president, the poet, and the general," Briarwood replied. "But who is this Abbott?"

"I am speaking of General Henry Livermore Abbott, Harvard class of 1860. He was brevetted to brigadier general posthumously by President Lincoln before his own death and confirmed by the United States Senate early in this year. Though only a major during the war, Abbott was forced into the role of commanding the Twentieth Massachusetts Volunteer Infantry in the midst of battle on many occasions.

"May I continue, Your Honor?" Nathan asked politely.

"Please do," the judge replied.

"To give you some understanding of the Twentieth, it was widely known as the 'Harvard Regiment' because its ranks were mostly Harvard graduates. There was no other Regiment from the entire Commonwealth of Massachusetts that took as many casualties as the Twentieth. This did not go unnoticed, for by war's end it had been nicknamed the 'Bloody Twentieth'. They were at Balls' Bluff at the beginning of war, and they were at Appomattox when General Grant mercifully concluded it, Your Honor.

"Between these two battles, there would be many more—and may God save me if I fail to do these brave men justice by misplacing the order of their occurrence. As I have already mentioned, there was Balls' Bluff, in which one third of the Twentieth would not live to see another day, and another third would be taken hostage before Major Abbott took over command to deliver the remaining third. Then there was The Seven Days', Antietam, Fredericksburg, Chancellorsville, Gettysburg, the Wilderness, Cold Harbor, Spotsylvania, and Petersburg... not to mention their many skirmishes.

"Allow me to highlight what I have discovered about Major Abbott's illustrious career, with an understanding that this account will be woefully inadequate in its detail. He was first wounded at Glendale during The Seven Days' in Virginia, but it is said he remained on the field until the following day when both sides had their fill of killing. He would miss the Battle at Antietam in Maryland, only because typhoid fever had weakened him greatly. Perhaps he was divinely afflicted with this illness just so he could return to the Twentieth for the poorly conceived march on Fredericksburg, Virginia. Abbott would take command once more when three officers and over sixty enlisted of the Twentieth would perish instantly in their attempt to dislodge a well-entrenched Confederate army sitting merrily on top of Marye's Heights.

"Then there was Gettysburg; this battle being just to our east was a possibility we Philadelphians, heretofore, thought inconceivable. What you may not know is that the Twentieth was put squarely in the middle of General Meade's line on Cemetery Ridge during Confederate General Pickett's mad rush to the Copse of Trees. Dare I say it again?

"Major Abbott was forced to assume command when ten of the thirteen officers lay dead or wounded. Gettysburg was a glorious victory for the North, but a bloody day for the Twentieth. Unfortunately, Major Abbott's gallant efforts would come to an end at the battle of the Wilderness in Virginia. While assuming command of the Twentieth after the wounding of his colonel, he, too, was mortally wounded and died on the field of battle. That was May of last year (1864); he was no more than twenty-two years of age, Your Honor."

Judge Briarwood and Nathan's father did not speak, having been mesmerized by the accounting of this brave young man's service to his country. Nathan broke the silence.

"I think of him more often than the three other Harvard alumni put together, if you understand my meaning, sir."

"I believe I do understand and will remember General Abbott as a great patriot," the judge responded thoughtfully. "Thank you for that fine testimonial, Nathan."

"It was my honor, Your Honor," Nathan replied with respectful lightheartedness.

"Now to the business at hand," Nathan addressed his father. "The school year has already begun, and I must be going back at once. That is why I am here. This is for you." Nathan handed his father the envelope containing the bank check. A quizzical expression came over the elder's face when the envelope was opened.

"What is this?"

"That is the total amount of money that I believed, and still believe, you should have paid for taking extreme advantage of Colonel Hillary after the loss of his mother and father... and yet Mr. Turner believes it should be returned to you."

"I did not ask for this."

"As I said, this was Mr. Turner's idea, not mine."

"Why would a man give up this much money freely?" his father replied suspiciously.

"Fairness, kindness, selflessness," Nathan answered. "I don't exactly know why, Father, but it was the action of someone I could admire."

"Well, at this rate, he will soon be out of his friend's money," his father said snidely.

"Perhaps," Nathan responded with tenderness. "In any event, I must say good-bye. I love you more than you know, Father."

\* \* \*

*I don't need to apologize to him for anything, Medal of Honor or not*, Emily thought.

She was upset with Nathan, but could not put her finger on the exact reason why. That didn't matter now because she was even angrier about having to get up so early to decorate herself with nothing to show for it. She was well aware of her good looks and charm. When applied generously, they had unlocked many closed doors and loosened many sealed lips. This was a setback.

*There is a story here. I can smell it*, she thought in the vernacular of the newspaper business. She quickly arrived back at her carriage, which had been waiting for her around the corner and out of sight; it was being driven by her uncle's servant.

"Daniel," she huffed. "You are certain Mr. Turner asked for nothing of my uncle except his forgiveness?"

"I was there from the moment Mr. Turner entered the house until he left the house, Miss Preston," Daniel stated categorically. "I have told you everything I know."

"And you truly believe he was being sincere?"

"I most certainly do, Miss Preston."

"Daniel," Emily began, using her sweet, manipulative voice this time. "You have been my uncle's butler for many years. I know you can read and have probably consumed his entire library by now. I know this because you cannot help but say things only an educated man would say. What do you think Mr. Turner's true motives were last night?"

"I think they were to receive forgiveness, Miss Preston," Daniel spoke earnestly.

"Damn men!" she snapped.

No longer able to hide her exasperation, Emily wrapped the coach blanket around her body more tightly than was necessary. There was something going on in this quiet, little town—a conspiracy—and she was going to get to the bottom of it. Not in this get-up, though; she would need to change outfits and return for more leg-work.

"Good-for-nothing weasels, all of you. Take me home!"

"Yes, Miss Preston," Daniel replied kindly.

After returning home and "un-decorating" herself, Emily still managed to meet up with her uncle at the breakfast table. Unfortunately, her uncle was so preoccupied with the day's upcoming agenda that, as hard as she tried, she could not extract a single piece of useful information with which to begin her investigation; that was until her uncle excused himself from the table. That was when the maid made a seemingly innocuous comment in passing that piqued Emily's ears.

"I heard there's gold out in them hills," the old woman said, as if to herself.

"Now what did you say, Miss Bessie?" Emily asked, knowing full well the information was intended for her ears only.

Miss Bessie was her uncle's black housemaid. She had kind of come with the house when her uncle bought it over thirty years before. If there was ever a rumor or juicy bit of gossip within the black community of Gettysburg, she knew about it. This was what Miss Bessie told Emily, with whom she had been sharing this type of talk since Emily was a little girl. Just yesterday, she had heard some talk about Samuel from a friend of a friend of a friend. The story had Samuel going out to the old doctor's property with the rich, young rebel and the Walker boy a couple of days before. When they got back to town, the rebel bought the property for $100,000, and it had something to do with rocks; big, shiny rocks the size of your fist or bigger. It was said the Walker boy had been out there before and took with him a couple of extra horses and pickaxes.

"If that don't sound like gold, I don't know what does, sweetheart," Miss Bessie stated confidently. "If you can find that old battlefield, you are gonna find a mine full of gold. Maybe when that handsome young boy, Nathan, gets rich in his own right, you and he can settle down and start a family of your own."

"Miss Bessie, who is Samuel?" Emily asked, ignoring the suggestion of marriage.

"Mister Samuel was a slave from down South. He escaped just before the war ended. He's a good Christian man, works hard, is all I know about him."

"Where can I find Mister Samuel, Miss Bessie?"

"Oh, I heard he and the rebel were going back down South to find his family, darling."

"He was leaving with Mister Turner?" Emily shot back. "But, I didn't see him at the train station this morning."

"So, that's where you went off to all prettied up," Miss Bessie answered. "Well, Samuel worked for Mister Duke. Why don't you go talk to him?" Emily sprang from her seat and gave the old woman a big hug.

"You are the best there ever was, Miss Bessie," Emily stated tenderly. "Who knows? The information might even prove to be accurate this time."

"Now don't you go forgetting Miss Bessie when you and Nathan get rich," the sweet, old lady said. "Then I'll be a-changing your baby's diapers just as I was a-changing yours. Oh my, how old I am."

"You are not old, Miss Bessie, and I will never forget you."

The journalist had her assignment and was on horseback headed back into town within minutes. Before speaking to Mr. Duchene, however, she used her influence as the judge's niece to uncover more reliable information from courthouse records, the banker, and the only law office in town that could handle such a transaction of real estate. The results of these visits clarified a few issues, like Mr. Turner paying $10,000 for the property, not $100,000, and the seller being none other than one of Nathan's father's investment groups. Then again, these same visits to the courthouse, banker, and law firm produced more questions than they answered.

*Why would Nathan's father give up property to a Confederate general if it was suspected of containing gold, or something else of extraordinary value?*

*Why would a Confederate general buy property at such an inflated price if it did not contain gold, or something else of extraordinary value?*

*Why purchase land and place it in an unbreakable document where it could never be altered or resold?*

Then there were the two bank accounts: one to which Mr. Duchene could gain access, and the other to benefit the locals by means of making small loans.

*What am I missing?* She thought hard.

*What does Nathan have to do with a benevolent Confederate general? Unless the rebel general was at Nathan's battle.*

As a result of the investigations for her *Pittsburgh Chronicle* article, Emily knew that Nathan's near-death battle occurred on this property, but she was never made aware of the two soldiers ever meeting.

*Why did he have to go and join the army and risk his life like that?* Her mind wandered involuntarily. *Did he not know how much that would have hurt me if he died?*

*Stupid boy... stupid, insensitive boy!*

These last two unresolved questions—and one unflattering commentary—always accompanied her run-ins with Nathan, but that was ancient history. It was time to pay the Duke and Duchess Hotel a visit. Emily never found it necessary to stay at the Duke, but Mr. Duchene was always kind and forgiving of the more mischievous children in his town, which had naturally included her. She also knew he did not partake in rumors and gossip, but would have heard more than anyone else in town besides the barber. If he decided to tell her anything, it would be the truth.

*Perhaps I can use Nathan as a way to loosen Mr. Duke's tongue.*

When Emily saw Mr. Duke sitting on a porch rocker out in front of the hotel, she gave her horse a good kick in the rear to prevent missing this golden opportunity. The animal and pedestrian traffic, although sporadic, appeared determined to stop her from ever getting a good head of steam. When she finally did reach the hotel's hitching post, her frustration must have been clearly visible.

"Good day, Miss Emily. Is there a fire?" The old gentleman joked.

"Hello, Mister Duke. There is no fire," Emily replied innocently. "Only a confused young lady, I suppose."

"And why is that young lady confused?"

"I am worried about Nathan and he won't talk to me."

"That is curious," Mr. Duchene replied warily. "It was just yesterday that Nathan used the same words of concern and endearment for you, my dear."

"There are certain things that I withhold from Nathan, but that does not diminish my affection for him," she replied tearfully.

"There, there... you are right, of course," the kind-hearted man responded, as he passed her his handkerchief. "It is clean. Now come sit down with me, and tell me how may I lessen your distress or calm your fears."

"I have an abiding fear that Nathan's life is in jeopardy, as long as he continues to listen to the surreptitious ramblings of a rebel against his own father's wishes and against the trained sensibilities of my uncle."

"I have met Mister Turner and have paid close attention to his actions," Mr. Duchene began. "I believe him to be a different man than what others have portrayed him to be. This would include the opinions of your uncle, whom I admire greatly."

"Then, why will Nathan not tell me what is really going on with this man and the property?"

"I do not believe they even know what is to be done with the property, my dear."

"Why would someone pay $10,000 for land they have no idea what to do with?" Emily asked, while keeping the handkerchief close to her face in an effort to wipe away a tear she hoped would present itself.

"As best I can understand it, your good-natured young man and Mr. Turner had some coming together in battle and, as a result of their mutual devotion and love for the late Colonel Hillary, have bonded as close as any kinsmen," the old gentleman offered without fear of misrepresenting the relationship. "It was explained to me that Colonel Hillary's body was buried on the field of battle by Nathan himself and remains there still."

"What about the rock, Mister Duke?"

*Well now, another reference to there being a rock*, Mr. Duchene thought.

"I know of no rock, Emily," Mr. Duchene replied firmly.

Noticing the slight hesitation and change in Mr. Duke's tone of voice, Emily knew she was being denied a full disclosure. This would not be an outright lie on Mr. Duke's part. He most likely did not have enough information about any rocks to offer a comment—that would be gossip or hearsay—but he had definitely heard something about a rock. While Emily was processing this information, so was Duke.

"My dear Emily, I have known you since you were a little girl, and I have seen that look in your eye before," he began. "Please, I have told you all I know so that you and Nathan can begin to trust one another again. I hope you will not use anything I might have said, or did not say, to go and do something rash or dangerous."

"My purpose for visiting you was to regain my sense of ease for Nathan's safety, which was lost when he became a soldier at sixteen," Emily answered more honestly than she intended. "Thank you for caring so deeply for Nathan and I."

"I noticed that you did not respond to my plea for restraint, but know that I do care, Emily. Please be careful."

Emily smiled nervously but said nothing. She returned the handkerchief, climbed atop her horse, and rode off toward home.

*Now, who can I get to ride out to Mr. Turner's property with me?* she thought.

It was a productive day of investigation. Emily had just enough time to wash up and meet her uncle for supper. Suppertime was usually a quiet affair; her uncle would continue his reading throughout the course of it, and Emily was more than willing to share the day's adventures with Miss Bessie as she served the meal. She knew well that if she said something so fraught with mischief and peril, it had a way of piercing through her uncle's considerable wall of concentration. Tonight would be one of those nights.

"Miss Bessie, would you happen to know of anyone that might be able to direct me to Mister Turner's property?" Emily asked calmly.

"Whatever do you want to go—?" Miss Bessie began but was interrupted.

"What is this about Mister Turner?" her uncle demanded.

"I was simply asking Miss Bessie if she—" Emily began but was also interrupted.

196

"Yes, yes, I heard that," he stated with some irritation. "What are you up to now, Emily?"

"I am up to protecting Nathan from harm, Uncle," she began. "You know my feelings for Nathan, and I suspect he is somehow being manipulated by that treacherous rebel."

"But why go out to the property?" her uncle inquired. "What do you expect to find there?"

"I do not know," she replied. "Gold, maybe."

"Gold!" the man cried out. "Who put that silly notion in your head?"

Emily looked at Miss Bessie and stifled a grin.

"What else could cause a man to buy up ten thousand acres so far away from his own home?" she asked in earnest.

"Do you think for an instant that if gold had been discovered on that property, I would not have heard about it?" her uncle replied. "The property was bought for sentimental reasons and for those reasons alone."

Emily allowed her fork to drop abruptly onto her plate and began to weep—or something like it. The man looked at Miss Bessie for help, but got a foreboding glare instead.

"What did I say?" he asked in disbelief.

"Were you not listening? And you call yourself a judge," Miss Bessie scolded him, as she moved quickly to comfort the child she helped raise. "Miss Emily said she wants to protect the man she has feelings for. Can you men be more witless?"

"And I am supposed to allow this careless behavior because of her affections for this young man?"

"You are still not paying attention. She will go whether you allow it or not," the wise, old women said crossly. "Have you forgotten how it is to love, Judge?"

He knew he was outnumbered and outsmarted, for this kind of rebuke was unassailable. The only remedy was to acquiesce and look for some way to mitigate the potential harm to his beloved niece. After more tears and more consoling from his maid, the uncle threw up his hands.

"Very well, I shall go with you, and you, too, Miss Bessie, and Daniel as well," the uncle proclaimed. "We shall make a short vacation out of it. I do not think the rebel would mind."

"You would do that for me, Uncle?" Emily asked softly.

"There is nothing I would not do for you my sweet, impetuous princess," her uncle stated tenderly. "The three of you shall make preparations for a three-day excursion to begin the day after tomorrow. I believe one full day of exploration will suffice once you have found nothing that would suggest any endangerment to your Prince Charming.

"Miss Bessie, have Daniel pack my fishing gear and include an additional rod and reel if he, too, is a fisherman. I remember Dr. Peterson having some of the finest trout streams not far from his house."

The following morning was a flurry of activity. It was agreed the night before that they would stay at the doctor's house. The judge knew its exact location and the open pasture that turned into a bloody battlefield should not be too far from there. He recommended they plan for the worst and assume the house to be dirty and uninviting. It would be much cooler in the higher elevation, so two rooms with fireplaces would need to be swept clean and readied for habitation. Both Daniel and the judge accepted responsibility for maintaining an adequate supply of cut wood for the fire, in between their fishing duties.

By noon, the judge managed to clear his schedule for the remainder of the day and the four days that followed. Before leaving for home, he slipped into the general store in search of anything that would improve his chances of catching more fish. It wasn't long before Mr. Duchene walked into the store in search of ink for his fountain pens. Curious to see the judge hovering over the small collection of fishing tackle, he began moving in that direction.

"I recommend the fly over the worm, and don't forget grease for the line; otherwise, it will sink along with your dinner plans," Duke warned.

"Good day, Mister Duchene. I agree with your assessment of the fly, and thank you for reminding me of the grease," the judge replied. "Do you have any recommendations on these artificial lures with the hook in disguise?"

"I was shown a lure similar to this one by one of my guests," Duke said cheerfully, while pointing out a white-bodied model with a white feathered tail. "He mentioned having success with pickerel and largemouth bass in still water."

"Any suggestion for trout?"

"Ah, planning a trip to the mountains, Judge?"

"I have agreed to accompany my niece to Dr. Peterson's property," the man sighed. "A concern for Nathan is what I am supposed to believe, but you and I both know Emily. It could be anything, really, and she would go it alone if I did not submit to her wild fantasies."

"When do you leave?"

"Tomorrow morning."

"Mind if I join you?"

"Your company would be a pleasure and greatly appreciated," the judge answered joyfully, "in the event I am besieged with more abstract feminine feelings."

"I shall be at your door at the break of day, then."

"Very good, very good indeed. I shall see you then."

Duke bought his ink and hurried back to the hotel to explain to his wife why she would be assuming command of the Duke and Duchess for a few days while he went fishing... for a rock!

## 12

# Reunited

Once the tree line was breached and the Parker farm was in plain sight, Turner could no longer be restrained. Without a word of explanation, he gave Courage a kick and a shout, and off they flew.

"We gonna try'n keep up, Mista Joseph, suh?" Samuel asked.

"Let him go, Samuel," Parker replied. "He sees no one but her now."

They watched as Turner's image became smaller and smaller. A faint ringing of the supper bell could be heard, but Parker knew that was not a call for many to wash up for supper. That was a call for only one, and that one was his sister.

Jane woke with a premonition that her sweet general would be returning that day. So, after all the morning chores were taken care of, she slipped on her prettiest dress and went about the rest of the day trying to find ways to occupy her mind while trying to keep it clean. She knew there would be no time for changing. She was engaged by brushing Topsy, her latest strategy, when the alarm sounded.

"He's back!" Jane screamed, as she dropped the brush and gave Topsy a big kiss on the muzzle. She ran out of the stable as quickly as her hiked-up, long flowing dress would allow. She hurried past several people without so much as a glance in their direction. They, in turn, made no attempt to distract her or impede her momentum; nor did they bother to follow her, knowing full well what the initial meeting of these two lovebirds might look like.

The front yard was empty when Jane came flying around the side of the house. There was no one on the porch, and the person responsible for sounding the bell was gone. This was about the same time that Turner exploded through the tattered gateway. From a bird's-eye view, it seemed as if neither had any inclination of slowing down and a terrible collision would occur shortly. That was until Turner pulled up on the reins suddenly, causing Courage to dig in all four heels and very nearly touch his rump the ground. In one fluid motion, Turner spun out of his right stirrup, off his saddle, and then out of his left stirrup and landed on the ground, running in Jane's direction. At this point, the distance between them was so precariously close that Turner had her swinging in his arms within seconds. He slowly put her back on the ground after several revolutions and they shared a long, passionate kiss.

"Oh, how I have missed you, my love," Turner said breathlessly. "Hours were days and days were years."

"And you were on my mind night and day, my darling," Jane replied lovingly. "Promise me you will never go up North without me again."

"I can do that, my sweet," Turner promised. "But I no longer consider it enemy territory. There is so much we need to talk about, but allow me to simply hold onto you for the few moments we have been given here."

"Yes, hold me tight," Jane whispered.

Joseph and Samuel backed down their horses' pace to a slow canter once they saw the two embraced and then to a lazy trot at the gateway. This was an effort to accommodate the love-struck couple, but they were on the only path leading to the house and could go no slower. When the approaching sound of eight clopping hooves hitting the ground failed to untangle the two young lovers, Joseph thought it best to say something. They were so close as they passed that his words could be heard without him having to raise his voice or even look in their direction.

"If you think I am going to avoid the front lawn just so you two can cling to one another like two cats caught up in a cottonwood, you are mistaken."

"Yo go on hug'n her, Mista Phil'p, suh," Samuel added instantly. "An' pay no nev'a mind ta Mista Joseph, ya hear?"

"Don't encourage them, Samuel, or they shall be here all day and all night," Joseph responded with a smile.

"Now, Mista Joseph, dey ain't hurt'n nobody," Samuel continued his good-natured defense.

"Samuel, have I miscalculated or have they been separated no longer than two short weeks?" Joseph asked in mocked seriousness.

"Nope, but dey cain't help demselves is all," Samuel answered as if he, too, were confounded by the facts of this reunion.

This lighthearted bantering about love and its ill effects on the human brain went on until both men were out of earshot of Turner and Jane. She felt so good in his arms that Turner needed no additional encouragement to maintain his embrace, but Joseph had a point.

"If I were to release you now, my love," Turner began softly, "would you mistake it to mean I could not cling to you all day and all night forevermore?"

"Let this be my reply," Jane said, while moving her lips back toward his.

This latest kiss was distinctly more subtle than the first, but with no less passion, and it answered every question on Turner's mind perfectly. They walked hand in hand back to the house where Jane would head indoors to freshen up, and Turner would head back to the stables to remove saddle and bridle before turning Courage loose. There was no fanfare, no ceremony for the valiant return of a war hero this time. Mr. Parker was in town on business, Mrs. Parker was in the house stitching up torn britches, and the two Parker brothers were in the large training corral working some horses: and each gave Turner one good wave when they saw him. This was a hard-working horse ranch and farm with plenty of daylight left. There would be no time for long-winded storytelling until suppertime. Unless Samuel had found something else to do, Turner would take him out to the fence line and pick up where he left off.

Turner understood how anxious Samuel must be to leave. After only a few weeks of separation, he had become desperate to see Jane again. Still, this expedition into the Deep South would require careful planning and the utmost diplomacy. There had been a sense of unease about this mission from the time Turner first offered Samuel his support. For a decorated Confederate general, the trip would normally be considered passage into friendly territory, but a trip to recover the family of a recently emancipated slave was another story. The properties of the once proud and powerful slave owners were being confiscated by the occupying Union army and then literally given away. The fortunes of those owners who were allowed to keep some of their property fared no better, for their crops withered and died from lack of a labor force to maintain and harvest them. Therefore, tensions would be perilously high and unpredictable.

Any chance of finding Samuel's family must also take into account the possibility of some interaction with his previous owner. It did not appear to make any difference which of these two slave owner categories this fellow fell into; Turner knew the contentious meeting had the potential to end badly. It was in times like these that he could sleep well before battle, knowing he would have Joseph by his side. Unfortunately, that would not be the case here; he and Samuel would have to put their endeavor—and their lives—in God's hands.

*The Lord did tell Samuel that He would bind Satan's hands*, Turner thought and immediately felt better about the situation.

Jane, now wearing more practical clothing, appeared at the back door. When she noticed Turner walking in her direction, she moved outside and patiently took a seat on the back-porch bench swing. In her eyes, he was the most ruggedly handsome man she had ever met, much less kissed, since giving such things importance. This preoccupation with Turner's masculinity caused her to completely overlook the saddlebag he was carrying in one hand and a crushed gift box with mangled ribbon and unbraided bow in the other. When he was in range, she offered him the spot beside her.

"We are in luck, my darling," Jane began joyfully. "Mother has asked Joseph and your friend to go slaughter a lamb for supper and my help in preparing it won't be needed for another hour." At this point Jane leaned over, kissed Turner on his scruffy cheek, wrapped her arm in his and gently laid her head on his shoulder. She continued.

"So, now, you have just come back from a great adventure. I have received but two short letters expressing your love and safety, for which I am truly thankful," Jane began tentatively. "But, if there is something else you feel you need to tell me that, if I should hear it for the first time while sitting at the table might cause me to lose composure or become faint, it might be best to tell me here."

"There is so much to be told, but I can think of two items that might best fit into that category, my sweet," Turner replied. "And I am glad we are alone."

Turner knew full well that such weighty topics deserved more than an hour each to explain and then discuss, especially with the woman he would soon call his wife; but there was not much he could do but proceed with the time he was given.

"As it turned out, Benjamin's estate was worth more than I expected... more than could be reasonably imagined, actually," Turner stated without emotion. "One hundred twenty-five thousand, seven hundred eighty-six dollars and twenty-five cents to be exact—in Northern currency— and I was named its sole beneficiary."

Turner could feel Jane's body go limp. He also sensed a desperate desire to speak, but she could not catch enough breath to express herself. He held her close and would say no more about it until she was able to speak again. It was a reaction not unlike his stifling reaction when the lawyer first gave him the astounding number.

"It's okay, sweetheart," Turner reassured her. "Take your time. We have an hour, as I understand it."

"What... did... you... say?" Jane asked in short, stammering outbursts.

"We have an hour?" Turner replied, knowing what he was being asked, but playfully giving the wrong answer.

"Before… that," Jane replied, now whispering in a faltering, almost sad, voice and without acknowledging Turner's levity.

"Oh, you mean the one hundred twenty-five thousand, seven hundred eighty-six dollars and twenty-five cents?" Turner stated jovially, as if to add a punch line to his fun.

Jane said nothing, but instead buried her head in Turner's chest and began to cry uncontrollably. Turner wasn't exactly sure what just transpired, but he was quite positive it was something he said or the way in which he said it. He was able to drag and kick his saddlebag close enough to get a hand on it without disturbing Jane's position on his chest. Using his one available hand, he brought the bag slowly up to the bench and dumped the contents until he found a clean handkerchief; this he gave to Jane. It would take several minutes for Jane to quiet her persistent sobs, but she continued to rest her head on Turner's chest in silence.

"Can you tell me what is wrong, my love?" Turner asked gently.

"I don't want the money," she replied hesitantly. "I want you."

"What do you mean? I am yours."

"You are rich now; it will change you—money like that changes everyone it touches. I love you the way you are."

"Oh, my tender flower, my sweet dream come true, my joy, forgive me for being so cavalier," Turner begged. "Tell me where to send it, and it will be out of our lives forever."

"You would do that?" Jane inquired between the intermittent gulps of breath.

"My affections are for you alone, not wealth or any other worldly thing that could distract me from you," Turner promised.

This seemed to relieve Jane's doubts and fears, and Turner was grateful this challenge to their young, vulnerable relationship was met head-on and in private. Even so, there was one more hurdle that was best addressed while they still had this valuable time to themselves.

"Are you able to talk about another somewhat difficult topic that will most certainly come up at the table tonight?" Turner asked, as sympathetically as he could manage.

"Yes. If we are to remain devoted to each other, we must be able to talk freely about such things," Jane said, with a renewed strength in her voice.

"I must go away again," Turner stated. "Only, this time, southbound."

"Would this have anything to do with your new friend?" Jane asked calmly and observantly.

"Yes."

"Then, tell me, why you would agree to another painful separation for this man?"

Turner proceeded to explain how he and Samuel met at the train depot. Then, with great care, he described Samuel's terrifying escape from his brutal master after the heart-wrenching sale of his wife and two young children to another unknown plantation owner or slave trader. He went on to say how much he admired Samuel for saving every penny he earned to go back down to Alabama to find his family, and how God spoke to him about protecting them from harm. Soon after receiving Benjamin's bountiful estate, Turner admitted, there was nothing else he could imagine doing with the money other than to help expedite Samuel's honorable and faithful quest. That help would require not just money, but his personal involvement.

"Was I wrong?" Turner asked earnestly.

"No, my sweet, kindhearted, young general, you were not," Jane said, with a few, freshly generated tears rolling down her cheek. "You need not try to justify this quest any further, for I have already come to the conclusion that you and Samuel were meant to do this wonderful thing together. Now, I believe I am out of tears, but is there anything else you would like to say before I am called away?"

"Well, there is this," Turner replied, as he reached under the swing and produced a tattered box, which he gently laid on Jane's lap. As with the parasol, Jane just sat there looking at the box in amazement.

"I am certain if your mother were here, she would say something like, 'I believe it was meant to be opened, dear,'" Turner said softly.

Jane wiped away what was left of the ribbon and bow, and then lifted the deformed lid, which Turner quickly took from her. With trembling hands, she reached under the crumpled, but clean, tissue paper and removed a beautiful new dress. She immediately stood up, held it to her body and made several alternating spinning motions. Turner stood and attempted to demonstrate how he had to guess her dress size by using his hands, as if they were holding onto her waist, but he was cut short. Without a word, Jane fit herself into his hands and kissed him hard on the lips. She removed herself just as suddenly, folded the dress haphazardly and threw it back into the box. Then, snatching the lid off the swing, she disappeared into the house with the whole disheveled heap. This left Turner standing alone and somewhat perplexed.

"Is that how it goes?" he asked himself plainly. "The very thing I thought she would find appealing, she found objectionable. The thing I thought she would find objectionable, she found appealing. And the manner in which she receives gifts is bewildering to me."

*What is a man to do?* He thought. *And we haven't talked about the rock yet.*

He slowly began repacking his saddlebag when Benjamin's Bible fell from a tangle of clothes. The idea crossed his mind that now would be as good a time as any to delve into the margins. Supper was at least two hours away, and he knew of a few good spots to hide, but his responsibility as a host had been somewhat lacking. To this point, he had yet to introduce Samuel to one single person.

*Who am I kidding?* he thought, as he set a course toward the closest hideaway. *Samuel will have everyone eating out of his hands by supper.*

The bits and pieces of information from Turner's trip up north had been circulating the farm and had everyone looking forward to suppertime. The fact that Turner was nowhere to be found only added to the suspense and anticipation. So it was only when the food arrived and everyone had taken their seats that they noticed Jane missing.

"She helped me set the table not ten minutes ago," Mrs. Parker said curiously.

At that moment, Jane appeared at the top of the stairs and all eyes became focused on her. Her face glowed like polished ivory. Her hair glistened, as it flowed effortlessly down onto her shoulders before being captured in the back by a single red bow. This arrangement, along with a simple silver necklace, accentuated her long, slender neck. Her smile sparkled between two perfectly matched ruby lips. The dress she wore dazzled the eye and quickened the heart; she was stunningly beautiful.

"Come, my dear," her father smiled and spoke pleasantly. "We wait for you."

"Coming, Father," she replied and glided slowly down the steps.

All the men rose as she approached the table, and Turner eagerly pulled out her chair.

"Is that a new dress, darling?" her mother asked fondly.

"Yes, Mother," Jane replied sweetly. "A thoughtful gift from a certain handsome general."

After the blessing, the act of actually eating became secondary to the requests for more and more detail from Turner. The barrage of questioning became so unintentionally acute that it required Mr. Parker's intervention in order that Turner might enjoy a few, uninterrupted bites of his roasted rack of lamb in between responses. This call for a moment of peace and quiet to savor one's food was short-lived, however, for it only redirected the rejuvenated conversation toward Samuel, who was now finding it difficult to return to his meal. That suited Turner just fine; in fact, to keep this new center of attention flowing away from him, he unashamedly joined in the questioning in order that he might take delight in a second helping of Mrs. Parker's cheese grits and corn pudding.

The only topic not discussed was the rock and its mysterious coming and going. There may have been other reasons at play for that topic to be passed over, but everything else seemed to fade away once the discussion turned to the rescue of Samuel's family. It was agreed by all that this journey to Alabama would be long, arduous, and fraught with every form of danger. Their destination would be Henry County, southeast of Montgomery and bordering the Georgia state line.

After supper and cleanup, the whole Parker clan retired to the sitting parlor to continue their discussion. Turner began by admitting to his unfamiliarity with their target territory, other than the names of the few main railroads that went west before turning south. His intricate yet optimistic plans were to use the South Side Railroad going west into Lynchburg, Virginia. From there, the Virginia and Tennessee Railroad headed south into Bristol, Tennessee, and then the East Tennessee and Georgia Railroad lead into Chattanooga, Tennessee. From Chattanooga, they would travel the Western and Atlantic Railroad into Atlanta, Georgia. From Atlanta, the Western Railway would take them west into Alabama.

"All of this will depend upon the condition of these war-torn railroads and what has been described as 'very near evil', the destruction of Atlanta by General William Tecumseh Sherman," Turner added hastily.

Parker's brothers, Joshua and Aaron, were in Atlanta during its bombardment and with General Hood's subsequent retreat to Lovejoy, Georgia. They were also at the battles of Chickamauga and Chattanooga back in September and November of 1863. Their accounts of the area were what one would expect—heavily damaged with little chance of improvement so quickly. Their assessment of Turner's plans, however, was supportive; there was simply no quicker way. Joseph stated his regrets for not being able to accompany them, but it was fall, and winter loomed. He was in agreement with the traveling plan and would take them to the Burkeville train station. With apologies to Samuel for being so blunt, he also suggested they begin their investigations at the Henry County courthouse for a bill of sale.

"You would have known if your wife and children went to a neighbor or stayed within your owner's extended family," Joseph suggested to Samuel. "And these types of movements would not normally be documented, but a sale to an unknown buyer most likely would be."

Samuel nodded but said nothing.

After giving this last unpleasant aspect the respect it deserved, Mr. Parker rose from his chair. Up to this point, he had been mostly quiet but remained keenly attentive. He was not asked his opinion on this subject or on any of the extraordinary experiences that his future son-in-law had gone through nor did he offer it. Now it was time to say his piece and retire for the evening.

"Philip, it is wonderful to have you back safe and sound," he began joyfully. "You continue to show a remarkable ability to humble yourself in the face of great misfortune and great fortune. That gives me some reasonable assurance that you will make a good husband and father someday, as well as being a good friend.

"Samuel... well, sir, I cannot imagine having lived in your shoes," he continued solemnly. "All I can say is, once your family is found, and I believe they will be—just as the Lord promised—you are welcome to stay here with us for as long as you like."

"Dat's mighty kine, suh... mighty kine, indeed," Samuel replied.

With that, Mr. Parker said good night, and he and Mrs. Parker went upstairs. Joshua and Aaron repeated their father's wishes for a good night and headed to their rooms. Feeling the time for sleep had finally arrived, Joseph stood and stretched.

"Samuel," he began, "unless you have something on your mind that cannot wait until tomorrow, let me show you to your room. Philip, I believe you know where your room is."

"Now Mista Joseph, suh, why y'all mak'n such a fuss?" Samuel replied gently. "I's happy jus' ta sleep out in dat fancy barn wit dem fine ho'ses."

"The hell you will!" Joseph barked. "You are our guest. Those days are gone, Samuel."

"Well, it's jus'... well, I's nev'a been treated so kine'ly in aw my bow'n days."

"Good night, Samuel," Turner said.

"Good night, Samuel," Jane echoed.

"Well, aw' righty den. Good night, Mista Phil'p, suh... Miss Jane, ma'am," Samuel replied graciously. "Nev'a in my bow'n days," Samuel whispered to himself, as he followed Joseph up the stairs.

Once they were alone, Turner spoke first.

"I can see it in your eyes, but you cannot come with us."

"Why not?" Jane snapped. "I can ride as well as you and know how to shoot a gun, too."

"I know that," Turner replied tenderly. "But if you were to come, all my attention would be focused on you. Can you see how that might put Samuel and his family in jeopardy?"

"But I want to be with you, always," Jane said, as the tears began to well in her eyes. "I want to be there if you get hurt."

"Let me bring Samuel's family back home safely, then you can protect me from myself for the remainder of my days."

"Must you save everyone?"

"I thought I did once, but not now," Turner said after a brief pause. "Grant me this one last mission, and then I will find less adverse ways to help those who are in need."

Jane walked over to Turner and kissed him gently on the cheek. She then wrapped him gently in her arms and rested her head against his shoulder.

"But I love you so much," she said, while still in his caress. Without another word, she released him and vanished up the stairs.

* * *

It had been five days since Turner's return home, and it was time to leave again. He and Samuel spent most of their days working on the fence, while the evenings were used to help define their plan around the supper table with the family's input. Each day, Jane would arrive with a basket full of goodies, and the three of them would eat, talk, or listen to her read poetry. Only one day's work was skipped to allow Turner to ride into Burkeville. This was to arrange for the transfer of $1,000 in Northern currency to the town's bank by the day of their departure. He did not mention this to anyone other than Jane, but the money was to be used in the event a ransom of some sort was demanded. He would also visit an attorney to have a quick last will and testament drafted, leaving his entire estate to Jane should he not return. This document would be given to Joseph in a sealed envelope before his leaving, in addition to his remaining wartime journals. Turner's only request was that the envelope not be opened unless he was known to have died and that no one, especially Jane, was to know of its existence.

In these last few days together, Turner decided it would be best if only Jane and Joseph were told about the rock that had once lain upon Benjamin's grave. If not for Samuel's eyewitness testimony, his claim of a rock that could not be moved suddenly disappearing on its own might have been hard to swallow. As it was, both Jane and Joseph acknowledged that there must be some significant, heavenly purpose for its arrival on that spot. Unfortunately, their subsequent prayers and conversations about the rock's supernatural qualities produced nothing for practical use.

Just before Turner climbed atop the carriage that would take him and Samuel into town, Jane took off the silver necklace she wore on his first night back and put it around his neck. Turner, in kind, presented Jane with a small, slightly used music box that played the first eight bars of Chopin's Nocturne Op. 9 No. 2. He had seen the box in the window of a consignment shop while visiting the bank earlier in the week and could not resist purchasing it. When the time came, they exchanged a prayer, a hug, a kiss, and a promise of everlasting devotion to each other... and then the carriage sped away with Turner on it.

The ride into town was anything but dreary and dispirited. Each man took his turn singing a song as loud as he could manage and still keep a tune. Each shared what he believed to be the most humorous or embarrassing story about himself. They joked and wisecracked and ribbed and generally behaved like pre-pubescent children until, before they knew it, they had arrived at the depot. Joseph said a short prayer and headed back home. Turner and Samuel purchased their boarding passes and claimed seats on the station platform for the hour-long wait. Turner excused himself to take care of some last-minute business in town and asked Samuel to watch the bags. Before long, Turner was back, and the two of them were on their way to Lynchburg.

The first thing both noticed was how agonizingly slow their train was moving compared to locomotives up north. This speed, or slower, remained the case as they were taken farther and farther south. The only good thing that could be said was that at no time was there a need to find another method of transportation because a mile of track was missing. In three days, they were finally sitting in a bleak Western and Atlantic passenger car as it struggled its way toward Atlanta. The torturous hundred miles from Dalton, in the northwest corner of Georgia, to Atlanta took two days—a distance that would have taken a half-day before the war. Turner was looking forward to spending one of those two days in Atlanta to catch a breath and unwind before heading into Alabama, but even his worst-case scenario had them at this point two days earlier.

Being two days behind seemed the least of his worries now, for as they approached the city of Atlanta, the locomotive slowed to a snail's pace and the devastation enveloped them. Everything upon which the conquering Union army could claim some paltry military purpose was laid bare, and that included Atlanta's magnificent Union Depot. Had Turner not known General Sherman showed some mercy to the churches and hospitals, he would have thought the man the devil in disguise. From this moment on, Turner could no longer use Richmond as a reference to express the outer limits of cruelty unleashed on a defenseless town and its vulnerable citizenry.

When the train finally came to rest, the passengers were let go in the middle of the freight yard and shooed away in every direction. Turner attempted to find out where he could purchase boarding passes for the Atlanta and West Point locomotive heading west, but it felt as though he and Samuel were purposely being shunned. Believing this to be nothing more than good, old-fashioned southern bigotry, Turner went off by himself. This proved to make little difference because he was still being ignored. When a few people did finally open up, it was not much more than to refer to him as a "carpetbagger", or worse, a "scalawag".

*So, that's it*, Turner thought. *These people think I am a Northern opportunist, perhaps by the way I am dressed; either that or a Southern traitor openly associating with a freedman by emancipation. They have been shell-shocked and are afraid of their own shadows. Who can blame them?*

Turner decided it was time to take charge. He climbed atop the nearest stonewall and addressed the crowd.

"Citizens of Atlanta, my name is Philip Turner," he shouted in a strong, confident voice. "Major General Philip Turner of the Confederate States army. I have brought with me my parole pass, should anyone care to question my word. I am proud to say that I commanded the best Virginia cavalry there ever was. We fought beside General Robert E. Lee at Sharpsburg and at Gettysburg, and we would have given him every last drop of our blood at Appomattox Court House if he had let us." This bold and surprising move had its intended effect, and most passersby stopped to listen. He continued.

"Has Atlanta lost all its charity?"

Turner allowed this provocative statement to settle in before continuing.

"Five days ago, my friend and I left Virginia bound for Alabama, where we hope to find his family. We are tired from the journey, but even more overwhelmed by the devastation you all have had to endure. We understand your sorrows, but is there one kind soul left in Atlanta that could help point us in the right direction?"

"I was at Gettysburg, Mister Turner," came a shout from the crowd. "I commanded the Fifteenth Alabama Infantry and would have won Little Round Top on the second day of battle if we had but one more regiment beside us. I don't recall your name, sir."

"On the second day of battle, my men joined Major General Jubal Early's Division of General Richard Ewell's Second Corps and pushed Howard's XI Corps back to Cemetery Hill," Turner called out, without knowing exactly where to direct his comments. "Whom do I have the pleasure of addressing?"

A dignified man in his late twenties or early thirties, with the right sleeve of his jacket pinned up to the shoulders, remained steadfast as the curious onlookers began to disperse. Except to take a quick glance at Samuel standing with the luggage, he kept a careful eye on Turner. When it was just the three of them, more or less, the man spoke again.

"My apologies for wanting a bit more evidence of your proclamations than a scrap of paper," the man stated politely. "Especially when broadcast by one so much younger than most major generals, sir."

"The decision to bestow such a lofty rank was not mine, and I assure you it had more to do with the bravery of my men than anything I could have mustered individually," Turner replied earnestly.

"Well stated," the man said. "Please, come down from your rocky podium, and tell me where it is you need to go."

The Good Samaritan's name was William Calvin Oates. He had lost his right arm in a skirmish near Petersburg, Virginia, and spent the remainder of the war reestablishing his law practice in Alabama. They exchanged a few more tales as a result of that battle in Gettysburg, including Turner's address to the General Assembly in Virginia for the return of Confederate dead that still remained there. This seemed to please Mr. Oates immensely.

"In the future, it would be my great honor to join you in this benevolent endeavor, Mister Turner," he said cheerfully. "Until then, tell me how I may assist the two of you today."

"Our destination is the courthouse in Henry County," Turner began. "I believe the railroad we are looking for is the Atlanta and West Point."

"I am afraid that railroad will put you too far north of your destination," Oates observed. "But you are in luck. My practice is in the town of Abbeville. This is the same town where the courthouse for Henry County resides. If it would please you both, you shall board the Macon and Western Railroad to Macon with me and on the second day, refresh yourselves at my residence."

"May da Lawd bless yo, Mista Oates, suh," Samuel said gratefully.

"Yes, we are in your debt, sir," Turner added.

"Charity, like courage, is what keeps our country strong," Oates replied. "We are all doomed should we forget to practice them both routinely."

For some reason, Macon, Georgia, had been spared from General Sherman's wrath in his hell-bent "March to the Sea", and thankfully, the trip into Alabama took on a much quicker pace. Oates was patient to listen to Samuel's story, which, along with the story of how Turner and Samuel met, took the entire train ride to conclude. Even prior to the war, Alabama had few slave-holding plantations when compared to the upper Southern states. That gave Oates reason to believe that, if the documentation did exist, it would not take long to discover. He would begin the search immediately upon their arrival.

"But it was quite unusual for a slave owner to be so cruel as to split a family," he stated curiously. "At least in these parts."

"Was your wife unhealthy, Samuel?"

"No, suh. Nev'a been sickly," Samuel replied.

"Could she have been considered a troublemaker?"

"No, suh. She done spent aw her time in da masta's house."

"Could she read?"

"Oh yes, suh. Helps teach'n da masta's chi'dren she do," Samuel answered proudly. "Aiding, too."

"Aiding?" Oates asked curiously.

"Adding," Turner answered. "Arithmetic. Samuel is quite the wordsmith."

"Yes, I have noticed that," Oates replied kindly. "Do your children read also, Samuel?"

"Yes, suh," Samuel answered, but now sensed something was wrong.

"There is your answer," Oates stated. "Intelligent house servants are assets. Their intelligent children are not."

"Da masta done sow'd ma fam'ly 'cause my chi'dren was smart?" Samuel asked gravely.

"Not because they were smart... because they could read," Oates corrected him. "You are smart, Samuel, but you cannot read. Your master may have overheard something your child said that could only have been gathered by reading it somewhere—quite innocently on your child's part; perhaps some bad news about the direction of the war. This would, of course, be good news among his slaves, especially among the younger men."

Sensing this hypothesis was having a negative effect on Samuel, Oates continued after only a brief pause.

"This should be considered favorable news, Samuel, because I doubt you will find your wife and children on another plantation. They most likely reside in an aristocrat's household, but some distance away."

Samuel gave Oates an appreciative half-smile.

They arrived in Abbeville on the second day, just as Mr. Oates predicted. Without having had a proper bed for seven days, Turner slept like a log. Samuel, on the other hand, prayed without ceasing that entire evening. It was long after midnight that sleep finally overtook him.

Turner and Oates were up early the following morning, having quietly listened to Samuel's tender prayers until they had both fallen asleep. For Samuel not to already be awake was quite unusual, and they suspected pure exhaustion to be the cause. This prompted them to take their coffee, jerky, and conversation outdoors in order to leave Samuel undisturbed. The courthouse would not open till 9:00 AM, and so they waited until 8:00 to wake him.

Oates was right about the number of slaves being sold in Henry County. There were only two names registered in the past year, five in the past two years, and none of them were members of Samuel's family. This left them with no other option but to pay Samuel's cold-hearted, former master a visit. Oates arranged for two horses, and Samuel provided the course of direction. They were standing at the entrance of the plantation's long, winding access road within the hour.

"Are you ready?" Turner asked.

"I been pray'n fo' dis time ta come," Samuel replied.

They proceeded at a slow canter, so as not to miss anything, or anyone, along the way. It was a mile of scattered forest and empty fields before they stood before the large, beautiful two-story mansion. They saw and heard nothing. Turner gave a shout while they remained in the saddle... nothing. The two dismounted and tied the horses to the hitching post.

"Stay with the horses, Samuel," Turner said. "Let me handle this... please."

Samuel nodded his agreement.

Turner walked carefully up the stairs while rethinking his decision to come unarmed. He knocked politely on the door and waited. After a minute, he knocked again. When this did not elicit a response, he banged harder.

"What do you want?" came a threatening shout from behind.

Turner spun around to see a tall, imposing man approach abruptly from the tree line beyond the horses. The man could see Turner clearly on his elevated position atop the stairs, but did not yet notice Samuel on the other side of the horses. Before Turner could answer, the man rounded the horses and literally ran smack into Samuel.

"Samuel? You're still alive?" The man asked in disbelief. "We can remedy that, you son of a whore."

Still holding tight to Samuel with his left hand, the man brought his right arm back as far as it would go and released a punch that sent Samuel crashing against the horses and onto the ground as if dead. This assault brought Turner flying off the porch full steam. By the time his feet landed on the dirt, however, the angry man had a long-barreled pistol aimed straight at his head. Turner tried to stop, but his momentum carried him to within a foot of the gun's muzzle. Without turning toward Samuel, the man spoke harshly.

"So, you thought this scalawag was going to help you, heh, Samuel?" the man taunted him bitterly. "To do what? Retrieve your family? Because of you, they have all abandoned me. Even my wife is gone. Now, I shall have my revenge and will begin with this traitor."

No sooner had the man released these words, he heard the distinct sound of a pistol being cocked close to his right ear.

"It do seem da two of us have revenge on our mine den, suh," Samuel stated calmly. "Now, I pa'fer da Lawd do'n my reveng'n, but dat's gonna be up to yo. Yo see, I got's me dis here... ah... now, Mista Phil'p, what ya'll call dis bitty thing again?"

"Derringer," Turner answered, without taking his eyes off the pistol that was still pointed at his head.

"Yes, suh, I got dis here dann'ger," Samuel began, but was interrupted by Turner.

"Derringer, Samuel."

"Dat's what I say'd: dan-n-ger."

"No, you are saying 'danger.' It's a derringer."

"Dat's what I say'd: dann'ger."

"Will you two shut up about the gun?" the man said angrily.

"Fine, have it your way," Turner said politely.

"As I was say'n, I got's me dis here gun," Samuel began again. "But, I truly rath'a be talk'n den shoot'n. So, let's yo jus' put dat big ol' gun back in dat holst'a… aw slow… like molasses in winna'time."

This jocular bantering made the man even more furious, but there was little he could do unless killing this man standing before him was more important than killing Samuel. He put the gun away. Turner spoke first.

"I am truly sorry to hear of your circumstances, but all we want to know is where we might find Samuel's family. I am willing to pay you a substantial sum of money for that information."

From the corner of his eye, Turner couldn't help noticing Samuel fiddling with his gun.

"Samuel, what are you doing?" he asked.

"Load'n my dann'ger," he replied calmly.

The angry man and Turner looked at Samuel and then at one another. Turner spoke first.

"Your gun was empty?"

"Not no mo' it ain't," Samuel replied. "If'n yo recaw, yo done told me yo'self not to keep it loaded so's I don't go shoot'n myself by accident."

"Yes, I do recall that," Turner said nervously. "But it's loaded now, right?"

"Yes, suh."

"All right then," Turner replied with a sigh of relief, and then turned his attention back to the angry man. "Just give us a name, and we will be on our way."

"Go to hell," the angry man snapped.

Suddenly, a child's voice rang out.

"Pa! Pa! Daddy!"

Samuel looked over at the corner of the house.

"Josiah! Josiah Mason, ma'boy!"

In his euphoria, Samuel inadvertently dropped the derringer and ran off in the child's direction. The angry man and Turner looked at the gun lying on the ground, and then at one another. This brought a slow smile to the angry man's face—that was, until Turner delivered a fast and powerful jab directly to the man's nose, which immediately produced a heavy stream of blood and snot. The man rocked backward a few steps and instinctively used both hands to cover his face. That allowed Turner to quickly remove the man's gun from its holster, place it in his own waistband, and send another solid punch to the man's kidney. That caused the man to drop to one knee and vomit more blood.

"Never mind about that name," Turner said, as he bent over to pick up the Derringer, which he unloaded—so as not to shoot himself by accident.

Among the joyful tears, it was quickly learned that Samuel's son was the only member of the Samuel's family at the plantation. Once this information was discovered, the three exited the property as if their lives depended on it.

# 13

# Morning Sunshine

B ack in Pennsylvania, the diverse expedition party left Gettysburg at the break of day, three on horseback and two in the horse and buggy: five people, five expectations for going. The estimated time of arrival to Dr. Peterson's property was shortly after noon, unless Miss Bessie required more than four rest stops. The buggy had a well-padded bench seat, a spring on every wheel, and a horse that was an excellent trotter, but this particular passenger could get awfully cranky at the five-mile mark. Miss Bessie was given the option of staying or going, but when would she ever have the chance to fill her pockets full of gold again? The judge preferred to ride in the buggy for its comfort, but insisted Daniel switch with him every so often when Miss Bessie's endless chattering became like a squawking crow in his ears.

The horses did not seem to mind the extra cargo that would hopefully make their stay more comfortable, so the party made good time. It had been several years since his last visit to the doctor's farmhouse, but the judge's keen sense of direction put them close enough to pick up the trail left behind by Turner and his party last week. After several switchbacks up the gentle mountainside, they finally arrived at their destination. What they saw, however, was nothing less than astonishing.

Instead of a country house abandoned and in disrepair, they were now staring at a dwelling in the same condition in which Dr. Peterson had it built. Not only was the structure like new, curtains hung in each window, and white smoke puffed lazily from all three chimneys. As the puzzled newcomers continued their watchful approach, the many chickens that occupied the front yard started clucking and dancing about nervously. Even the odd-shaped goats that plucked away at the leaves of the low-hanging branches began to bleat their opinions of this intrusion.

"This is the doctor's house; of that, I am certain," the judge surmised. "But how and when it was remade confounds me."

The front door opened unexpectedly, and out walked a tall, trim, middle-aged woman. She wore split-skirt buckskins for riding and a plain, soft cotton blouse. Her long blond hair had a hint of silver in it and was pulled up by means of several clips and barrettes. These fasteners were applied haphazardly, suggesting haste was more important than vanity or a mirror. Still, with all these slight imperfections, one could imagine her being as lovely as Emily in her prime. When the unassuming woman reached the edge of the front porch, a wide, bright smile came to her graceful face, and she spoke.

"Welcome. I've been expecting you."

"Have you now?" the judge responded crossly.

"Why yes, let's see if I can remember correctly," she began cheerfully. "You're here to fish Doctor Peterson's legendary streams while Miss Bessie—sitting next to you—hopes to find a stray nugget or two, preferably gold. Young

Daniel there hopes these three days away from your desk will give him enough time to demonstrate to you how well versed in the realm of jurisprudence he has become—"

"Is this true, Daniel?" the judge interrupted. Daniel began coughing, as if something large had suddenly lodged itself in his throat.

"Come now, Daniel, this isn't the time to hide that brilliant mind of yours," the lady prodded.

"I had hoped to ask for your guidance, sir," Daniel stated meekly.

"That's better," the lady said approvingly. "Now, where was I? Oh yes, Mr. Duchene came to find a rock—a special rock that has the power to bring mortal enemies together—and then there's Miss Emily." At this point, she stopped talking and simply looked intently at Emily. She shook her head a few times and continued. "My, my, my, you are a beautiful thing, aren't you?"

"That is very kind of you to say, Miss," Emily replied, with little reaction to the compliment. "I'm sorry; I don't believe you have given us your name."

"*Mon nom est le Soleil Du Matin,*" the lady replied.

"That's your name?" Emily inquired, having no understanding of the French language.

"*Monsieur Duchene?*" the lady was now speaking to Duke.

"Her name is Sun, or Sunshine," Duke answered.

"*Très bon, Monsieur Duchene,*" she said. "*Est-ce tout?*"

"Sun, or Sunshine... of the morning," Duke added. "Morning Sunshine is her name."

"You may call me Sunny, but I do love the morning sunshine best, don't you?" she asked rhetorically, while turning her attention back to Emily. "So, you're responsible for all of us being here? And why have you come, my dear?"

227

"If it is not too much to ask, Miss Sunny," Emily stated coyly, as if putting the intriguing woman to the test, "I was hoping you would tell me."

"Very well," Sunny agreed. "You're here to get back at someone who has hurt you deeply."

"That's not true!" Emily protested vehemently.

"Now see here, you needn't be cruel," the judge interjected.

"I beg your forgiveness, my sweet child," Sunny apologized earnestly. "I do have a way of saying the first thing to pop into my head. Well then, let's get you all inside where it's nice and cozy. I have supper almost ready."

"We are going nowhere until you can tell me what you are up to, madam," the judge fired back.

"I'm up to making your short vacation here more comfortable, Judge," she answered. "And don't you worry about chopping wood; there's enough to last the entire winter."

"How do you know our names and so much about our trip?" the judge continued his cross-examination.

"My, my, my, you are full of questions, aren't you?" Sunny asked sweetly. "They will all be answered soon enough; I can assure you of that. Well, then, I'll be inside should you choose to join me. If not, I suppose my goats will have no qualms eating your supper for you."

With that, Sunny disappeared inside the house, and Miss Bessie began her slow, painful descent from the buggy.

"And where are you going?" the judge huffed.

"I am going inside," Miss Bessie replied boldly, as the feeling of solid ground under her feet brought some relief to her aching bones. "Miss Sunny was kind enough to invite us in twice. I do not need to be asked a third time."

"I do not see the harm, Judge," Duke added as he, too, climbed down off his horse. "I had a suspicion something mysterious was at work up here, and we have two more days to discover what that something is."

Emily, still reeling from the woman's accusation, leaped from her horse, grabbed her bag, and Miss Bessie's, and the two went inside. The men carried the remainder of the gear and provisions to the front porch. The horses were relieved of their saddles and harness, and then released into a large grassy corral behind the house. All four horses took one quick lap around the fenced perimeter and then began grazing happily, alongside the other two horses being held there. Upon reaching the back door, the men suddenly heard a stern voice call to them from inside.

"You better not come in here with those dirty boots on. You may bring them inside once they are off your feet. The house shoes are for you." Each man looked to the other to make certain they were following the procedures given to them: first, the boots come off, then they may enter, and then they should find some suitable replacement for the boots.

Once inside, they found a short-legged latticed bench with a pair of women's boots resting on top. Three pairs of Indian-style moccasins sat on the floor in front of it. They added their boots to the bench and slipped on the moccasins, which were lined in rabbit fur and made them feel as though they were walking on a cushion of air. The back door led directly into the kitchen, and the smell of bread being baked in the brick oven was intoxicating. A large copper pot with a dense, savory stew simmered over an open flame in the fireplace. Again, each man looked to the other in an effort to find some way to get that bread dipped into that stew without being caught. These thoughts were not allowed to advance beyond mere desire, however, because there soon came another warning call from within the house.

"Don't even think about it. Supper will be ready shortly."

"How is she doing that?" the judge asked out loud what the other two were thinking.

The evening proceeded amicably, especially after that supper and the travelers' realization that they had a warm, safe place to sleep. Sunny addressed all their questions, and yet never really seemed to answer any of them. There was no satisfying explanation for how the doctor's house was made inhabitable once more, or how Sunny could know what she did about her guests. These things just were. No more was said about their personal expectations, except that Miss Bessie's ideas about deep shafts lined with gold were sadly dispelled. The only event that could have been described as a potential disruption to an otherwise pleasant evening would have been the goats eating all the food that was left out on the front porch—and that was enough to feed five people for two more days. This caused Sunny to exhibit a slightly embarrassed smile. She promised them no one would starve, for there was fresh milk, eggs, and butter in the springhouse, salted meats in the smokehouse, and canned fruits and vegetables in the root cellar.

"Besides, I'm looking forward to cooking up some fresh trout tomorrow evening," Sunny predicted. This statement prompted the three men to turn their conversation toward fishing and the three ladies to discuss everything else but fishing. It was not long before the idea of getting a good night's sleep entered both conversations. The sleeping arrangements were two persons to a bedroom, and there were three bedrooms. That put Emily and Miss Bessie in one room, Duke and the judge in another, and Daniel to himself.

"If there are but three bedrooms, where will you be sleeping, Miss Sunny?" Emily asked, more out of concern than the ulterior motive of a journalist. By now, Emily had put their initial encounter behind her and had grown curiously fond of this beautiful and clever woman.

"Oh, don't you worry about me, dear child," Sunny replied without further elaboration, again addressing the question, but not answering it.

Sunny did, however, offer a prayer of thanksgiving for God's glorious presence in that house that night and His great love for each of her guests. Immediately following this invocation, she slipped into the kitchen and was not seen for the remainder of the evening. A hostess's disappearance from the sanctuary of her secluded home in the middle of night would have normally generated some concern, but this was Miss Sunny; it simply added to her quirkiness. The guests made their way to the upstairs bedrooms, unbothered by it. The two large Franklin fireplace stoves on the main floor kept the frigid night air at bay, and sleep came easily.

* * *

At some point that night, Emily awoke to see Sunny standing patiently in the bedroom doorway. The door had been opened to its fullest, but only allowed the faintest amount of light to penetrate the blackness of the room. Perhaps it was the peaceful, indifferent way in which Emily had returned to consciousness that caused her to see Sunny's likeness in the doorway as something between real and surreal. Unfrighten by the image, Emily sat up slowly. She took a quick glance over at Miss Bessie's sleeping form and then back to face Sunny. It was not until Sunny reached out her hand and spoke that definition came to her body.

"Come," she said tenderly. "I have something to show you."

Without a word, Emily brought her feet out from under the covers and into the soft moccasins that lay beside the bed. At the foot of the bed, she grabbed the robe draped over the bedpost and put it on rapidly. The two glided down the stairs and directly to the front door.

"But we will freeze," Emily stated and stopped at the door.

"You must trust me, dear," Sunny replied gently.

To Emily's amazement, the moccasins and the light-weight robe over her nightgown were all that was needed to keep her warm, even though a dense cloud of steam was produced with each breath that she exhaled. As soon as they reached the tree line, the pounding sound of gun-fire and terrifying screams was non-stop. In an instant, the star-filled sky turned to daybreak, and men in uniform came rushing through the dense forest from every direction. Sunny held tightly to Emily's hand, as these frantic men passed them with death in their eyes.

"They cannot hurt you," Sunny reassured her.

It was not long before they were passing the dead and dying. The scene was so horrific that Emily found it difficult to stand, much less continue walking, and the urge to vomit was ever-present. The barbaric events that were taking place all about them did not have an effect on Sunny, and if not for her hand, Emily would have crumbled to the ground at the first sight of blood that spurt and pooled from so many disfiguring wounds.

"Let me go back, please," Emily pleaded. This request for compassion must have been granted, because they came to a stop.

"You have arrived," Sunny stated and let go her hand.

Though still in the grips of shock, Emily could not help but notice that the gunfire was now sporadic and far off, and the voices were now a mixture of those barking orders and those in the agonizing moments before death. As her overwhelmed senses gradually returned, it also became apparent that the only ones left standing wore gray, and she, too, stood in a sea of bodies dressed in blue. No longer able to look upon the bloodbath that surrounded her, she covered her face with her hands. That gesture only made her sense of hearing more acute, and she immediately recognized Nathan's voice cry out.

"Stay away from him! Stay away from him, or I'll shoot!"

A sudden rush of strength and determination took control of Emily's body, and she quickly dropped both hands. Carefully scanning the battlefield, she caught a glimpse of a young man in blue that could be Nathan, but he was facing away from her. He was kneeling and holding tightly to another man in blue with one hand. In the other hand, this same young man pointed a shaking pistol at the towering man in gray that stood before him. Without hesitation, Emily began running towards this occurrence as fast as she could.

It was Nathan, and the soldier in gray was speaking to him with kind words.

"Put the gun away, son. It's done... it's over."

"Put the gun away, Nathan!" Emily screamed, but no one heard her.

"Philip Turner," the man in blue being held by Nathan called out.

"What did he say?" the man in gray asked, as if stunned by what he just heard.

"He said, 'Philip Turner,'" Nathan replied and lowered his gun. "He has been calling out that name since he took the bullet. Can you please help him? I don't want him to die. Please, sir, save him." The man in gray knelt down to look at the Yankee colonel's wound. He took Nathan's free hand in his and applied it to the wound.

"Keep pressure on it until I return. Do you understand me, Private?" he commanded Nathan.

"Yes, sir," Nathan replied tearfully.

The man in gray stood up and spoke to the first soldier he saw.

"No one is to disturb them. That's an order, understood?"

"Yes, Sergeant," the soldier replied.

With that, Joseph (the man in gray) set off in search of Colonel Philip Turner. Once he was gone, Emily moved in front of Nathan and knelt down. She looked deeply at Nathan's dirty, innocent face and thanked God for sparing his life. At that moment, all her convoluted reasons for wanting him to hurt, just like she hurt, vanished. She watched him go from kneeling to sitting in order to free up the hand not covering the wound. Upon request, Nathan received a clean rag from the rebel guard and began to wipe the sweat off Colonel Hillary's face with this free hand. She listened as he spoke to this badly injured and incoherent man with endearing words about how important he had become in his life, and how that life would be so much better if only he were his father. Then, Nathan began to sing softly:

> Amazing Grace, how sweet the sound,
> That saved a wretch like me.
> I once was lost but now am found
> Was blind, but now I see...

Emily joined Nathan in singing the next five stanzas and then listened to him speak to God in prayer. She watched as Nathan's hand turned dark red in a vain attempt to keep the blood from spilling out of his commander's body, and she wept with him. She moved in closer, wishing only to hold Nathan close to her and never let him go.

"I love you," she whispered in his ear, just as Colonel Turner arrived. That was the last thing she remembered.

\* \* \*

At some point that night, Duke was awakened by some commotion going on outside his window. He removed himself from the bed and spread opened the curtains with the back of his hand. Below, he saw Sunny dressed warmly and sitting atop her horse. She was holding onto the reins of his horse, which had already been saddled. He got dressed as quickly and quietly as he could, so not to wake the judge, and dashed down the stairs. His boots, coat, gloves, and hat were waiting for him at the front door.

"*Bonjour, Monsieur Duchene,*" Sunny greeted him. "*Êtes-vous prêt à monter?*" *Are you ready to ride?* Duke translated in his mind.

"*Pourquoi parlez-vous français?*" Duke inquired, as he took the reins from Sunny and climbed into the saddle. Translated: *Why do you speak French?*

"*Est-il pas la langue votre pays d'origin?*" Translated: *Is it not the language of your homeland?*

"I am an American now, Miss Sunny," Duke stated proudly. "Let us speak the language of my new homeland."

"Very well," Sunny replied and sighed. "I so enjoy speaking French, though."

"Where are we going?"

"To the place where Nathan buried Colonel Hillary," Sunny answered, without bothering to explain how she knew of either Nathan or Colonel Hillary. It was a short ride, and Sunny slowed once they reached the open pasture.

"Careful; this was a battlefield, remember," she warned.

There was only the light from a waning moon by which to guide the horses, but Duke knew their destination immediately. The large, white rock located several hundred yards within the open field was unmistakable. It was faintly illuminated and projected an array of color within itself that would come and go imperceptibly as they approached. Duke circled the rock twice before dismounting and could detect no dark side to it—yet it did not cause any shadows on its own; that is, there was light but none of the effects of light.

"You may touch it," Sunny stated before dismounting herself.

"What is it?" Duke asked, as he put his hand on it and walked around its entire smooth, rectangular body.

"It's a rock, Mister Duchene," Sunny replied. "The same rock your three friends saw when they came to visit a few days ago."

"Does it cast spells?" he asked, not referring so much to witchcraft as science.

"It's indestructible and immovable, as your friends discovered," Sunny said and gestured to the two broken pickaxes. "But it doesn't alter the mind."

"And where is Colonel Hillary buried?" Duke asked without taking his eyes off the rock.

"Colonel Hillary lies beneath the rock."

"But how?"

"Quite logically, the rock arrived after Nathan buried his colonel," Sunny stated. "And it was taken back the morning after your friends arrived here."

"Logically? How logical was it for a rock of this size to appear, stay for a year or more, and then disappear? And I take it to mean this was accomplished of its own accord?" Duke asked in astonishment. "What purpose would that serve?"

"That has yet to be determined," Sunny replied, "as Mr. Turner pointed out to you upon his return to your hotel."

"So, we know for whom this magical rock was intended," Duke concluded. "But who provided it, Miss Sunny?"

"The rock yields no magic, and it didn't come with a return address, Mister Duchene," Sunny responded whimsically. "I can tell you this: it comes with a special purpose, and you're being shown this for a reason. Now that you've seen what you hoped to see, I believe we can go—for this rock will do nothing more than any other rock would do."

"What is your hurry, Miss Sunny?" Duke stated, as if he had her backed into a corner.

"Stay if you wish, but tomorrow is certain to be a busy day," Sunny answered politely and climbed into her saddle.

"Okay, okay, I'm coming."

Silently, they trotted back in the direction from which they had come. Just before rejoining the path through the trees, Duke turned back to look upon the rock once more. It was gone.

"Just like that, huh?" he whispered to himself.

\* \* \*

At some point that night, the judge sat up and maneuvered his feet off the bed, and there he sat. He had been made to feel welcome and comfortable the entire evening—and he was—but his unsettled mind would not permit him a wink of sleep. Not wishing to disturb Duke and his sleep, he located his moccasins with his feet and exited the room as quiet as a mouse. When he shuffled himself to the top of the stairs, he saw a considerable amount of light coming from the direction of the kitchen on the main floor. He heard not a sound, but thought an investigation was in order; besides, that was to be his first stop anyway. Once he descended to the foot of the stairs, he heard the distinct sound of pottery smashing against the floor. He quickly altered his path to include a stop by the fireplace, where he would grab the first wrought iron instrument he touched, which happened to be the tongs. He would have preferred the poker, but this tool had some weight to it. He approached the kitchen with all the stealth he could muster and popped open the door with the tongs.

"Miss Sunny?" he noted in a low voice. "What in blazes are you doing up at this hour?"

"I had to occupy my time somehow, and putting dishes away sufficed," Sunny replied sheepishly. "Did you come downstairs to tend the fire, Judge?"

"Never mind that," the judge snapped and lowered the fireplace tongs to his side. "This is when most people occupy their time sleeping. May I inquire as to why you are occupying your time in the kitchen?"

"I was waiting for you, Judge," Sunny said, without bothering to look up from sweeping together the bits and pieces of a broken dish.

"Waiting for me? In the middle of the night?" The judge laughed. "What an absurd thing to say." Sunny shrugged her shoulders but said nothing. "And for what purpose have you been waiting, dear lady?"

"To take you to the battlefield," Sunny replied in all seriousness.

The judge smiled and waited a moment for the finish to this wisecrack, but received nothing more. With a sigh, he set the tongs down on the table and plopped wearily into the nearest seat. Sunny went to the icebox and pulled out a pitcher of fresh milk. She poured a glass half full, set it in front of the judge, and took the seat across from him. There was nothing left for him to do but accept that he had walked straight into another feminine trap.

*And where was Duchene? Was he not invited to assist me in these matters?* The judge thought in annoyance. *And how did she get a block of ice way out here?*

"Thank you," he said politely and finished the cool beverage in one long string of gulps. "I have a feeling I will regret asking this, but you have given me little choice. So please, explain to me if you can, why I should have any interest in visiting the battlefield in the middle of the night?"

"There will be a fresh new college built on those hallowed grounds, and you shall be its first chancellor," Sunny stated unequivocally.

"Poppycock!" The judge exclaimed and rose from the table straightaway. "You have gone too far this time, Miss Sunny... if that is your true name. I am going back to sleep. Good evening, madam."

"Good evening, Judge," she replied with great gentleness and remained seated.

The judge quietly grumbled to himself from the time he parted company until the time he flopped back onto his bed, whereupon he grumbled some more.

"A new college?" he murmured quietly. "We have a perfectly fine college already, Miss Sunny!" He had never heard of such blatant lunacy. As he saw it, nothing could be proved by looking out over an empty field in the middle of the night.

"Chancellor?" he whispered cynically and rolled over onto his side. "Who is she to tell me what I am going to do!" From this irritated state, he moved into a sitting position on the edge of the bed. His mind overlooked the fact that he was still wearing his robe and moccasins.

"The nerve of that woman!" he uttered defiantly and stood upright. "I have a good mind to call her bluff on this one!" With a strong desire to put an end to this chicanery, the judge began to retrace his steps back toward the kitchen. It would come as no surprise to him if he were to see Miss Sunny somewhere along the way. That moment came when he was halfway down the stairs. There, standing by the front door, Sunny held open a men's full-length, bearskin coat pointed in his direction.

"Quickly, we haven't much time," she said with some urgency. "The buggy is out front."

"Of course it is," the judge muttered under his breath and walked himself into the heavy coat without resistance.

In the short amount of time it took to make their way through the dense forest of tall pines and hardwoods, the dead of night became the break of day and the narrow, rarely used path they were on turned into a wide, deeply rutted utility road. The scene that came next could not have been more astonishing, for what should have been the serenity of a countryside pasture, was now the makings of a vast construction project. To the east and along the ridgeline stood three magnificent brick buildings of great dimension and one partially completed building. Long rows of brick, large piles of wooden timbers, and a countless number of army-style wagons filled with all kinds of building materials occupied the entire center of the pasture; that is, except for the lone statue contained safely inside of a small corral. To the west was built a small town of temporary housing, and an abundance of mules and horses grazed in every direction. Suddenly, a bell rang out, and a multitude of young people came streaming out of one of the buildings and funneled back into another building.

"What is going on here?" the judge asked in stunned disbelief.

"What does it look like?"

"Is this your college?" he asked without turning from the scenery.

"No, Judge. This is Colonel Hillary's college, and you are to lead it."

"I never wished for this, or dreamed of this, or aspired to do this thing you are speaking of," the judge stated as a matter of fact.

"Some folk glide through life; some plod through it; some desire this or that to happen, but some are chosen," Miss Sunny replied, as if this challenge was somehow predestined.

"But why me?" the judge asked, just as he saw Daniel exit the building with a small group of mixed-race, mixed-gendered students. The judge immediately dropped the reins, leaped from the buggy, and began shouting joyfully.

"Daniel! Daniel! Over here, my boy... over here!"

"He can't hear you, Judge," Sunny remarked passively.

As soon as her words were spoken, the judge stopped his frantic gesturing and turned abruptly.

"I will ask you once again," the judge demanded. "What is going on here?"

"You're being given a wonderful opportunity, Judge," Sunny replied calmly. "Should you choose to accept it, Daniel will become the first student to earn a law degree from this place—class of 1870, unless you dawdle."

"How is that possible?" he inquired, hardly containing his amazement or his emotions.

"With men, it would be impossible, Judge," Sunny reminded him. "But with God... all things are possible."

"I understand that part," the judge acknowledged.

"What you see before you will all be accomplished through Mister Turner, but he will need help," Sunny continued. "You remember Mister Turner, don't you, Judge?"

"Yes, I remember him," the judge replied, suddenly feeling very small.

"Then you know how difficult it is to forgive a person a little," she added somberly, "without first knowing you've been forgiven much."

"Yes, yes, I understand that part as well," he confessed. "I will look forward to meeting with Mister Turner again soon. Perhaps I will be the one asking forgiveness this time."

"You will make a fine chancellor, Judge," Sunny stated affectionately. "It's time we go back."

* * *

The following morning, the entire house awoke to the smell of bacon, except for the coffee drinkers, for they were greeted first by the smell of coffee. Not knowing of the others' midnight ventures, each new arrival to the breakfast table looked at Sunny to see if his or her personal experience would be acknowledged in some way. When that did not occur, they all looked to themselves, and it was plain as day. The three that were taken away the night before had been transformed by their experience, and their silent, awkward behavior did not go unnoticed by Miss Bessie.

"What have you all been up to?" she asked observantly. "Cat must have gotten to everyone's tongue this morning."

"Now, now, Miss Bessie, can we not begin a meal in silence every now and again without being accused of some mischief or wrongdoing?" the judge asked playfully.

"No!" she replied candidly. This response brought a smile to everyone's face, except for Miss Bessie's... and Emily's.

"All right then, we shall begin our table talk with you," the judge suggested. "What would you like to do today?"

"Well, since Miss Sunny here won't let me cook, clean, or so much as lift a finger, I am bored to tears," she began earnestly. "I was hoping Miss Emily would take me with her to look at that little battlefield everybody's been talking about."

This innocent request brought with it another moment of silence, as everyone looked to Emily. She had been uncharacteristically demure since waking and poked at her food without eating a bit of it. She felt no desire to revisit the scene of so much pain and sadness. In fact, her experience was so traumatic that she had actually developed a deep sense of appreciation for Nathan's father because of it. Who knew how much more killing a sweet, sixteen-year-old boy from Philadelphia could handle, especially without his beloved colonel's guidance? She knew better than to let that darkness fester inside of her, however, and for the first time that morning she smiled. Emily glanced at Sunny and then turned towards Miss Bessie.

*I do need to see the battlefield again... as it is now*, she thought.

"I would love your company, Miss Bessie," Emily said gratefully.

"Now that that is settled," the judge stated thankfully, "Daniel, what can you tell me about the Supreme Court case of *Marbury v. Madison*?"

Daniel was grateful that he had been given such an easy case with which to begin his dialogue with the judge. This was a well-known case, but certainly not a case easily recited in precise detail at the breakfast table—except for those with exceptional recall capabilities.

"Well, sir," he began confidently, "it is my understanding that William Marbury was nominated and confirmed as a justice of the peace in the District of Columbia by our great nation's second president, the honorable John Adams. When our third president, the honorable Thomas Jefferson, took office, he ordered his secretary of state, James Madison, to hold that commission, as well as many others. Mr. Marbury sued Mr. Madison in the Supreme Court, and arguments began in February of 1803. Two weeks later, the

Court held that Mr. Marbury had a right to the commission; however, the law giving him that right, Section 13 of the Judiciary Act of 1789, conflicted with Article III Section 2 of the United States Constitution, which made it unconstitutional. It would be the first time an Act of Congress was declared unconstitutional. The latest instance of that occurring was just recently in the case of *Scott v. Sandford* back in 1857."

You could hear a pin drop. Daniel went back to eating, as everyone else stopped and stared at each other in utter amazement—except for Sunny, who broke the silence.

"Anyone for more coffee?" Sunny asked placidly.

"Yes, please, Miss Sunny," Daniel replied, still unaware of the hush he created.

When the reaction to Daniel's scholarly discourse slowly began to wear off and the morning meal was complete, the guests were given permission to come and go as they pleased. The men were asked to clean and wrap, in butcher's paper, any fish they wished to be included with the evening meal and place it in the icebox. There were no plans for an afternoon meal, so the kitchen would remain open for whatever a person could find to satisfy his or her hunger. The freshly baked apple pie, however, was for supper and therefore off-limits. After these simple instructions were made clear, Sunny disappeared into the kitchen, not to be seen again until suppertime.

The beautiful autumn day went by eventfully, and each person had a story to tell at the supper table. Before long, it was time to rest up for the long journey home the following day. There would be no intrusions to a peaceful night's sleep, and everyone woke refreshed. Another magnificent breakfast awaited them in the morning, and more than enough provisions were produced for the trip back home. It was agreed beforehand that Daniel would start out riding with Miss Bessie in the buggy to give the judge some uninterrupted time to think on matters. When the time came to leave, each guest gave their hostess a declaration of gratitude and a big hug. Sunny remained on the front porch until they were out of sight.

"Moccasins!" the judge exclaimed a short distance down the road. "Miss Sunny gave them to us, and yet I left mine under the bed. I shall never find another pair more comfortable. Go on at this pace, and I shall catch up quickly."

With that, the judge turned and galloped back. He arrived in no time, but the house he now looked upon had little resemblance to the house they had just left and lived in for the last two days. Gone were the chickens, the goats, the smoke from the fireplaces, and the curtains. In fact, it was the house he had expected to see when they first arrived: uninhabited and in some state of decline. This transformation was so inconceivable, even the horse rose up on its hind legs when given a slight tug on the reins to stop.

"There, there, it's okay, boy," he said calmly and leaned forward to pat the horse's neck.

"Well now, it appears we left just in time," the judge mused as he looked about. "I'm going to miss those moccasins."

There was not a sound, other than the soft breeze as it rattled the water-starved leaves that refused to drop from the trees. The judge was about to return to the others when he caught a glimpse of something lying on the slightly buckled front porch. His approach was slow and cautious, but altogether unnecessary because the object was nothing more dangerous than a pair of moccasins.

"Thank you, Miss Sunny," he called out. "If that is your true name!"

# 14

# Proposals and Propositions

"You must not show yourselves until I can get you safely on that steamboat back to Tallahassee," Oates (the man harboring Turner, Samuel and now Samuel's son), exclaimed breathlessly.

Oates had just rushed back from his law office in town, where he had noticed three unfamiliar men on horseback who would stop from time to time to ask a passerby a question or two. There was no hostility in their manner, and he might not have given them a second glance, except the one doing the asking wore bandages across his face and stared ominously from behind two swollen black-and-blue eyes. Having been told the story of Turner's meeting with the slave owner the night before, Oates intentionally deviated his path so that he might overhear their questioning. The next thing he knew, this bruised man on horseback was asking him if he had seen a white man, a black man, and a black youth traveling together.

Oates brought this encounter to Turner and Samuel's attention, and then proceeded to describe the short conversation that ensued.

"'I have not seen that particular combination of travelers,' I answered them. 'But I am a lawyer here in town, and if there was a grievance, perhaps I can help you gentlemen,'

"'That will not be necessary,' the bruised man answered peacefully.

"Being curious of their intentions, however, I continued my probing," Oates went on.

"'If you have been abused in some way, I would be willing to escort you to the sheriff's office,' I offered.

"'That will also not be necessary,' was this man's curt reply.

"That was the end of our conversation, for they continued their slow pace through town," Oates stated. "If I were a gambling man, I would bet the friendly behavior was a ruse, and these three seek nothing more than revenge on their own terms.

"With that being said, it may be in our favor they have decided not to include the law because of the pounding that man took at your hands, Mister Turner... not that he did not deserve it. Therefore, we must get you back across state lines and, preferably, on that boat without anyone being the wiser."

The steamboat to Tallahassee that Oates was referring to was the boat ridden by Samuel's son, Josiah, twice before. Josiah was hesitant to share his precarious story with two white strangers, until his father assured him there was no danger in these two men and that he could speak openly. This set Josiah's mind at ease, and he began describing how they were sold to a slave trader first, and then to a college professor and abolitionist from Tallahassee, Florida. Once the purchase was complete, the four of them traveled by steamboat down the Chattahoochee River from Fort Gaines, Georgia, and then into Florida on the Apalachicola

River. From what Josiah was told by his mother, their new owner was a kind and upright man. He had been antici-pating the end of war in the North's favor and went about the South spending every Confederate dollar he owned (soon to be worthless) on liberating educated slaves. His idea was to bring as many of these intelligent people as he could afford into Florida's capital to help form some system to educate the freed slaves. The state of Florida had the fewest number of citizens in the Confederacy, but half of that population consisted of slaves.

Josiah recalled standing in the streets of Tallahassee on May 20, with his mother and sister, as Lincoln's Emancipation Proclamation was being read by General Edward McCook and then watched as the United States flag was being hoisted above the Capitol Building. It was on that day he told his mother that he would earn his way back onto that steamboat to find his father.

Josiah then described how, with the professor's help, he was taken on as a porter on the steamboat in exchange for passage to Fort Gaines. When he arrived back at the plantation, he was told by the few remaining former slaves that his father had escaped, not to be seen again; that was three months ago. Since then, he ate and slept where he could, but maintained a constant, hidden vigil over the plantation in hopes of his father's return.

"I wasn't going anywhere without my daddy," Josiah said, with all the bravado a twelve-year-old could muster.

This declaration brought with it a determination to make it out of Alabama unharmed. The plan was to leave for Fort Gaines the following morning by buckboard. Turner, Samuel, and Josiah would be traveling among some fake cargo in the back and kept hidden under a canvas blanket. The unhurried trip was no more than twenty miles and it took less than two hours without hindrance. Mr. Oates would take no compensation for his generosity and immediately started back home. On the second day, Tallahassee became the site of yet another great celebration, when Samuel's family was reunited once more and the Lord was glorified.

"Praise da Lawd!" Samuel cried out and fell to his knees before his wife, Rosie, and his daughter, Jasmine. "I be praise'n His name till da end o' my days... Jesus is Lawd... Jesus is da King o' Kings!"

That night, Rosie, agreed to begin their new life in Gettysburg and doing whatever the Lord had planned for them there... as long as it didn't involve freezing to death. It took another day in Tallahassee for Turner to develop an alternate route north that would keep them as far away from Alabama as possible. That new strategy would begin at the Tallahassee Train Depot and take them east. The Pensacola and Georgia Railroad would take them to Live Oak, Florida, where a short branch line heading north connected it with the Atlantic and Gulf Railroad at Lawton, Georgia. They would head east into Savannah, and Turner could reassess their traveling strategy going north from there.

With the railroad companies pulling up rails from their minor routes to rebuild their major routes along the eastern seaboard, Turner could not have chosen a faster route. They would reach Petersburg, Virginia, in half the time Turner expected. He would not have complained, even if it had taken longer, because of the enjoyment he received from listening to Samuel's family talk among themselves. With so much joy and laughter, it was hard to believe they once lived as slaves.

What intrigued Turner most was Rosie's depiction of the man who had bought them out of slavery. She carefully painted the picture of a man who not only wanted to teach slaves to read and write, but more importantly, he wanted them to experience how faith in a loving God could give a person true freedom. The beginning of that freedom was forgiveness; this was a concept Turner thought Benjamin would have immediately embraced.

"Unfortunately, the professor has little hope that will occur in the public domain without a strong man of faith, like Mister Lincoln, in charge," Rosie pointed out. "He feared if reconstruction was left to the politicians, it would be nothing more than legalized retribution and a hindrance to the healing of our country."

"Do you believe that, Miss Rosetta?" Turner inquired.

"If I cannot forgive others, how am I to expect my Lord to forgive me, Mister Philip?" she confided without hesitation. "But then, the professor's compassion was much bigger than his bare money purse. I'm afraid it will take the government to educate so many people, even if it turns their hearts away from God. I believe the professor was on the better of the two paths."

"And you believe this is your country?" Turner continued his inquiries.

"My husband and I were born here. My two children were born here," Rosie replied kindly. "To what other country do we belong?"

"Yo' as right as rain, Rosie darl'n. Dis is our home an' we is betrothed to it, but only while we in d'ese earthen bodies," Samuel proclaimed and then quoted Philippians 3:20: "Our conversation (citizenship) be in heaven; from whence we look fo' da Lawd Jesus Christ." Now Mista Lincoln was a fine man, sho' 'nuf a great man. An' da Lawd done used him up fo' good. Now we gotta git aw used up."

Since Rosie's reaction to her husband's response was a quiet watchfulness, Turner guessed she was waiting for more. This restraint was not new to Turner; he had interrupted Samuel a few times in the past, only to discover the best part was yet to come. So, he, too, waited... silently alert. Their patience paid off.

"Think not an' say of yo own self, 'We has Abraham as our father,'" Samuel quoted John the Baptist from the Gospel of Matthew. "'Fo' I says ta yo, God is able of d'ese stones ta raise up chi'dren o' Abraham.'"

Samuel continued somberly.

"What happen ta po' Mista Lincoln was a crime worth griev'n, but his murder done set ta motion da professor. An' mo' folk besides him... wit money o' no. An' jus' as da professor was caw'd upon down so'th, we bin caw'd to dat land up no'th. An' if aw we does is till dat soil ta help fill empty bellies, I'm a will'n. An' if we is ta build a mighty teach'n school ta feed hungry minds an' help bring up chi'dren o God—use me, Lawd!"

"Samuel, my friend, you have done it again," Turner cried out in amazement. "Why did I not see it sooner?"

Turner reached into his luggage and pulled out Benjamin's Bible. He opened it and flipped furiously through its pages. Having come to the third chapter of Matthew (the chapter Samuel had just quoted), he read from the margins:

> Having been born into a Christian family and raised a Christian, I often come back to these words and ask myself: Was I given a birthright into God's Kingdom? No! Thankfully, I am but one of these stones God raised up. Praise the Lord!
>
> If only there was a school that took ordinary stones and instilled in them a trust in God's

love and forgiveness as well as West Point
instills the trappings of war.

"It would seem we are to build a school, Samuel," Turner
gleaned from what he just heard Samuel say and what he
just read from Benjamin's hand. "A mighty teaching school.
Don't ask me how, but I am confident we will be given the
answers in God's time."

Turner made the decision to delay their passage from
Petersburg into Burkeville one day to allow the telegram
he sent requesting transportation to be received by Jane.
This would be the first communication back home since
he and Samuel set off on their journey, so he was sure to
include the fact that he now had three more guests... all
in good spirits.

It was not Turner's intention to spend the night in
every major Confederate city left in ruins by Union forces,
but it was inevitable since all fighting had taken place on
Southern soil since the battle of Gettysburg. Fortunately,
Petersburg had not suffered the devastation on the same
scale as Atlanta or Richmond, even though it encountered
siege-like harassment and numerous Union attacks from
June of 1864 to its ultimate surrender in April of 1865.
General Grant had even hosted President Lincoln in that
town on April 3; that was only days before Grant left for
Appomattox Court House and accepted General Lee's sur-
render of his Army of Northern Virginia on April 9.

The following morning, five anxious travelers hopped
aboard the South Side Railroad and headed west. It would
be a slow-moving train ride from what was reported, but
it would be the final leg of their extraordinary three-
week journey. Turner had hoped to use most of that time
dreaming up ways to make a college out of nothing but
land and hardly enough money. His intuitive mind had not

yet gone beyond the notion of constructing a railroad to the property when Josiah approached him.

"My sister would like to know if she can call you Uncle Philip," he said boldly. Everything Josiah said, he said boldly.

Turner glanced beyond Josiah to where Jasmine was seated. She was playing happily with the doll he had bought her in Tallahassee, but she did not look up. This was the same little girl that had not said two words to him since they met and immediately rejected the doll when he first presented it to her. He had given Josiah a set of marbles at the same time. The gifts were meant to comfort and entertain them during the long trek into the unknown, but he had not seen Jasmine with the doll until now, and the marbles were a useless toy on a train. To remedy these two dilemmas, he had found a used set of dominos from a second-hand store in Savannah; this cheered them both up immensely. Still, Jasmine remained aloof. He could not imagine the turmoil that was going on in that pretty little head of hers, so he did not press it. But he was sure to give her a tender smile whenever he caught her staring at him.

"You may tell your sister that I would be honored if she would call me Uncle Philip, but she must do one thing," Turner stated matter-of-factly. "She must first give me a hug so tight that I will be forced to cry 'Uncle' three times!"

Once Josiah relayed the message, Jasmine screamed and came running toward Turner as fast as she could go. With only a few feet left before contact, she threw her doll above Turner's head so that he would have to reach up to grab it. With his arms outstretched, Jasmine wrapped her arms around his unprotected chest as they collided, and she squeezed.

"Uncle! I give up! Uncle!" Turner hollered in mock distress.

"One more," Jasmine said, while intensifying her embrace.

"Uncle!" he huffed breathlessly, as he brought his arms down around her slender body and returned the hug and the doll. "I believe I have just saved your friend from being crushed like a bug."

"I knew you would catch her, Uncle Philip," Jasmine said with a grin. She would remain on Turner's lap for almost an hour, talking about everything a precocious ten-year-old girl could imagine.

Turner enjoyed every minute of their conversation, but when Jasmine was called away, he immediately went back to his thoughts on using a locomotive to bridge the gap between Gettysburg and the new school. The best-case scenario would be to have the Baltimore and Ohio Railroad extend its service from the Gettysburg Station to the proposed new school. If they refused, he must build his own line. It was not uncommon to have two or more railroads owned by different parties servicing the same town, but it would require its own station with a wheelhouse at each end. The cost could be reduced substantially if the rail and the locomotive were purchased in the south and brought up north. In the south, there were whole sections of track and equipment not being used. Unfortunately, B&O used four-foot, eight-and-a-half-inch gauge rail, and southern rail was five-foot gauge, making this option a less-than-perfect solution. There was much to think about.

Of course, none of these thoughts took into account the foreboding cost of designing and constructing the school itself. Turner only knew that if God wanted it built on that hillside in Pennsylvania, it would be built on that hillside in Pennsylvania. His primary focus (and his strongest suit) was the creation of a system that could transport architects, construction workers, and materials to the property as efficiently as possible. There was only enough time to recall the names of a few railroad men who might be willing to sell him twenty-five miles of rail before they arrived at their destination.

To Turner's utter amazement and joy, there, standing next to Joseph on the station platform, was Jane. Without a second thought, he sprang from his seat, exited the service door at the end of the passenger car, and leapt onto the platform before the train had come to a halt. It was not an extremely large crowd, but there was enough smoke and enough people milling about on the platform to mask Turner's sudden and unanticipated flight from the moving train. This presented him with the opportunity to sneak up behind Jane and softly place his hands over her eyes.

"Make a wish, my love," he whispered in her ear.

"That you not leave me to worry another three weeks ever again," came the cool response as she turned slowly, gently wrapped her arms around his body and then allowed her head to rest contentedly on his chest. Knowing how painstakingly drawn out these meetings were, Joseph spoke next.

"I think I will go and welcome Samuel and his family to Virginia," he said, as if to himself. "When the train finally comes to a complete stop, that is." When his friend had gone, Turner spoke.

"I will endeavor to do better than that," he said tenderly and dropped to one knee. From his pocket, Turner produced a small box, which he raised as high as his arms would reach, whereupon, he opened it. "Marry me, Margaret Jane Parker, and I shall not leave your side again."

By this time, Turner's actions were starting to attract a few curious onlookers. The box contained a simple silver ring lying on a bed of cotton, but it instantly placed Jane into an immobilized state of enchantment. This was not the acceptance of an umbrella or a dress, so Turner was quite willing to wait for as long as it took. Evidently, some in the crowd believed that reasonable amount of time had come and gone. Finally, a nicely dressed, elderly woman walked up to Jane and spoke warmly to her.

"It's all right, darling. You take as long as you need. But this poor man's arms have got to be getting tired." This concerned observation snapped Jane out of her trance, just as Jasmine appeared at Turner's side.

"Uncle Philip, I'm cold."

"Okay, sweetheart," Turner replied without standing or lowering his arms. "We can find you a nice warm coat as soon as I'm finished proposing to Aunt Jane, all right?"

"Okay," she said and ran off.

"Uncle Philip? Aunt Jane?" Jane asked, while taking Turner's hands into hers, box and all, and lifting him up.

"It's a long story," Turner answered with a smile.

"Yes," Jane stated in her delayed response to his original question. "I will marry you, John Philip Turner."

"The Lord has brought you into my life to make me whole," Turner vowed and kissed her gently. "In return, I give you all my love forever and then forevermore."

"You have been put through fire and brimstone, my sweet, kind general. Where a weaker man would have caved in and used the Lord to back his vengeance, you have remained strong and righteous," Jane professed. "It would be my privilege to care for you and to love you into eternity."

"Then it will be my fondest moment to ask your father for your hand in marriage as soon as we are back," Turner proclaimed. "But for now, let us go hunt down a coat for our newly adopted niece and whatever other apparel that will be necessary for a family to make it through a long Virginia winter."

When as many top coats, britches, dresses, boots, hats, scarves, gloves, and blankets as could be found in Burkeville were purchased, they headed for home. Samuel and Josiah drove the carriage with Jane, Rosie, and Jasmine seated in the back under a warm blanket. Turner and Joseph rode horseback. This arrangement gave all a chance to connect, or reconnect, with each other during the ride back: and what a lively ride back it was, especially when Samuel and Josiah began singing the spirituals that would have emanated from the cotton fields, and Philip and Joseph broke out in songs that were heard from the many campfires between battles.

It was dark by the time the travelers had reached the Parker farm, but the ringing of the bell could be heard as soon as they transitioned from tree line to open field. They were greeted merrily from the porch by Mr. and Mrs. Parker and their two sons. Samuel's family was shown to the large guest room on the first floor that Turner had occupied when he first arrived. This, they were told, would be their living quarters for as long as they wished to stay. Having already witnessed the breadth of the Parkers' generosity, Samuel merely expressed his utmost gratitude; Rosie, however, burst into unrestrained tears. Turner was told he would bunk with Joseph through the winter, without any further discussion about sleeping outdoors like an ill-treated soldier.

Because they were expected back earlier, it was necessary to reheat supper, but no one seemed to mind. Rosie wore the new dress that Samuel had acquired when he and Turner passed through Hanover, Pennsylvania. With Mr. Parker's blessing, it was announced that Jane had accepted Turner's proposal of marriage; a toast was offered by Joseph, who suggested it was all his doing. He also took the opportunity to inform Turner that he, too, had been seeing a young lady with remarkable qualities, to which Turner made a grand toast.

Josiah quickly became the newest center of attention and found it difficult to take two bites in succession without having to respond to his heroic efforts to find his father. Samuel and Turner took great pleasure in this, as they went about stuffing themselves with baked ham and candied sweet potato without a care.

After the table was cleared and the dishes were cleaned and put away, Mr. and Mrs. Parker excused themselves for the evening with a blessing for each person present and for the memory of their lost son, Caleb. Joshua and Aaron also excused themselves, for there was much to be done before the snows fell. Josiah and Jasmine were washed up and tucked into their beds without much resistance, for they could hardly keep their eyes open. That left Joseph, Philip, Jane, Samuel, and Rosie to spend a few minutes discussing what the future might look like. Joseph went first.

"While away, you have received several correspondences," Joseph began, as he handed Turner a collection of mail. "I opened those with Southern addresses and responded promptly, as was your request. They were all letters from your men or their families wishing you well. Of those with Northern addresses, one was marked urgent, and I felt obliged to open it since it arrived soon after you left. I responded by saying you were on business down South without giving a date of return. The envelope without an address is the one you asked me to hold for you in your absence."

"Thank you, Joseph," Turner stated wearily. "I will look at them tomorrow with a fresh pair of eyes. For now, I would like you all to consider what I have come to believe was the reason why Benjamin and I bonded like brothers, why I became the lone heir to his estate, and the purpose of the rock that could not be moved... at least by man."

Knowing how tired everyone must be, Turner dispensed with the particulars and went straight to the point.

"I believe we are to build a school—a college—to the glory of God."

"A college," Jane repeated the words. "Is this to be a seminary?"

"No, my love," he replied. "It will teach great literature, higher mathematics, and the marvels of science primarily, but the students will always know they are covered in God's love. And the composition of the student body will be male and female, white and black, rich and poor, believers and nonbelievers... if that makes any sense."

"It does, coming from your lips," she said with a touch of sadness.

"Do not let this worry you, my sweet," Turner responded with tenderness. "This is not my calling. I am to remain here with you, in the South." Turner then looked toward Samuel and spoke.

"I believe this is meant for you and Nathan and whoever else God lifts up to support you. What say you, Samuel?"

"Well, suh, what goes on in dem classrums, I be leav'n ta others," Samuel stated after some careful thought. "But I reckon I can see to it dat things git taken care of, proper like, 'specially with dem young folk. Dey gonna know dat da Lawd lov'em... no matter who dey are or what dey done.

"I jus' might plant me some roses, too. Ain't nobody dat don't likes ta smell 'em. An, whenever I goes wander'n, I be reminded o' ma sweet Rosetta." This proposition caused Rosie to lay her head gently on her husband's welcoming shoulder.

"Joseph," Turner said, turning his attention to his soon-to-be brother-in-law. "You look puzzled, my friend. What is it?"

"I am curious," Joseph began. "Am I to understand that you have had no contact with a certain judge by the name of Douglas since your return from up north?"

"Judge Douglas?" Turner answered with astonishment. "While in Gettysburg I went to his home seeking forgiveness, but received only enough so not to be shot. Why do you ask?"

"Well, the letter marked urgent," Joseph continued, "was from Judge Douglas offering his full support for your new school."

"What did you say?" Turner asked in disbelief.

"Colonel Hillary's college, I believe he called it," Joseph replied.

# 15

# Strength to Forgive

"Emily, what are you doing here?" Nathan asked joyfully while, at the same time, wondering if this unexpected visit to Harvard was a good thing or something he would soon regret. "And Miss Bessie... is that you inside all those coats?"

"Yes, young man, it is," Miss Bessie replied with chattering teeth. "Do you have any other ideas for staying warm up here?"

"Now, Miss Bessie, it's not half as cold as it's going to be," Nathan remarked, "but let me pull a chair up nice and close to the fireplace and see if we can't start unbundling you."

"That would be right nice, Nathan," she moaned in an effort to garner more sympathy. "And a hot cup of tea with a spoon of honey and a dash of cream, if it's not too much trouble. Oh, my bones ain't so thick as they used to be."

"I'm afraid you have summoned me to the administration building, Miss Bessie," Nathan replied apologetically. "But give me a few minutes to see what I can find in the professor's sitting parlor that might help to warm you up."

"Thank you, child," Miss Bessie said sweetly, while reluctantly removing her hat and scarf.

Nathan headed toward the door, but turned suddenly as if he had forgotten something.

"Emily, can I get you anything while I'm out?"

"No, thank you," Emily said politely and watched as he exited the door. Turning to Miss Bessie, she spoke.

"And what was that all about, Miss Bessie?"

"To give you time to think about what you are going say, that's what," she said in her normal speaking voice. "Don't think I don't see that look in your eye, like you got that poor boy on a string and he can be tugged and talked to any which way. Do you love him or no?"

"I do," Emily answered honestly.

"Good, because Nathan's a fine, young man who could have been shot through and through on that battlefield, according to your own words," Miss Bessie stated firmly, and then softened her tone. "My dear sweet child, the Lord saved that boy for someone, and it might as well be you. Say what you come to say, but try using them words that lie closest to the heart."

Nathan returned sooner than expected with a silver tray in hand.

"As luck would have it, my story of a long, ghastly journey with the grim potential for pneumonia to set in fell upon sympathetic ears, and I was given this tray," Nathan stated happily, as he carefully set it down on the hearth in front of Miss Bessie. "It had just been prepared for another, but my needs—perhaps being slightly embellished—may have come across as being more worthy. It appears to have all that you requested, Miss Bessie, except there is granulated sugar instead of honey. However, I see that a few cakes were left on the tray. I am willing to go back if sugar is not to your liking."

"That will be fine, Nathan," Miss Bessie replied, as she gave Emily a glance and a discreet smile.

"Now, to what do I owe this pleasure?" Nathan asked, while looking from Miss Bessie to Emily.

"I'm sorry," Emily blurted out. "There, are you happy now?"

"Perhaps a little closer to the heart, my dear child," Miss Bessie stated softly, just before taking a sip of her tea.

"Sorry?" Nathan asked with a genuine lack of understanding. "For what?"

"I was there," she replied, a little closer to her heart. As the battle scene crept back into her mind, tears began to trickle down her cheek. These were not the feigned tears used for manipulation, but rather the heartfelt and sincere kind that could not be withheld even if she tried. "I saw you; you were so brave and noble. I just wanted you safe. I just wanted you back. I just wanted you to hold onto me and say you would never let me go. Nathan, I do love you. Will you ever forgive me?"

"Emily, it is I who should be asking you for forgiveness," he insisted and gathered her into his arms. "I know I hurt you. I let my anger for my father overshadow my love for you, but I was young then and did not fully understand these things. I cannot say I will never make another mistake, but I will never let you go, my sweet, my love."

After holding her tightly for some time, Nathan slowly moved himself away just enough to kiss her on the forehead, then place another kiss on the tip of her nose, and then another kiss on the lips, which appeared to be the true destination of his affection.

"Well, well, well, if only Miss Sunny could see you two now," Miss Bessie stated softly before taking another sip of her tea.

"Who is Miss Sunny?" Nathan inquired of the one he held in his arms. "And what did you mean when you said you were there and you saw me?"

"Oh, it's just my best story ever," Emily professed, while repositioning her head on Nathan's chest. "But you are going to have to hold me a little longer before you get me to tell it."

\* \* \*

He could not help but read it before going to bed, and it was the first thing Turner thought of when he woke up the following morning. The letter from Judge Douglas was one of those "about-face" maneuvers that had you shaking your head and looking for the subterfuge. It was the way in which war was played. From the first sentence, whereby the judge wished he could retract every unkind word spoken and sought some temporary forbearance until a more permanent forgiveness could be gained in person; it was pure military deception. It took a letter from Duke Duchene (the second letter Turner opened) to relax this initial skepticism. Both men offered their support for an endeavor that had not yet been conceived in Turner's mind until after their letters were sent. The third letter read from his bedside was Nathan, claiming to be engaged to be married to Miss Emily.

"What has this world come to?" he mouthed to himself. "I could not ask for better news than this, and yet I am baffled by it all."

It was still early morning. Turner's roommate's bed was empty, but he could hear Joseph speaking from downstairs. On his nightstand lay a dozen or more letters that would, most likely, take most of the day to open, contemplate, and respond to in some intelligent fashion. Turner dressed himself and made his way quickly down the stairs with the fistful of letters. He found the entire Parker clan in the kitchen, finishing their coffee and finalizing plans for the day.

"Good morning to all," Turner offered, as soon as he was through the door. The greeting was quickly responded to by all.

"Mister Parker, sir," Turner began, with as much courage as he could muster. "Would you find it objectionable if I were to kiss your lovely daughter good morning, sir?"

"I would find it troubling if you did not, my boy," the elder replied, without looking up from his morning Scripture meditation.

"Missus Parker…" Turner began but was interrupted.

"I do not think a kiss would offend anyone in this room, my dear," she said, without turning her attention away from the boiling pot on the fire. She had a point; the three Parker boys went back to their planning immediately following the greeting and showed little interest in Turner's inquiries.

Now that they were engaged, it was as if Turner and Jane were not as interesting as they once were. That suited Turner just fine, as he walked across the room unheeded and kissed his bride-to-be eagerly.

"You are more beautiful each time I see you, Missus Turner," Turner whispered into Jane's ear.

"That's funny… I have many fond memories of us, but I do not remember a wedding, my darling," Jane whispered back.

"We shall soon remedy that," Turner pledged lovingly.

"Joseph, my good man," Turner called out, "you have been invited to a wedding. That is, if you will accept his apologies for waving that loaded pistol at you."

"And who would that be?" Joseph asked without a clue, for he had had many loaded pistols aimed at him.

"Private Nathan Walker," Turner replied cheerfully. "He will be marrying Miss Emily Preston in the spring, after he graduates from Harvard University."

"Little Nathan Walker is getting married," Joseph stated kindly. "But is this the same young lady who libeled and defamed him in a newspaper article she penned not long ago?"

"The very same," Turner responded with a smile.

This sordid little anecdote had everyone, including Mr. Parker, in the room popping their heads up in an effort to catch more of the intriguing story. Unfortunately for the eavesdroppers, this conversation ended as Samuel walked in.

"Good mon'n. Sho' is a lovely day," he said pleasantly. The greeting was quickly responded to by all.

"Now, Mista Parker, suh," Samuel spoke candidly to the father. "My boy an' I is ready ta go ta work as soon as yo gives da word."

"Uh oh, here it comes," Turner whispered to Jane.

"Balderdash!" the old man exclaimed. "Samuel, you and your family are guests in this house. Show me a man who would put his guest to work, and I'll show you a no-good snake-in-the-grass."

"Samuel, do not resist. You shall soon find out that the Parker family's hospitality cannot be outdone," Turner kindly interrupted. "By the way, you have been invited to a wedding."

"Who's weddin' is dat, Mista Phil'p?" Samuel asked, while taking Turner's advice not to insist on pulling his weight around the farm, at least for now.

"Nathan intends to wed Miss Emily in the spring."

"Yo don't mean dat young woman who done made him kiss dat frog?" Samuel countered.

"One and the same," Turner replied.

The addition of this new titillating piece of information caused everyone to look up again but, to their dismay, no more was said, and everyone concluded their preparations and then left. Only Turner and Samuel remained. Jane offered to show Rosie and the children around the farm after the morning chores and breakfast. This would give Turner and Samuel a chance to meet and discuss God's plan for the making of a college—Hillary College.

Until then, Turner planned to sit at the writing desk in the sitting room and get through as much mail as possible, beginning with those posts from his men. Joseph had retained Turner's journals while he and Samuel were down South, and was able to respond to each of these letters promptly, but that was to serve as a temporary measure to counteract any delay. They were addressed to Turner, and they would receive a response from him.

Breakfast was a madhouse. It was only made manageable with the help of Rosie and the kids, who would insist on being made useful. Jasmine was familiar with the henhouse and returned to the kitchen with every egg that was laid. Josiah accepted and attacked every chore that would help build his muscles. It was his intention to become a fighting soldier, just like the men in the 2nd and 99th United States Colored Troops he remembered passing through Tallahassee earlier that year. Mrs. Parker and Jane found Rosie's company most delightful while preparing the morning meal, for they soon discovered all three were admirers of Charles Dickens and each of a different book: Mrs. Parker preferred *The Christmas Carol*; Jane, *The Tale of Two Cities*; and Rosie, *Oliver Twist: The Parish Boy's Progress*.

After breakfast, Turner and Samuel adjourned to the sitting room. Three stacks of letters sat neatly upon the writing table: one with southern addresses, one with northern addresses, and one with outgoing addresses. It would take another day for Turner to complete the correspondence to the southern addresses, because each recipient was very personal to him. Among the northern addresses, there were many official-looking letters from his banks, his lawyers, and various investment companies wanting to do business with him. Turner would come back to those. For now, his purpose was to make Samuel aware of the contents of the letters from Judge Douglas, Duke, and Nathan that he had already read.

In addition to offering their unconditional support, these three letters also detailed how Emily had been taken back to the battlefield, how Duke had touched the large, white rock that covered Benjamin's grave, and how the judge had witnessed the construction of at least four magnificent buildings on that site. All three letters were cautious in trying to explain how this was accomplished, but there was no doubt in the minds of the authors that something glorious was at work.

Turner understood that Samuel was no architect, no master builder, no engineer, no literary scholar, no adept administrator... he could not even read. However, he also understood that the colossal project set before them would not succeed by man's effort alone; that was where Samuel came in. Next to Benjamin, Samuel was the most righteous man Turner had ever met, and his input was not simply desirable, it was essential. After reading the three letters out loud, Turner waited for Samuel's response in silence.

"Don't dat beat aw?" Samuel quipped. "I reckon it cain't be made no plainer... 'less da Lawd was ta take us aw by da hand, Mista Phil'p."

"Yes, I see that, too," Turner said with sadness in his voice. "But four 'magnificent' buildings in the middle of nowhere, transportation, people, payroll... where will it all come from? The amount given to me by Benjamin isn't half of what is necessary for such an undertaking. And I have made other promises: bringing home our countrymen from the Gettysburg battlefield, rebuilding the South, helping Jane's parents, raising a family."

Turner slowly lowered his head into his hands. His attempts to rein in his fears and his tears were to no avail. He had finally met his match; he had come to the end of his rope. There was no hope of accomplishing what was being asked of him. He had failed Benjamin... he had failed his Savior. He spoke again, each word being more painful than the last.

"I can't do it, Samuel. God chose the wrong man."

Samuel stood up and walked over to his broken friend. He grasped onto Turner's shoulders tightly and began to talk to God.

"Lawd, I don't believes none o' it," Samuel stated boldly. "'Course he cain't do it. Dey ain't no one alive dat can do what Yo be ask'n dis man ta do. Dat don't mean he's da wrong man, no suh.

"Lawd, I believes Yo done picked Yo'self da right man, but he is weak... jus' like every oth'a man dat's ever been bow'n is weak. Da devil got's him a think'n Yo ain't strong 'nuf ta raise up fo' tiny build'ns out a noth'n if'n Yo wants to.

"In Jesus' name, I ask's Yo ta give dis man da stren'th ta rebuke dat devil an' aw his cruel an' thiev'n ways. Stand with'm, Lawd. He cain't do nothin' by himself. He cain't do noth'n with men alone. He needs Yo, Lawd. He is will'n. I am will'n. We needs Yo now, Lawd."

* * *

The telegraph requesting his return home to Philadelphia as soon as could be arranged had a touch of urgency to it. The only other communication Nathan had with his father since their meeting before heading back to school was the announcement of his engagement to Emily, which received no response. Mother, on the other hand, had not stopped with her joyful yet constant stream of communications with regards to said engagement. If this meeting with his father was to be some sort of warning as to how the Walkers were to react to the intrusion of an outside—and perhaps hostile—family, then it would be a very short visit.

The return home was a pleasant journey, and Nathan entered the family's country home as unceremoniously welcomed as he had been on his last visit. His calls of greeting echoed through the house but went unanswered. He walked down the long hallway, popping his head inside each room as he went along. The only room for which the door remained closed was his father's study. On this door, he knocked.

"Come in; it is unlocked," he heard his father say.

"Good day, Father," Nathan offered cheerfully. "The house seems to be deserted."

"Welcome home, son," his father replied with uncommon warmth and affection. "Yes, your mother and Missus Preston have been busy as beavers lately. Which reminds me, I hope for the very best between you and Emily. She is a charming young lady, and we welcome her with open arms."

These verbal expressions without the usual stern, abrasive quality to them were an immediate cause of concern.

"Are you dying?" Nathan asked earnestly.

"Well, if you are speaking of the final act that all living creatures must submit to, yes, of course," his father responded. "But if you are asking if I have developed a disease which could take my life prematurely, I am aware of no such illness."

"Then why have you called me away from school so suddenly?" Nathan asked.

"Have a seat, and I will tell you," his father began. "Do you remember Judge Eugene Briarwood, the man you met not a month ago?"

"Yes, of course."

"When you left the room that day, he told me he had a fatal illness, and that death would come soon," his father said solemnly. "His funeral was the same day I sent you that telegram."

"I am truly sorry. I know you were close to him."

"For a time, we were as close as brothers," his father recalled with affection. "Some would say that Gene took the high road, and I took the low road, and there is truth to that."

"You need not be so hard on yourself," Nathan said, in an effort to comfort his grieving father.

"No?" his father asked sorrowfully, as he rose from his chair and wandered to the windows. "Let's see if you still believe that."

With his back to Nathan, he began to reminisce about his growing up with his best friend, Gene. If he got himself into trouble, Gene was there. If he got himself into a scrape with a bully twice his size, Gene was there. If he were to get into debt, Gene was there. If he needed to hear a kind word, Gene was there. Never once did Gene withhold his friendship... never once. For the most part, Nathan's father remembered having returned this friendship, although he could not recollect Gene ever asking him for anything of significance or importance. At this point, Nathan's father turned to face his son.

"He never asked anything from me, until that day when he sat where you are sitting now," Nathan's father admitted, now barely containing his tears. "And do you know what he asked me for?"

"What?"

"Forgiveness," his father revealed. "Can you imagine your best friend, who never did you wrong, asking you for forgiveness?"

"You forgave him, of course," Nathan replied, as if this were a foregone conclusion.

"I couldn't," his father said flatly, before burying his face in his hands in shame and remorse.

"But why?" Nathan exclaimed in disbelief.

Nathan's father stumbled back to his seat, as if pierced by his son's words. There he sat, trying to keep his emotions intact long enough to get through this terrible business that he promised himself he must do. After a few much needed breaths of air, he continued.

"After you left the room, we continued reminiscing; then Gene shared with me the true purpose of his visit. He described to me how his heart ached because of his apathy towards my salvation, and that it was not something you withhold from those you profess to love.

"Underestimating the importance of these remarks, I merely laughed.

"'If that was all you came to tell me, Gene, go without burden because all religion is bunk to me,' I said. But he persisted.

"'The life and ministry of Jesus Christ is true. I stake my reputation on it,' he said, hoping to see some weakness in me. I was not without sympathy, but I did not return his hope.

"'If legends and myths give you solace, my friend, then do not let me stop you from imbibing them,' I said coldly.

"'Then forgive me for not being more forceful when I had a chance with you, my dearest, truest friend,' he asked in the most decent fashion.

"'Why should I forgive you for something I do not wish upon myself?' I replied angrily. That is when he pleaded with me to forgive him and impressed upon me that it was necessary for him to hear me say those words of forgiveness before he left this world..."

Nathan's father was forced to stop because he could not wipe the tears away fast enough, and he gasped for air. Nathan ran around the desk and wrapped his arms across his father's trembling shoulders, and gently rocked him back and forth. When Nathan's father was finally able to catch his breath again, he spoke softly.

"I sent him away, Nathan. I sent away my dearest friend in this world without giving to him the only thing he ever asked of me. What kind of monster would do such a thing?"

"You are not a monster," Nathan said lovingly. "You are a sinner, just as I am a sinner, just as your good friend was a sinner. That is why we all need a Savior."

Nathan released his father and perched himself on the edge of the desk.

"I believe your anguish is a good sign, Father," Nathan continued. "It proves, without a shadow of doubt, your humanity. It may even come to pass that Judge Briarwood started a good work in you; something more precious than benignly consenting to a request for forgiveness if there was no truth in it. That good work may provide you another opportunity to forgive him—to thank him—in person."

"Thank you, son. You have grown wise."

"Heredity, I suppose," Nathan quipped.

"I shared my story with you because I do not want to die without knowing you have forgiven me."

"But why, Father? You have given me food, shelter, education, love... in your own way," Nathan answered with sincerity.

"I just need to hear you say it... and mean it," his father asked politely. "Please."

"I forgive you, Father," Nathan replied honestly. "I will always forgive you."

"Thank you," his father replied in relief. "Now, I have something for you... well, not for you exactly." With that, he removed an envelope from his desk drawer and handed it to Nathan.

"What is this?" Nathan asked, while pulling the slip of paper out its protective sleeve.

"What does it look like?"

"A banker's check for two hundred fifty thousand dollars," Nathan exhaled and leapt from the desk. "Issued to John Philip Turner. But why?"

"Son, my world is made up of scoundrels and swindlers," his father confessed, "of which I am the best. Whereas the vast majority of my business 'associations' deserve to be swindled, Colonel Hillary's parents did not. That check represents the balance of the profit my holding company made reselling their property, plus interest.

"I have also been hearing of many kind and benevolent things occurring wherever Colonel Hillary's rebel friend has shown himself. Maybe it's time I forgave him, too, huh?"

"You truly have changed," Nathan spoke softly, as if to himself and then addressed his father tenderly. "Thank you, Father. You do not know how much this means to me. You have given me reason to bear the Walker name proudly. You have given me back my name."

# Notes

## Chapter 1 – The Battle

Fort Sumter – Battle of 1861 (April): Davis, William. The Battlefields of the Civil War. Salamander Books Ltd. (2003)

West Point during the Civil War. Crews, Dick. The Cleveland Civil War Roundtable (2008)

Gettysburg – Battle of 1863 (July): Davis, William. The Battlefields of the Civil War. Salamander Books Ltd. (2003)

Chancellorsville – Battle of 1863 (May): Davis, William. The Battlefields of the Civil War. Salamander Books Ltd. (2003)

Jackson, Thomas J. Stonewall (1824 – 1863): Earns nickname at Battle of First Manassas (First Bull Run), 1861 (July): Davis, William. The Battlefields of the Civil War. Salamander Books Ltd. (2003)

## Chapter 2 – End of War

Appomattox Courthouse (1865): The Surrender Meeting. Publication by National Park Service (updated 2015)

Union and Confederate Engineer Operations in the Civil War: O'Connell, Daniel. Virginia Center for Civil War Studies; Virginia Tech

#### Chapter 3 – Peace and Joy

Wilderness – Battle of 1864 (May): Davis, William. The Battlefields of the Civil War. Salamander Books Ltd. (2003)
Starvation Balls: Reaction to the Fall of Richmond. Feature by Civil War Trust

#### Chapter 4 – Turner's Journey

Antietam (Sharpsburg) – Battle of 1862 (September): Davis, William. The Battlefields of the Civil War. Salamander Books Ltd. (2003)
Mobile Bay – Battle of 1864 (August): Davis, William. The Battlefields of the Civil War. Salamander Books Ltd. (2003)

#### Chapter 5 – Fire!

Uncle Tom's Cabin; or, Life Among the Lowly: Stowe, Harriet Beecher. John P. Jewett publisher (1852)

#### Chapter 8 – The Rock Won't Move

Romeo and Juliet, play: Shakespeare, William. Originally published in 1597.
Life of Joseph, Son of Jacob (Israel): Book of Genesis (Old Testament); Chapters 37–50

## Chapter 9 – Hallowed Ground

Gettysburg Cemetery: Civil War Era National Cemeteries: Honoring Those Who Served. Publication by National Park Service, nps.gov

## Chapter 10 – Homeward

Fredericksburg – Battle of 1862 (December): Davis, William. The Battlefields of the Civil War. Salamander Books Ltd. (2003)

Hollywood Cemetery: Hollywood Cemetery and James Monroe Tomb. National Park Service, nps.gov

The Underground Railroad: National Park Service Network to Freedom. The Colonial Williamsburg Foundation (2017)

## Chapter 11 – The Prince and the Princess

Confederate advance on Philadelphia (1863): The burning of Columbia- Wrightsville Bridge, civilwaralbum.com

Harvard's Secularism: Kendrick, Anna. The Harvard Crimson (student newspaper) article dated March 8, 2006

Henry Livermore Abbott (1842 – 1864): Wikipedia

## Chapter 12 – Reunited

William Tecumseh Sherman (1820–1891): Scorched Earth: Sherman's March to the Sea. Feature by Civil War Trust.

Chickamauga and Chattanooga – Battles of 1863 (September and November): Davis, William. The Battlefields of the Civil War. Salamander Books Ltd. (2003)

Atlanta – Campaign of 1864: Feature by Civil War Trust

William Calvin Oates (1835 – 1910): Biography by Civil War Trust

## Chapter 13 – Morning Sunshine

Marbury v. Madison (1803): Wikipedia
Scott v. Sandford, or Dred Scott case (1857): Wikipedia

## Chapter 14 – Proposals and Propositions

The state of Florida and the Civil War: The American Civil War: State by State – Florida. National Park Service, nps.gov

Florida in the Civil War: The Battle of Natural Bridge – 1865 (March); also see, The War Ends: Surrender, Occupation, and Emancipation – 1865 (May). Division of Cultural Affairs, Florida Department of State

Petersburg – Third Battle of 1865 (April): Two Days in April: Breakthrough at Petersburg. Feature by Civil War Trust

## Chapter 15 – Strength to Forgive

Charles Dickens (1812 – 1870): Author: Oliver Twist; Richard Bentley, London, publisher (1839). A Christmas Carol; Chapman & Hall, London, publisher (1843). A Tale of Two Cities; Chapman & Hall, London, publisher (1859)